Trefoil

M C Moore

To Dennis
Thanks for
all your support

MC Moore

DEDICATION

Celine-for all you support through this project.

Bronwyn-for all your editing help.

Mom-for believing in me.

CHAPTER 1

The dreams had started about ten days ago. A single woman running through a forest, as if she were being chased by an invisible attacker. There is a sense of fear and urgency in her movements. She felt no need to pause for the tree limbs or brush that impedes her progress. She was heading for a single point in the trees, an arch of branches. Then with one fluid motion she puts something in her mouth and disappears. Meckenzie knows who the woman is, she would know her anywhere. Even if it had been eight years since she had seen her. The woman was her mother.

As always, Meckenzie awakens to find herself in her room, feeling out of breath with a killer headache. Always she wants to cry and sometimes she does. Meckenzie stumbles into the bathroom to splash water on her face. Sleep has been elusive. Running a brush through her golden blond hair, she decides returning to bed will only encourage the dream to return.

So Meckenzie pads quietly down the stairs to the first floor of the grand home that has been in her family since it was built in 1887. It is one of the few homes surrounding Central Park that is still a single family residence. She was always impressed that her great grandmother had taken so much care in designing the home with the architect. The hand carved baluster that ran along the circular stair case through all seven floors. The stained glass of the top floor that allowed rainbows to dance upon the walls throughout the day as the passing of the sun made its way across the sky. Her grandmother had loved so much having her whole family in residence when she was alive, that is why the house was so large.

Meckenzie had explored every nook and cranny with her brother and sister. Many adventures had taken place here. One would enter the home on the ground floor which housed the living room, dining room, kitchen and a parlor. The circular stair case ended in a dome at the top, allowing light to flood down all the floors to the entryway. The terrace floor was one down from the ground floor and housed the art gallery, ballroom, and a terrace complete with garden. One floor down from that was the gym and swimming pool. Their father had a room and a library on the second floor. Her brother Taggart's room and the media room were on third floor. Meckenzie and her sister Kellan had rooms on the fourth floor. There was a fifth floor that had a guest room and parlor. Meckenzie had always felt like the house was too big for her family, especially after her mother had vanished.

Being the first born of triplets, Meckenzie was always the first one up, so it surprised her to find her brother Taggart making coffee.

"You're up early."

Startled, Taggart dropped the coffee grounds on the kitchen floor.

"I have a Physics exam this morning, just trying to get in some extra cramming. You look like crap, trouble sleeping?"

"Thanks!" Meckenzie growled at Taggart.

"No really, are you okay?"

"Just been having some weird dreams, well I should say a weird dream. Is there anything for a headache in this house?" Meckenzie and her siblings had never had to take any kind of medication. While other kids struggled with colds and the flu, the Desmond trips, as the triplets were sometimes referred to, had perfect attendance for eight years running. The only thing that had kept them home was that fateful spring after their tenth birthday when their mother had disappeared.

Taggart gestured behind him, "I think dad has some stashed in the drawer by the sink."

"You look; I'll get the broom and clean up your mess."

Taggart was only a minute younger than Meckenzie, but she always felt like the older sister. Always trying to clean up after him and keep him out of trouble. Not that Taggart was prone to any trouble that was all Kellan. Being the youngest of the three, Kellan always seemed to find trouble.

After sweeping the floor and downing some aspirin, Meckenzie went to wake up Kellan for their morning run.

Knocking softly, Meckenzie opened the door to Kellan's room.

"K, wanna run?"

Kellan mumbles, "Mmphh?!"

"K, I didn't sleep well. I need to run, so get up."

"Ok. Be ready in five."

Meckenzie changed into her running clothes and pulled her hair back. With any luck, they could do five miles through Central Park before needing to get ready to make it to school on time. That was if Kellan was really getting ready.

Throwing on her running clothes, Meckenzie slipped her iPhone around her arm, setting the run app so it would count her miles and play her run playlist. She made sure she had the pepper spray she kept in a hidden pocket of her running shorts.

As she came out of her room, Kellan started down the stairs, iPod in hand.

"Think we have time for five miles."

Kellan laughed, "I do, but you might not be able to keep up."

"Keep up? I'm not getting any slower, I think maybe you're getting faster."

Kellan took off down the stairs and shouted over her shoulder, "Race you then."

Passing the second floor, Lawrence Desmond smiled at his daughters as they dashed down the stairs. "You girls be careful and stick together if you're going into the park at this hour."

The sun barely had a hold on the morning sky as the girls started their run. They had been running in this park for years and had mapped out a five mile path that led right back to the house. Kellan took it slow at first, letting Meckenzie keep up, but eventually she started to pull ahead. By half way through the second mile, Kellan was far enough ahead that Meckenzie would lose her around bends or bridges. By mile three, she was nowhere in sight.

Meckenzie listened to Arcade Fire play as she jogged on. As she approached the Trefoil Arch, Meckenzie thought she saw someone hiding in the shadows. It would be just like Kellan to try to scare her, but being cautious, Meckenzie reached for her pepper spray.

As if the arch entrance was covered with a thin layer of water, it shimmered ever so slightly with the light of the rising sun playing off its surface. Meckenzie thought her mind must be playing tricks on her. The shimmering stopped and the shadow within the shadows was gone. Surely it was lack of sleep and the lingering headache that created this illusion.

Meckenzie stopped before the arch entrance. Slowly turning 360 degrees, she observed the area around the entrance to see if the person had exited into the grass. No one was around, not even Kellan. Spooked, she began running again. Picking up her pace with the goal of just getting home.

The burn in her legs felt good, but it reminded Meckenzie of her dream once more. The frantic nature of the woman's run plagued her thoughts. What was she running from? Or maybe, she was running to something. Lost in her deep thought she almost ran into traffic. Meckenzie startled, stepped back up on the curb just in time to avoid the town car with a blaring horn. She crossed at the light, with only the safety of her home and a warm shower in mind.

Meckenzie found Kellan in the kitchen elbow deep in a bowl of some sugary breakfast cereal. She thought maybe Kellan had seen something at the arch this morning. "Did you see someone under Trefoil Arch?"

Kellan laughed, dribbling rainbow colored milk from her lips. "You mean like a troll? Did he ask you to answer his riddle before he'd let you pass?"

"Never mind, it must have been the sun."

"Not a troll then?"

"You are a dork. Why would it be a troll? It looked like a person, there one second gone the next. They had to have been there when you jogged through." Lack of sleep was throwing Meckenzie into a bitter mood.

"Nope."

Meckenzie grabbed a banana and headed up to her room. She needed to wash the morning off of her and get her head cleared. This was turning out to be a long day and she hadn't even made it to school yet.

Meckenzie stepped into the bathroom, shedding her iPhone and pulling her hair out of the ponytail she had pulled it up in. She began slowly running a brush through her hair staring blankly at the mirror. Suddenly Meckenzie had a feeling she was being watched so she turned around to see if anyone was behind her. No one was there. As Meckenzie turned back to the mirror, she could've sworn that it shimmered like a pool of mercury. Meckenzie reached out and touched the mirror, not really knowing what she expected to find.

She sat the brush down on the counter and decided that the lack and sleep and headaches were really getting to her. Maybe a shower would solve all those problems. Meckenzie had no way of knowing that her problems were just beginning. No way of knowing that the day was just going to get longer and more complicated.

CHAPTER 2

The walk to Darian academy was only a few blocks. Taggart had left early to get a few minutes of lab time in. He was well on his way to medical school, and his acceptance into Harvard, which had come before school had started, was the first step. Knowing what you wanted to do from a very early age was a blessing and a curse. Taggart had been singularly working toward the goal of getting into Harvard since he was seven. This means he had very little social life, no girlfriend, and very few friends. He always said he didn't need many friends because he had a perfect set of bookend best friends in Meckenzie and Kellan. He also claimed that when he was ready he'd have no problem getting a girlfriend, because what girl didn't want to marry a doctor.

Meckenzie had very little clues as to what she wanted to do with her life. She had considered the possibility of becoming a writer. She exceled at school politics, though she thought that might be in part to her being pretty and part of the schools trendy triplet population. Meckenzie thought it would be easier the closer she got to college. Kellan had always been the athlete, and had been recruited to play basketball at Stanford, Connecticut, Texas, Tennessee and several other schools. She had done several basketball camps in the last four years that had gotten her national exposure. Not to mention Kellan seemed to be getting faster and stronger the last couple of years.

Meckenzie had several acceptance letters in her room, but still had not decided which school she would attend. The thought of being separated from her siblings was a troubling one, but she knew that after this year, her senior year, they would all be going their own directions to start their adult lives. Meckenzie thought it might be worth it to go to NYU and just stay at home with her dad. He would be all alone in that big house once the trips went off to college.

The warning bell rang as Kellan and Meckenzie jogged up the steps. First period was the same for the trips; a Humanities block that involved English and Government. They slipped into their table in the back next to Taggart, and waited for class to begin.

As Mr. Humphries started the lecture involving the writing of Plato and the fact that the government was a republic and not a true democracy, the door opened to the class. Meckenzie felt him before he entered the classroom. It was a dull ache in her head that felt malevolent. The intake of air from the female population of the class could have sucked the oxygen out of the room. His tall, lithe body was clothed in designer fashions, dark hair framed a finely chiseled face, and the icy cold blue eyes staring back at Meckenzie could not be real.

As he handed Mr. Humphries a note, he scanned the class. Meckenzie flinched as a buzzing sound like a horde of bees began in the back of her head. She must have instinctively looked behind her. Kellan asked, "What's wrong?" Taggart reached over and touched her arm, the buzzing stopped.

Mr. Humphries mumbled, "This is highly unusual. Well, it seems we have a transfer student. Students welcome Tynan Rabe. He'll be joining us for the rest of the year. Though it is highly unusual to get a transfer mid semester, we'll try to make you feel welcome. You can take a seat in the back; I believe there is an opening at the Desmond table next to Kellan. Raise your hand Kellan."

Tynan snaked his way through the tables. Everyone watched him except for Meckenzie. She only felt a sense of dread and sickness.

As he sat down he smiled at the triplets, "Hi, I'm Ty."

Kellan not privy to Meckenzie's growing apprehension introduced them. "I'm Kellan; this is my sister Meckenzie and my brother Taggart."

Ty smiled and gave a little chuckle. "You all have Celtic names and an English surname." He said without expecting a reply. "My name is Celtic also, but my last name is German, it means Raven. I'm a bit of a language aficionado." Arrogance dripped from his last sentence like tar.

Meckenzie's head began to buzz again and instinctively she touched Taggart. The buzzing stopped. She focused on Mr. Humphries droning lecture at the front of the room and prayed for time to move a little faster.

When the bell rang for class change, Meckenzie thought that she might have to go home sick. As soon as she reached her next class, math or calculus as it was evilly know as, the buzzing had stopped completely. Meckenzie couldn't be for sure, but it seemed as if Ty had inflicted this debilitating buzzing upon her. It had started when he arrived and was gone when he had disappeared into the halls.

At lunch Meckenzie spotted Kellan headed for the front door.

"Kellan! Wait!"

Kellan flipped around "Hurry, I need to run home and grab my assignment for Ms. Thompson's class. I left it on the printer."

As the girls flew down the streets of New York headed toward Central Park, the buzzing started in Meckenzie's head. She slowed down a bit and looked around. She spotted Ty across the street staring at them. Kellan realized belatedly that Meckenzie had stopped. "Come on Meckenzie, are you ok?"

Just then, Ty turned and headed into a coffee shop. Meckenzie could have sworn she saw him laugh.

"Meckenzie, what are you looking at?"

"Did you see Ty over there? He was staring at us. I don't like this guy at all."

Kellan stopped and looked across the street, "I didn't see anything, now hurry up I have to get back to class. You sure are jumpy today."

"I just get this sick feeling and a buzzing in my head when he is around. Maybe it's lack of sleep."

9

"Or maybe it's a crush."

Meckenzie flinched in horror. She knew for sure there were no feelings of lust, love or even curiosity for Tynan Rabe. He was simply and most definitely evil.

CHAPTER 3

The rest of the day went smoothly and Meckenzie rushed home after the final bell to meet with the party planner her father had hired for their eighteenth birthday party. Kellan was working out with her Basketball coach and Taggart had decided to put in an extra hour in the lab. So it would be up to Meckenzie to make the basic decisions about the party.

As she turned the corner she saw Ty hanging out in the park. He was talking with a guy and a girl who looked similar to him. All three stopped and turned to look at Meckenzie at the same time. Then like a wave of nausea, the buzzing started. She hurried along to her front door and rushed in.

After locking the door behind her, she went to the front window to look across the street to where Ty had been with his companions. No one was there but a dog walker and about six mixed dogs ranging in all shapes and sizes.

Just then the doorbell rang and startled Meckenzie. She was unsure of answering the door, as no one else was home. As she looked through the window, she could make out one of the assistants to Doreen the party planner.

Doreen McDonald party planner extraordinaire traveled with a posse. Two assistants trailed in behind her as well as a man in his late twenties who gasped as he entered the entry way. The unknown man mumbled, "Fabulous," and brushed past the two assistants.

Doreen began introductions, "This is Adam Smith, he will be designing the flowers and other table pieces for the party. You remember Jen and James my assistants."

Meckenzie nodded, "Let's go down to the parlor and ballroom so you can see the space Adam."

Meckenzie led the group down the spiral stair case, pointing out all the fine architectural detail for Adam's amusement. "The home was built in 1887 by my great grandparents. My great grandmother designed the home with the architect, specifying room layout. She hand-picked many of the art pieces you will see in the home. She lived to be 106. She was 20 when the house was built and never lived anywhere else for the last 86 years of her life. She especially loved this floor. The ballroom has been used to hold weddings, birthday parties, and even her funeral. As you can see by the design, it will easily hold 100 guests and will fit our needs for the dinner and dancing portion of our evening. The parlor will be able to hold the gift bags and function as a sitting area for the after dinner festivities. Now to my great grandmother's favorite part of the house, the garden."

There were many agreeable noises coming from Doreen and her assistants. Adam giggled and followed close behind Meckenzie. Just as she was showing the group the garden, Taggart strolled into the room. "I'm not too late am I? Meckenzie hasn't decided to use streamers and balloons for our decorations."

As Adam turned to see Taggart come in, Meckenzie was aware of the sharp intake of air. Adam had found himself a new object for his admiration in the form of Taggart.

Taggart had always commanded the attention of everyone when he walked in a room. His boyish charm was hidden behind the body of a man. He's lean muscular build was draped upon a 6'3" frame and his blue eyes could make you dream of the ocean. Topped with stylish trusses of blond hair that resembled in every way Meckenzie's own hair except for the length.

In every way, Taggart should be dripping with girlfriends. Yet, Taggart had chosen to throw himself into his studies instead. He was pre-accepted in to

Harvard and he had every intention of going to medical school after. Meckenzie had no doubt that Taggart would succeed. He was driven.

Adam stepped forward, "I have not, nor will I ever use streamers and balloons for decorations. Now let's talk theme."

"Masquerade," said Taggart and Meckenzie simultaneously.

Adam about wet his pants with excitement. "So colors?"

"Gold, white and navy," Taggart was taking control of the decisions. Meckenzie was relieved; she had not really wanted to make all these decision anyway. Her head still hurt and she was as tired as she could possibly imagine being.

Adam squealed aloud when Taggart described decorating the garden with white silk and pillows and couches. Dorian and Meckenzie used this opportunity to discuss menu while her assistants began measuring every square inch of the ballroom and garden. After an hour of discussion, Kellan came bounding down the stairs.

They all decided on the final menu options from choices Meckenzie had made and the meeting was over. The triplets escorted the group to the front door and made plans for another meeting in a week. With a short four week time frame, things had to move fast.

"I'm going to get a shower." Kellan said as she bounded up the stairs.

As Taggart turned from the front door, he reached out to touch Meckenzie's shoulder. "So you want to talk?"

Meckenzie was confused, "About what?"

"I love you like a sister you know." Taggart laughed at his own joke

Meckenzie giggled, "I hope so, since we did share a womb."

"I know something is going on with you. You seem distant and moody."

"You mean because of what happened in Humanities today. I'm not sure what's going on. The new kid was just weird." Meckenzie didn't want to sound crazy because she thought Ty was causing a buzzing sound inside her head.

"He freaks me out too."

Meckenzie paused for a moment and decided to give her brother the whole story.

"I don't know what is going on right now. I have these dreams where I am this woman running in a forest. It's as if someone is chasing me, but I turn and no one is there. Then I toss something in my mouth chew a couple of times and then just disappear. I don't know if it is invisible chewing gum, I don't know who's chasing me. I just know I wake up tired and with a headache. Every night the dream comes and every night it's the same thing. And every night, the woman is mom."

Taggart looked worried. He opened his mouth to speak, but Meckenzie held up her hand.

"Then today, when that Tynan guy came into class, my head started buzzing. I know it sounds crazy. It was like there was electricity humming in the back of my head. You touched me and it stopped. Then he came to our table and it started again. I don't know if it is real, but I touched you again and it stopped...again. Later I saw him across the street and the buzzing started again. He actually seemed to know it was happening because he laughed out loud, but when I got around the corner it stopped. On my way home he was in the park in front of our house with some friends, he just stared at me, but the buzzing came back. The guy freaks me out."

Anger flashed on Taggart's face. He seemed to be breathing faster. "I knew something was off with that guy. He just seemed weird. Do you think he's stalking you?"

Meckenzie paused, why would the new guy stalk her. He had only been at the school for a day. It seemed impossible that he would have really taken that much interest in her in one morning.

"I don't think so. But maybe you can run with us in the morning. Kellan never waits for me to keep up."

"I guess it is probably time for me to take up running again. I won't always be able to keep my boyish figure without some kind of work out."

Meckenzie giggled, knowing full well that Taggart worked out every evening in the house's built in gym that resided in the basement. They made their way into the kitchen where they were greeted by their housekeeper and cook Isabel. She stood over the sink washing fruit and singing to herself. Isabel was like part of the family, having started working for their family right before their mother's vanishing. She had functioned as a nanny of sorts for the trips.

As best as Meckenzie could tell, Isabel was in her mid to late forties, though there was no way to know for sure, because Isabel didn't talk about her age. Isabel's wavy brunette hair was usually tied back with a ribbon or clip, which showed off her soft feminine features. Her eyes were a chocolaty brown that had always made Meckenzie feel comfortably safe. Meckenzie and Isabel were about the same height, which made them the shortest people in the house. Though in most situations, Isabel's personality made her seem taller than she actually was.

After their mother disappeared, their father had been adamant about Isabel walking the kids to and from school. Since they had turned fifteen he had let them walk themselves, being that the walk was only a few blocks from their house. Isabel had always been here when they got home, with snacks and homework help. Though Kellan was really the only one that needed homework help.

"You guys want some fruit?"

Taggart hopped up on one of the bar stools that sat around the island in the kitchen. "Sure. What's for dinner tonight? I may need to skip it to go to the library."

Isabel made a negative clicking sound with her tongue and shook her head. "I'm making pot roast with mini potatoes and carrots. I also baked fresh rolls. You surely can't miss your favorite dinner for the library?"

Taggart smiled knowing that he would stay for dinner. As Isabel had definitely made his favorite dinner. She tossed him an apple and smiled knowing her trap was laid.

Meckenzie grabbed a pear and headed up to her room. She wanted to get her homework done before dinner so she could watch some TV tonight. Maybe some mindless humor from Monday night sitcoms would relax her. Meckenzie considered running to the store and getting something to help her sleep, but she didn't know the first thing about medicine and definitely didn't want to start some kind of dependency on pills to get her to sleep. Maybe an evening work out would allow for some much needed sleep to come.

Everyone settled down for dinner at six, as was the custom in the Desmond house. Their father had made sure to always be home for dinner. He often would leave after dinner to go handle business or meet clients for drinks, but he was almost always home for dinner at six.

"How was the meeting with the party planner?" Lawrence Desmond asked.

"I think we have everything set. They will be sending out the invitations as soon as you give me a list of people you would like to invite. I will email all the addresses to Doreen and her assistants will take care of it. We have the menu selected. Taggart and the designer Adam have tightened up the plans for decorations and table settings." Meckenzie laid out all the plans that had been made that afternoon so her father could feel like he was a part of the planning.

Their father turned to Kellan, "And what input do you have?"

Kellan laughed, "I helped with the menu. I was working with Coach Swanson for most of the meeting. I think Meckenzie likes being in charge anyway. I will just show up and look pretty."

Their father laughed one of his whole body laughs. He loved his children. You could see by the smile on his face that nothing they could say would change that. For a moment his face flashed with a sudden darkness.

"Well, I guess this is as good a time as any to have this conversation." Lawrence paused, "Your mother left instructions for you on your eighteenth birthday."

All three of the trips dropped their silverware and stared dumbfounded at their father.

"Your mother left letters for all three of you and a key to a safety deposit box to be given to you on your eighteenth birthday. I have been keeping them in the safe in my office. After dinner, we'll go get them and we can decide what to do."

Kellan was the first to react, "So for eight years you've been sitting on a letter from mom and never thought we might want to know?"

Their father's eyes flashed with a sadness that had lived there for the past eight years. He had truly loved their mother. Still to this day as far as the trips knew, he had never dated or shown interest in another woman. "I did as she instructed me to do in my letter."

Kellan stood up from her the table, "We should just do it now. I know I'm not in the mood to eat anymore.'

"Kellan, it'll still be there after we finish dinner." Taggart stated.

Meckenzie looked at her father and thought she saw the beginning of tears in his eyes. "Come on Kellan, let's finish dinner."

So everyone ate in silence not knowing what the next hour would hold for them.

CHAPTER 4

After dinner everyone moved into Lawrence Desmond's study. He paused before the wall safe hand poised in the air like he was about to defuse a bomb.

"I just want to say that I feel very wrong about this. I have struggled for the last eight years trying to decide what the best course of action was in regards to raising you three. I love you more than anything, and I never want to see you hurt. When your mother left it was the worst hurt we could experience. I know it was even worse for you three growing up without a mother. I was angry for a long time. She asked me to keep her leaving a secret from you guys. I knew she had gone of her own accord. She said that it was very important that we not come looking for her. It hurt me not to run out and try and find her. I loved her."

Meckenzie rose from her chair and went to hug her father. She knew this had to be hurting him. She loved him so much for being the strong person that he was. Her father had always held this family together with his love, understanding and strength.

"We know dad. Let's just get this over with so we can get back to our normal lives." Kellan's anger had not subsided one bit over dinner. It stung through the words she spoke.

Their father punched in the code to the safe and withdrew three letter size envelopes and one even smaller envelope.

"They are addressed to you individually. There is a key in this smaller envelope along with the bank address and box number. Do you want me to stay with you guys or do you want to be alone?"

The trips looked at each other; Meckenzie knew that asking him to leave at this point would crush him. Taggart smiled at Meckenzie knowing she would make the right decision. Kellan just shrugged, as she stared at her envelope.

"You can stay. I think we should each read our letters to ourselves and then decide what we want to do from there."

Everyone agreed. Lawrence Desmond sat down behind his desk to wait and began shuffling papers. He knew this was going to be a long evening. He had intended to go back to the office, why had he chosen tonight to address this issue, he thought to himself.

Meckenzie stared in disbelief at her envelope. Could this really be a letter from her mother? She never expected to hear from her again. She and Kellan had made up stories about where her mother had run off to when they were younger. It always involved some secret mission for the government or being a secret spy who was going to get caught if she stayed in the United States.

Kellan had already torn into her letter and was reading intently. Taggart like Meckenzie had a bit of trepidation regarding the letter. Finally they both looked at each other and tore the envelopes together.

As Meckenzie began to read, she thought she must have fallen and hit her head and this was all a dream. Maybe her mother was insane, because what was written here was unbelievable.

Dear Meckenzie,

I know this letter must come as quite a shock to you. I have over the last few weeks thought long and hard about what I would tell all of you, my darling children, in these letters. Each of you so unique. Each strong of spirit. Each of you so pure. I love you more than anything in the world and that is why I must leave. I must protect you from the evil of my world spilling into the innocence of yours.

I have left you a present that will give you more information about my family's history. You will be able to retrieve it with your brother and sister on your eighteenth birthday. Each of you is special. Not special in the way that every mother thinks of her children as special. Each of you has a gift. The gift will begin to develop around your eighteenth birthday. I have some ideas as to what each of you will be blessed with, but not a concrete idea.

Kellan will be of sound body. It might be that she is able to run fast, or that she is strong, or she may be extremely agile. She may be able to jump higher than others of her own build. She might even be able to grow larger when she feels threatened.

Taggart will be pure of soul. This could mean he will be able to make people feel what he feels. Or he might be able to convince people to do what he wishes. He might be a healer, which is to mean he can direct the evil spirits from a person's body.

You, Meckenzie, will be pure of mind. You could be extremely smart. You might be able to move things with your mind. You might be able to read minds, or control minds. It might be that you have influence over people.

These are all parts of the Trefoil. That is your destiny. The reader, the healer, and the warrior. You are fairies.

There will be lots of questions. I have left someone to help you. Someone who will report to me on occasion. Someone to watch over you. Isabel will be able to help you. She is my cousin and was placed here for your protection.

Know that I love your father. I adore him like no one I have met before. I knew he had part Fae blood in him when I came to find him. I had never expected to love him, but I did. I hope that over the years he will understand why I have to leave. In the safety deposit box is a letter you should give him. I know that he will understand why I left when he reads his letter.

I hope to see you again one day. I know that you won't trust me when I say I never wanted anything but the best for you. Unfortunately that means me leaving you in order to protect you. I love you.

Forever your adoring mother,

Deidra

Meckenzie couldn't understand what could possibly have driven her mother away from them. The letter had only created more questions. And Isabel, her cousin? She looked up to find Taggart staring at her. Kellan was seething.

Taggart was the first to break the silence. "Well, I'm not sure if that helped."

Their father sat silently, waiting for someone to include him in the knowledge that was obtained from the letters. His eyes darted to each of his children, a protective wave of emotion emanating from him.

"Did you know that Isabel was mom's cousin?" Kellan said without really addressing anyone.

Taggart laughed, "That's what you bring out of your letter. Isabel?"

Kellan wadded up her letter into a tight paper ball, "That and the possibility that our mother was looney."

From their father's dumbfounded expression, it would seem he was not aware of the familial connection. He whispered almost inaudibly, "No."

Meckenzie stood up from her chair and handed the letter to her father. He began to read, slowly absorbing the information from the letter.

Meckenzie stood staring at nothing, wondering if she understood any of the things in the letter. Was it possible that her mother had gone crazy before she left? Fairies? And with special gifts?

Meckenzie felt a headache sneaking into the back of her head. She had never been sick a day in her life and for the last two weeks she had been plagued by headaches.

Taggart came to stand beside her, lightly placing his hand on her back. Almost instantly the pain in her head subsided. Meckenzie flipped around, unbelieving, could it be that Taggart was a healer.

"What?" Taggart said.

"You're a healer."

"Do you really believe this? I mean do you believe that you can read minds."

Meckenzie flipped her head back and forth from Kellan to Taggart. "Think about it, you have wanted to be a doctor as long as we can remember. I was getting a headache, you touched my back and it went away. Kellan is faster than she was six months ago. I mean she can almost beat me by a mile when we run five. Kellan, I bet you have noticed a difference in your strength and speed."

Kellan didn't respond, but her eyes told the truth. There was a difference.

Their father sat in silence. He's mind working overtime. As he struggled with the new found knowledge, he began to rummage through his desk. Like a man possessed, he threw papers everywhere. He then went to the bookshelves on the fire side of the room. They held all of the antique books our great grandmother had collected over the years. Lawrence Desmond searched frantically through every title on the shelves. He stopped at one very old leather bound book with gold leaf lettering.

As he pulled the book from the shelves he turned to his children.

"When I was younger, your great grandmother used to read me stories from this book. I remember sitting in the garden and looking at the beautiful pictures with her. She would tell me all the tales of the Fae, the fairies. I remember one about the clan of the water fairies. These fairies had every few generations the blessed gift of a triple birth. Three children blessed with extraordinary gifts."

He stopped and flipped through the book. Finding what he was looking for, he went over the leather sofa and sat beside Kellan; encouraging Meckenzie and Taggart to join him.

"I had always assumed they were fairy tales." At this he laughed. "But I believe she may have been speaking about her family." Meckenzie sat down beside her father.

"Your great grandmother was larger than life. She had this whimsical nature that was contagious. She could tell stories that would enthrall you. We would sit in the garden and she would bring out this book." He patted the cover of the leather bound volume.

"She would tell the story of a set of triplets that were destined to save the land of Aquinas. The land of the water fairies. They were each gifted with talents that were part of the legend of Trefoil." He flipped the book open and found a brightly colored page. The art work was intricate, drawings of waterfalls and forests, all surrounding a castle that perched on top of a cliff overlooking the sea.

Their father wistfully sighed, lost in his own thoughts. "I have heard the story from her lips a hundred times. The Legend of the Trefoil. It was a story about a set of Triplets that ruled the land of Aquinas. The castle was attacked by the Clan of Tine. The fire fairies of the South. They wished to control all the Fae kingdoms. They had intended to kill the younger two of the triplets and take the older prisoner. The battle that ensued would kill over half of both clans. His plans never came to fruition though and as a final act of vengeance, the clan leader of Tine climbed the walls of the castle and snuck into the bedroom of the oldest of the triplets. He planned to assassinate her in her sleep. She had dreamed of him coming and been given the gift of future sight. She was told to transfer her and her siblings' gifts into a necklace of three hearts that when combined made a three leaf clover. The necklace in its clover form would be given to the heir to the throne, her daughter. Each heart was forged of platinum and a heart shaped sliver of the stone of souls. The stone of souls was a crystalline formation found deep in the caves of earth fairy territory. There were legends that the stone held the magic of all of the Fae. So the stone was set into the lockets, and when their gifts were transferred to it, each stone would take on the color of one of the triplet's power. Green for the pure of body, red for the pure of soul, and blue for the pure of mind. The process of transferring the gifts had left her weak. She knew that her death was coming, so in an act to save all of Fae kind, she produced a great spell that would render her assassin and his clan powerless for seven generations upon her death. So with a swing of his sword, his power left him, but the strength of her spell and her life given was enough to bind all of the Fae's powers. He was killed immediately by the guards waiting outside the door. And with her sacrifice, the queen of the North ensured her progeny powers with the possession of the necklace. Every generation chooses an heir to the necklace from the children and children's children of the Trefoil, as the triplets would be known for all eternity."

He paused and flipped the page. "The legend is that in seven generations the Trefoil will be reborn. To protect the people of Aquinas from the revival of the Tine. I believe your mother believes that is you three."

Kellan threw her wadded up letter across the room. She retched as if her insides were being torn apart. "I'm going to my room." And with that Kellan stood up and stormed out of the room.

Taggart and Meckenzie sat in silence, their father flipping the pages of the big book slowly. He stopped at one page with a detailed drawing of three hearts of the necklace. In the center of each was a beautiful intricately carved gem. The lower part of the drawing showed how the three could be placed together forming a what seemed to be a three leafed clover. Meckenzie felt as if she had seen the locket before.

Her father spoke, "Your mother wore this."

Then in an instant Meckenzie had flashed back to a memory. Her mother sitting in the garden, humming softly to herself. The necklace catching the sun light and creating rainbows. "I remember." Meckenzie said softly.

Taggart stood up and walked to the windows of the study that overlooked Central Park. "Do we have to wait till our birthday to go to the safety deposit box?"

"I believe we should talk to Isabel first," their father said.

With that the three of them left the study. As Meckenzie and Taggart made their way up the stairs, Taggart took Meckenzie's hand. "I think we should go talk to Kellan. She seems to be taking this awfully hard."

"Let's go get her and take her to the garden. I feel like being in the garden."

Meckenzie knocked on Kellan's door. Kellan didn't respond so Meckenzie opened the door and called her name, "Kellan?"

Kellan sat at her desk staring at her laptop. She looked as if she had been crying.

"Kellan, let's go down to the garden. We can talk about it or not. Let's just get some fresh air."

"Why did she have to go? What could possibly have been so bad that she would leave us? I just want to scream at her."

Taggart strolled across the room and began rubbing Kellan's back. He looked like he was going to cry too. "I don't know what is real, or what to believe, but I do believe she thought she was protecting us. Let's get some fresh air."

The trips headed downstairs to the garden. It seemed like days since they had been down there with the party planners, though it had only been earlier that afternoon. The party seemed like such a foreign idea. They had all been so ready to celebrate their eighteenth birthday. Ready to come of age and to get started with the adult lives they were planning. Now there seemed like more questions than before and more uncertainties.

They sat quietly for a while just taking in the night air that was scented with night blooming jasmine, roses, and other flowers.

Meckenzie finally broke the silence. "I've been having these weird dreams. I've been getting headaches. I hear a buzzing in my head whenever that new guy Ty is around. Do you think these are all part of the gifts?" She said to no one in particular.

Kellan shifted uneasily in her seat, "I ran 100 meter in 10.52 today. The world record is 10.49. My coach about wet herself. I benched 275 the other day. It's weird but I jump higher too. I don't know if this is real, but something is really weird about my speed and strength. I think the coach secretly wants to test me for steroids."

Taggart laughed. "Maybe we should just get some sleep. Are we still running in the morning?"

Meckenzie nodded. They all headed up to their rooms. Meckenzie hoped she would be able to get some sleep, two or three hours a night was not cutting it.

CHAPTER 5

The girl running through the woods was in Meckenzie's dream again. She ran for her life, something glittering around her neck, something familiar. She dodged branches, leapt over broken trees and bushes. Her breathing heavy, her face contorted into fear, she ran. Then she grabbed some flowers off a plant as she ran past. The flowers, pinkish-purple in color, were immediately consumed by the woman. As she chewed, she continued to run. She came to an archway, no not an archway, a place where the tree branches had grown together in a way to make it look like an archway. As she ran through the archway she disappeared.

The dream didn't stop there as it normally did. The woman appeared again, but now she was under the Trefoil Arch in Central park. The woman stepped out into the park, looking over her shoulder. The light was fading out of the sky in the distance, it was twilight. The woman headed down the pathway towards the streets of New York. As she walked under a lamp in the park, her necklace sparkled. The hearts from the legend of Trefoil hung around the woman's neck in a perfect three leaf clover. And as if in recognition of Meckenzie's discovery, the woman looked up.

Meckenzie gasped awake. "Mom." The woman in the dream had been Meckenzie's mother, Deidra. She had been running and she had the lockets.

What was she running from? Where was she going? And when had this happened? Or had it even happened at all, maybe it was just a dream and Meckenzie had substituted her mother into the dream. Meckenzie flipped on the light next her bed, suddenly aware that she was sweating and short of breath. It was like she had been running along that path with her mother. She crawled out of bed and headed to the bathroom. As Meckenzie splashed cold water on her face for yet another night, she knew she needed more than anything to talk to Isabel.

If Isabel was really her mother's cousin, then maybe she would know if the dream were true. Was this Meckenzie seeing the past, or was she seeing the future. Perhaps it was all some subconscious illusion that her mind was creating due to lack of sleep.

Meckenzie climbed back into bed hoping to get a few more hours sleep. As she lay in the darkness, memories of her mother came flooding back. Deidra had always seemed very young, never a wrinkle on her face, always a twinkle in her eye. There was something so beautiful about her mother. The way her hair, golden and flowing, had created a gossamer effect. Only more enchanting were her eyes, like the clearest blue of the purest water. She had seemed tall, but tall to child could sometimes not mean tall to a teenager or adult. Her thin frame was strong enough to carry two of her three children on her hips at a time. Even when they were older, Meckenzie could remember being lifted off the ground by her mother so that a kiss could be placed gently on her nose or cheek.

It had seemed like a lifetime ago since Meckenzie had heard her mother softly singing in the garden, or the family had gathered in the sitting room to play games, or she had experienced the love of her beautiful mother. It had been eight years since her mother had sat in this very room braiding Meckenzie's hair or listening to Meckenzie tell stories of her day.

Then one morning without warning, Deidra was gone. When the children had awoken to start their day, their mother was gone without a goodbye. Gone to protect them, but from what?

With this last question, Meckenzie drifted off to sleep. She was not awoken by the dream again this night. She woke instead to the sound of Kellan calling her name.

"Meckenzie, it's time to run."

Meckenzie rolled over to look at the clock in her room. Six a.m. She had slept through most of the night, and she felt alive and well rested. Meckenzie leapt out of bed and quickly changed into her running clothes. Grabbing her iPhone and headphones she headed downstairs.

Kellan and Taggart were waiting for her in the kitchen, already stretching out their muscles.

"Good morning sleepy head." Taggart said with a smile. "How did you sleep?"

Meckenzie smiled, "Amazingly well thank you. Though I did have the dream again. It played out a little more; we can talk about it later."

Taggart and Kellan both seemed surprised that Meckenzie didn't want to recap her dream right then and there. Meckenzie just smiled and stretched some more.

Kellan laughed, grabbed a her iPhone and headphones. "Any of you slackers think you can beat me today," she said as she bounded for the door.

Taggart laughed and headed after her, with Meckenzie right on his heals.

The trips headed into the park. The sun was rising over the horizon. Before long the city would be a bustling lit metropolis. But for now, the trips were alone with the other early morning joggers, pounding their way into another glorious day.

They started their run together, all jogging at a reasonable pace along the trail. Meckenzie could tell that both Kellan and Taggart were holding back to her own pace. Taggart tapped Kellan on the shoulder and motioned for her to go ahead if she wanted. With that, Kellan took off at a much faster pace clipping along through the park almost at a sprint.

Taggart smiled at Meckenzie, "She really is getting fast."

"Yeah, she has been leaving me behind for months now. I would definitely say something is up. Whether we have some kind of super fairy powers, or she has been hitting the juice, Kellan is faster."

Taggart laughed out loud, "Juice? Kellan is way too proud to juice." He paused, thinking to himself. "You want to talk about the dream?"

"When we are all together." Meckenzie stopped. She knew that the revelation that their mom was the woman in the dream would make her seem slightly insane. She really hoped that Isabel would be at the house before school. It wasn't her normal routine to come before the trips went off to school, but somewhere in her mind, Meckenzie wished that Isabel would know that they need answers.

Before Meckenzie knew it, they had clipped out three miles of the run and were heading into the fourth mile. Meckenzie saw the Trefoil Arch up ahead. Taggart was lost in his own iPhone, so Meckenzie tapped him to get his attention. She pointed to the arch ahead. Taggart looked up and shrugged his shoulders.

"I saw someone under the arch yesterday. They were gone by the time I got to the arch though, but I felt like I was being watched."

They both looked at the arch again. Just as they did, something or someone moved in the shadows. Slowing down, they glanced at each other again. Taggart looked at her and back to the arch. He then sped up almost sprinting toward the opening. Meckenzie tried hard to keep up, but was losing ground fast.

While they were still sixty yards away, someone stepped out of the shadows. The stranger was wearing a long flowing cape making their face impossible to see. The person reached next to the arch then grabbed something from the bushes and fled back to the shadows of the arch.

As Taggart reached the entrance to the tunnel under the arch, he stopped. Meckenzie came up behind him gasping for air.

"There is no one here." Taggart managed to say between the gulping of air.

"Did you see them though? Did you see whoever it was come out of the arch and grab something out of these bushes?" Meckenzie leaned over the bushes next the opening of the arch. There to her amazement were the same flowers she had seen in her dream. "Oh my gosh!" She exclaimed.

"What?" Taggart jumped. "What is it?"

Meckenzie broke some the flowers off the bush, holding them in her hand, examining them.

"What? It's just Heather." Taggart responded.

"Let's go back to the house. I'll explain there. This plant was in my dream."

Taggart shook his head and started jogging through the tunnel under the arch. The two of them headed home. Meckenzie knew this was a weird coincidence. Hopefully Isabel would be at the house to help clarify a few things. There were so many things that Isabel needed to tell them, things she had known all these years and kept to herself. Meckenzie hoped she was ready to share her secrets and maybe help them discover the truth in all of this.

CHAPTER 6

When they arrived back at the house, Isabel was not there yet. Meckenzie suggested they get showers and get ready for school. She only wanted to tell her story once, and she wanted both her siblings and Isabel to be there.

Meckenzie ran upstairs, the flowers of the Heather plant still in her hand. She sat them on her dresser and got her things ready for a shower. She knew there was only a small window of time to get ready for school and possibly speak to Isabel. Meckenzie wanted more than anything to blow off school, that way she could just go through all the events from last night and this morning with Isabel.

Climbing out of the shower she heard Kellan calling her name.

"In here."

Meckenzie grabbed her towel and headed for the bedroom. No one was in the room. She stuck her head out the door of her bedroom thinking that maybe Kellan was in the common room their two bedrooms shared. No one was in this room either. Meckenzie got dressed and put her hair into a pony tail. She grabbed her school books and bag. She decided to check Kellan's room before heading downstairs.

She knocked, but there was no response. She knocked again calling out her sister's name, "Kellan."

"Meckenzie!" She heard it loud this time coming from behind her. She turned, but no one was there. Meckenzie opened the door to her sister's room, she searched for the light switch in the darkness, flipping it on and illuminating the empty room. Kellan's bathroom door was open and dark inside. Meckenzie quickly ran across the room and flipped on the bathroom lights as well, but no one was there.

She headed for the stairs thinking that maybe Kellan was already in the kitchen. Meckenzie couldn't understand why she had heard her sister's voice so clearly, as if she were in the same room or at least on the same floor.

As Meckenzie passed Taggart's room on the third floor, she knocked on his door and told him she would meet him in the kitchen. She passed her father's study on the second floor; he sat behind his desk talking seriously on the phone. Meckenzie waved and headed down to the kitchen. She reached the kitchen only to find that no one was in this room either. Where had Kellan gone? Meckenzie decided to check the two lower floors for Kellan.

The lights were all out on the garden level. Meckenzie took a quick peak into all the rooms anyway, but no there was no sign of Kellan. As she reached the sub terrain level, the lights were burning in the gym area.

"Kellan?" Meckenzie shouted over the music playing on the speaker system. There was no response, but all the lights would be out if no one were down here. Surely Kellan had been down here at some point. Meckenzie stuck her head into the changing room that the family had added for all the swim parties the kids had thrown over their childhood.

"Kellan?" There was still no response.

Meckenzie headed to the weight lifting area to see if Kellan had possibly been too busy to hear her sister's beckoning. As she rounded the leg press that Kellan had begged her dad for during their freshman year, Meckenzie saw Kellan lying unconscious on the floor. Her right forearm lay at an odd angle and seemed to be bleeding.

Meckenzie quickly opened her cell phone and dialed Taggart's number. She ran to Kellan, grabbing a towel off one of the pieces of equipment hoping to stop the bleeding. Quickly she checked Kellan's pulse.

"Kellan can you hear me?" Moaning Kellan stirred, but did not open her eyes. Her pulse seemed fast. Lying across Kellan's body was a free weight pole and several weights were scattered around the floor.

Just then Taggart answered the phone, "Why are you calling me and why aren't you in the kitchen?"

"Kellan is hurt in the gym. Get dad and come downstairs."

"What happened?"

"I don't know, it looks like a broken arm and she is bleeding."

Taggart yelled up to his father, "Dad, Kellan's hurt in the gym."

Meckenzie could not hear her father's response, but Taggart was yelling back at him the same things she had previously told him about Kellan's injuries. Then Taggart hung up the phone.

Meckenzie lifted the pole off her sister and sat it to the side. She couldn't decide if moving Kellan would hurt her more, she just knew she needed to get the bleeding stopped.

Taggart came bounding down the stairs, "Meckenzie?"

"Down here." Meckenzie was gently pressing the towel against the open wound created from the bone piercing the skin where it had broken. She tried not to move the arm afraid she would cause more bleeding. Taggart slid in beside Meckenzie and removed her hand from the towel.

"Has Kellan been unconscious since you found her."

"Yes."

Taggart lifted Kellan's army gently and tried to evaluate the damage. Their father rushed down the stairs with Isabel behind him. As Taggart touched Kellan's arm trying to clean away any blood, a strange thing started to happen. The bone seemed to be sliding back into the skin.

Lawrence Desmond turned pale as he rounded the corner into the weight area. He blocked the path for Isabel who was trying to get around him.

"Lawrence, you have to move so I can get to Kellan." Isabel prodded him out of the way and came to kneel on the other side of Kellan.

"Taggart, what are you doing? The bone is moving back into her arm." Meckenzie said.

Isabel lifted Kellan's shoulder and rotated her arm to match the angle of the broken bone. "If we line the bones up, and Taggart places his hands on top of the bones, I believe her arm will heal."

Taggart said nothing, he simply moved the forearm into place and then placed his right hand on top of the exposed bone. As they sat there for what seemed like an eternity, Kellan began to moan.

In less than a minute, Isabel removed Taggart's hand from Kellan's forearm. Meckenzie couldn't believe her eyes. There was no visible sign of trauma except for the blood that had begun to dry on her arm and the floor.

Kellan's eyes fluttered open. She jerked up out of everyone's hands. Sitting amongst them, all silent, all confused, Kellan examined her arm with unbelieving eyes.

Before she could say anything, Isabel spoke. "I think we should all go up to the kitchen and have some breakfast. I'll explain what I can."

Taggart drained of all color, stumbled to get up.

"Taggart will be a little weak from the healing. Maybe he should take the elevator." Isabel suggested. And with that, their father took Taggart by the arm and helped him up. Their father helped Kellan off the floor, and then they headed for the elevator. Meckenzie stared at Isabel, unable to process what had happened here this morning.

Isabel offered Meckenzie her hand to help her off the floor. As Meckenzie reached out to take it, there was a flash of blinding light in her mind. It was like static electricity pulsed directly from Isabel's fingers into Meckenzie's brain. She jumped back. "What was that?"

"What dear?" Isabel asked.

Meckenzie, untrustingly, looked into Isabel's eyes. Her eyes were the same color of blue as Taggart's. Her hair was darker then the triplets, it was brown, but had streaks of blond in it. Without pause, Meckenzie asked, "Are you our mom's cousin?"

Isabel laughed, "Well, I can see that cat is out of the bag. Let's say that we are kin. Cousin is a term we could use. I'm more like a great-great aunt though. I am Deidra's great aunt. I was your father's grandmother's cousin. You'll find that our family tree is an interesting twist and turn of events. Let's head up stairs and I'll fix you guys some breakfast. Taggart is going to need some special herbs to regain his strength."

As they headed up the stairs, Meckenzie tried to grasp the full extent of what had happened in the last twenty-four hours. It seemed almost impossible that they had met with the party planners yesterday. That the new kid Tynan had only started class yesterday morning. That they had just read their mother's letter last night. How was it that so much had changed in such a short period of time? Meckenzie didn't know how much more she could take till she would need to check herself into a mental institution. She was obviously going crazy if she believed all this was true and happening.

Isabel set to making breakfast by pulling out eggs, fruit, and bagels. "Maybe you should ask any questions you have now while I prepare breakfast or would you prefer I tell you story of how I ended up here?"

"You said that you are our great-great aunt? How old are you?" Meckenzie asked, Isabel didn't look much older than forty-five, so how was it possible for her to be their great-great aunt?

"I'm in my late forties. My father was married twice and I came from the second marriage. I was not really planned, so I was born only a few years after your mother. I was sent to live in the castle where your mother grew up. We were very close even with our ten year age difference. Diedra trusted me, so she sent for me when you were young, to help protect you. Then her brother was assassinated and she had to return to rule Aquanis. So I was then responsible for protecting you and helping to raise you."

McKenzie spoke first, "I don't know what to make of all this but maybe we should tell you what we know. Also, I think maybe I should tell everybody about the dream I've been having. I don't know how much time we have before school, maybe with everything that's going on today we should call in sick. I think we really need to figure out what's going on before we put ourselves in the public eye."

At this Lawrence Desmond went to the phone. He dialed the number to the school and waited patiently pushing buttons that he must have been prompted to push by the schools automated phone system. He then explained that his children would be staying home today due to a family emergency. After he was done he placed the phone back in the cradle and went back to his barstool silently, he stared at his three children.

Kellan had yet to speak since this morning's incident. Taggart seem to be lost in his own thoughts still looking pale and drained from his morning's experience. He sipped on tea that Isabel hadslipped in front of him.

Isabel spoke first, "I take it that the letters have been read."

"Yes, after dinner last night we sat down and read our letters." Kellan looked at her hands as she spoke. "I, for one, am hesitant to believe anything in them."

Taggart looked at her shocked, "Even after this morning?"

"I don't know what happened this morning. I was setting up the free weight bar, then I woke up and everyone was there."

"Kellan, your arm was broke. The bone was sticking out. You can see that you bled all over the place and Taggart healed you. I don't know how you cannot believe what was written in the letters now. Everything points to them being true and why would Mom lie to us?" Meckenzie said the last sentence with pain in her eyes. She was hurt by her mom's leaving, but she still didn't think that her mother would lie.

"Why would she leave us?" Kellan looked at her arm, "I just don't know."

Isabel interjected, "So let's say for the arguments sake that the letters are true. Let's also say that Taggart healed your arm this morning. And that each of you has a special gift that was bestowed upon you through your family lineage. You must understand above all else, that your mother loved you and if it was not for the war that is waging now in our land, she would be here. Diedra would never want to hurt you. She would never lie. Now, let's hear your dream Meckenzie. I think I can help explain a few things."

Meckenzie began to recount her dream. Explaining that it had been happening for weeks and that until last night it had ended when the woman had placed the Heather plant in her mouth and disappeared. Then she went on to tell them about last night's dream. The fact that it was their mother in the dream and the fact that she exited the Trefoil Arch. Meckenzie also explained how she had seen the lockets around her mother's neck.

Isabel set plates of food in front of the family. She paused a moment after Meckenzie's story. Trying to find the words to explain what Meckenzie had seen.

"Your gift allows you to see the past, it would seem. You have seen your mother's journey to this world before you were born. Diedra came through the passage at the Trefoil Arch. She came here to find you," she said pointing at Lawrence. "Your grandmother had left Aquinas to start a family amongst the humans. She knew that the time of the war would be upon our people in less than a century. Her idea was to come here and start a family so that the blood line might live on, even if our people were destroyed. Several families did this."

"She brought a fairy tale book, we saw it last night." Taggart added.

"Yes, though to us, it is not fairy tales as you would think of, it is our history. The war that began the incubation of gifts was fought over power. The Clan Tine, also known as Fire Fairies, have long coveted the land of Aquinas. It was once the High Kingdom of all fairies. There King Treigold ruled all the clans. He was a fair and just king, but his son only wanted power. He set out to acquire an army, and from the Clan of Tine he drew much of his warriors. He wished to rule, though his father was still King. When he marched upon Aquinas, the king met his son on the hills with only a small contingency of soldiers. He banished him from Aquinas and threatened to bind his powers if he did not leave and never return. The fight never happened, and King Treigold separated the Clans into four distinct governments set to rule themselves. The Water clan, which you came from, held the land of Aquinas in the North and has lived there ever since. The Tine Clan, or fire clan, was relegated to the south. The Earth clan, or the Talamh clan, took the land to the west. The Air Clan, or Aeris, took the east."

"Each clan built their strongholds and began to brace for the eventuality of war. The Talamh built fortress of earth in the mountains. They have a beautiful city built upon a cliff that is only accessible through a series of tunnels that run deep into the mountain. The Aeris can control the wind and are quite ingenious. They have built floating islands that dwell among the clouds. The Tine have built their homes of fire and metal, using the hottest volcanoes to forge the metals to build their fortresses."

"King Treigold's son, who was known as Trienan Raven, dwelt with the Tine. He stroked the fires of their jealousy by claiming that Aquinas should belong to them. They forged weapons and armor and trained to kill. This was new to the fairies, as it was never our way."

"Trienan created an army that would march across the land killing out whole villages that refused to join his new kingdom. During this time, King Treigold died. The kingdom was then passed to Trienan's sister, Evelyn. She had never intended to rule the kingdom. Her gifts lay in healing, not leading. She had three children, triplets, two girls and a boy. They were being groomed to rule the Water Fae as a Trefoil, a balance of power."

"Evelyn had taken to healing all the refugees who had entered the land due to Trienan's war. She would heal dozens in a day. And as you can tell by Taggart's state, healing takes its toll. Every time a fairy heals someone, a bit of their essence leaves them."

"Evelyn had gotten herself so worn out, that she could not even eat or drink. She instructed her children to prepare to take the throne as she would die soon. The oldest of the three had the ability to see the future. She foresaw her mother's death and the path that the three must take to bring peace."

"So they set forth to rule the kingdom in a threefold plan. One they would build an army. The youngest, Sarah, was a warrior, she was strong of mind and body. Sarah raised the army and trained them for the inevitable fight. The middle triplet, Johan, was a healer, he set to building up the stocks of healing remedies and healers into a centralized location. Johan set up a sort of a fairy hospital. The oldest, Katirin, created a think tank of mind readers and future seers, together they consulted the future and sought out the paths to peace."

"Trienan, hearing of the new government had an idea to grab the throne and the power. He would assassinate the two younger triplets and take the older one hostage. He would then marry his niece and take the throne. Katirin had a dream to this effect."

Meckenzie interjected, "This is the part that we have read, this is when the necklace was created and the powers were bound."

"Yes," said Isabel, "and for generations, the fairy have been without powers, but some powers have come back over the last few years. Everyone in Aquinas believes the war will come back to our doorsteps soon. That is why your mother went back. The descendants of Trienan have begun building an army."

"Do you have powers?" Taggart asked Isabel.

"No, I have been trained in the art of espionage and self-defense though. So I was volunteered to come and stay with you while your mother was away. I have always been here to protect you."

"So when Deidra hired you before she left, she knew she was leaving. You worked for us for two years before our mother left."

"I was being trained to come to protect you since before you were born. It was known then that there would be a Trefoil. You three were the first triplets born to a royal family in eight hundred years. Your mother was never intending to leave you, her brother was assassinated and she had to return to rule."

Meckenzie suddenly stood up. "Wait. You said you were our great grandmother's cousin and our mom's great aunt, does that mean that mom and dad were related?"

Isabel laughed, "In a way."

"Ewwww." Kellan said.

"It is not as close as you would think. Your family tree is a direct line from King Treigold. His daughter Evelyn's son Johan was the only surviving child from the original Trefoil. His son Tristan had two son's Sedric and Josiah. Your mother is the great-great-great-great granddaughter of Josiah. Your father is the great-great-great-great grandson of Sedric. Which makes them fifth cousins."

"It may seem strange to you, but the Fae have a tendency to marry their cousins, many human royalty do the same thing. It is just the way life is. Your parents' marriage was, although probably not known to you Lawrence, destined. When your grandmother came here, it was to protect the lineage so that one day, one of the line of the kings could come here and have the Trefoil in another place. So they might be protected from assassins. Your great grandmother Katirin was full Fae, and her son Taggart, whom you are named for, married a full Fae. Your father married a full Fae. Now your blood line is only fractional human. It was the only way to make sure that the powers were passed on, and yet protected." Isabel continued "You are royalty among the Fae and will be welcomed back as royalty should."

"Wait," Lawrence interjected, "Welcomed back? You mean to take my children to a place that is in a state of war."

"That was always the plan." Isabel said.

"No! I will not allow it. I will not allow you to drag my children into a war that they are not a part of."

"I am afraid that the war will come to them if we don't take them back. It is only a matter of time until someone figures out they are here."

Kellan angrily spoke from behind tears that had begun to fall down her cheeks. "Will we see mom?"

"Yes."

Meckenzie couldn't believe what she was hearing. She was expected to go with Isabel, who she had known almost her whole life, but who had been hiding her true identity. Could she really trust this woman? Was getting to see her mom enough for her to march off into battle for something she knew nothing about?

42

"What could we possibly do to help with a war? We are not even eighteen yet." Meckenzie added.

"You have more power than you know. Your simply being there will uplift the spirits of all of Aquinas. Plus, I will begin training you. You all have much to learn about what your powers can do."

"Will we go soon? Will we get to finish high school? There are only eight weeks left, I mean I have plans. I was accepted to Harvard and I want to be a doctor." Taggart interjected.

"I don't know when we will go. I do know that we have some time. I hope that we can hold out for a year. I need to train you as much as possible. Luckily you are all very smart and physically fit so you should be able to catch on pretty fast."

Lawrence Desmond stood up and left the room. He knew he was losing his children and he didn't know what to do. So he decided to go, he thought he might be able to clear his mind if he was away from them for a while. He needed to stop this, but he could tell his children were being swept up in this new found adventure. He could not lose them too. He didn't think his heart could take it.

Isabel and the trips watched him silently leave the room. They had seen the look on his face before when their mother had gone and knew he needed some time to himself. He had lost so much in his life, letting him leave was all they could do.

CHAPTER 7

After the day's events, everyone decided they were a little tired. Taggart headed off to his room to lie down. Kellan decided to swim to clear her mind, since Isabel thought it too soon for her to lift weights again. That left Meckenzie with Isabel. Meckenzie had so many questions. Where should she start?

Isabel motioned for Meckenzie to follow her. They headed to the garden, fresh air was definitely what Meckenzie needed. She was stuck in a swirling vortex of information that she could not wrap her mind around. Everything kept popping in and out of her thoughts, it was a serious case of information overload.

Isabel sat in one of the patio chairs and motioned for Meckenzie to sit opposite her. Isabel sat motionless and stared at Meckenzie; it was a little bit unnerving at first. Why had she brought her here Meckenzie? Then Meckenzie began to relax. A wave of relief washed over her as her mind cleared of all the thoughts that had been swirling about.

"What are you doing?" Meckenzie questioned.

Isabel smiled, "While I don't have any powers, I have been trained in the art of spell casting. One of the spells I'm most proficient at is a *ciúnaigh* spell, it is a calming spell. It should allow you to focus a bit of that energy you have buzzing around you."

Meckenzie felt wonderful. She hadn't been this calm in months. Not since the dreams started. "Can you teach me that?"

"Soon. Let's talk a bit about your dream. When did they start?"

"A couple of weeks ago. It was only once a night for a while. But now every time I close my eyes to sleep the same dream comes. It went the furthest it has ever gone last night. I had never seen the part of my mother coming through the archway to New York before. I can't remember seeing the necklace in the dream before last night either, and the heather plant. My mother grabbed heather before she vanished and then appeared here. I had not noticed the plant until last night. This morning on our jog, I saw some heather beside the Trefoil Arch. Right before Taggart and I got to the arch we saw someone grab some off the plant and walk into the arch and then disappear."

Isabel looked shocked. "When was this?"

"This morning right around sunrise."

Isabel stood up and began pacing around the garden. She looked very worried. "No more running in the park. If someone knows the three of you are here, they could snatch you at the arch and take you back to Aquanis. If it is the Tine Clan then we would lose you forever. They surely have spies amongst our people. I think it is best that we send a message to your mother."

"How will you do that? I'm sure there is not cell phone reception in Aquanis. I'm sure you can't just text her, or email her. How will you get her message?"

"The same way I've been doing it for years. We have curriers that travel between both lands exchanging messages for our people that have come to this world to live without the threat of war. We have the need at times to hide things in this world as well. I'll call the currier and have him come here. Let your siblings know that if they want to send a message to your mother to write it out and I'll include it."

Meckenzie sped downstairs to find Kellan. She was floating in the pool on her back staring at the ceiling.

"Isabel is going to send a message to Mom. She said we could write her a note and she would include it."

Kellan looked at Meckenzie and shook her head. "I don't have anything to say."

"Don't miss this opportunity because you are being stubborn."

"I'm not being stubborn. I just don't know what to say yet, I need some time. I need to know what I want. I spent most of my life relegating myself to not having a mother. I planned a future and I threw myself into my sports. I want to play college ball. I want to work in sports. I don't want to fight a war." Kellan said the last part and thrust herself under water so she missed Meckenzie's next statement.

"I don't think any of us want to fight a war. I think we will have to though."

With that Meckenzie headed upstairs to find Taggart. She knew Taggart would want to send a message. He was always more level headed than Kellan. Always forgiving.

Taggart was lying on the sofa in his sitting area reading a book. He had this intense look of concentration on his face. Meckenzie remembered that look from when they were kids and would play games. Taggart always trying to figure out the easiest way to win. He had always been frustrated at Meckenzie's ability to win games, once she started winning, there was no defeating her. Meckenzie was a born strategist. She could look at a problem like a puzzle and work out the answer.

"Isabel is sending a message to mom. She said we could write a note and she would include it."

Taggart looked up from his book. Without saying anything he stood up and went into his room. Meckenzie climbed the stairs to her own room and went in search of a pen and piece of paper. She sat down at her desk and began to write.

At first she wrote Dear Mom. Then she wadded it up and took another piece of paper. This time she started Dear Deidra. That sounded way to impersonal. She had to decide what she wanted to say with this letter. Did she want to be forgiving or confrontational? What good could come from confrontation in a letter? So she started again.

Dear Mom,

It is so weird to write that. I don't know what to say really. I have always wondered what I would say if I ever saw you again. I have had those conversations a million times in my head. I guess the one I had most often was the one where we rushed into each other's arms and cried.

I miss you and it is hard not having a mother. I am sure it was even harder leaving your children, but I am grateful we had dad. He is doing well by the way. He is lonely I think and works way too much and I think he still misses you.

I know we will see you soon. Isabel has told us that much. Kellan isn't taking this well. She has so much to lose by leaving this world, Taggart too. I still haven't decided what to do with my life, but it seems that destiny has decided for me. I don't know what else to say, so for now I'll say I love you. I miss you and I can't wait to see you.

Love Always,

Meckenzie

Meckenzie folded the paper and headed downstairs. She met up with Isabel in the kitchen and handed her the letter. Isabel placed it into a wooden box along with two more folded pieces of paper.

"Kellan isn't going to write a note."

Isabel shook her head. She then placed small white flower in the box. She closed it and said some words that Meckenzie couldn't understand. As Isabel did this, she began tracing her finger on the box. It sounded as if she were scratching something into the wood. Then Meckenzie noticed the gold writing that was appearing on the box where Isabel had traced her finger. The symbols were not anything that Meckenzie had seen before. Isabel began getting louder and louder, the box seemed to hum with the energy flowing through those golden letters, then it stopped.

When she was done, Isabel turned to Meckenzie.

"That is a protection spell. Your mother and I have a specific way we relay messages about you. The box is protected by the spell and if it is opened by anyone other than your mother, the flower will turn to flames and burn the letters. She also knows that notes from me always come with a white flower. Sort of secret Fae code."

"So do you often communicate with mom?"

"Not as often as we would like. There are spies everywhere, in Aquanis, in New York. We can't risk the enemy finding you, so we send messages only in an emergency. I haven't actually received a message in months. I better head out to the park, which is where the messenger will meet me. You stay here; I can't risk someone seeing you with me and the messenger."

Isabel headed out and left Meckenzie with her own thoughts. What did she really know about her history? Just one story. Meckenzie went to the front windows just in time to watch Isabel head into Central Park. As she sat there lost in her own thoughts, she caught movement in the trees directly across from the window. Meckenzie could swear someone was there watching her.

Meckenzie closed the curtains and decided to run upstairs to her father's balcony. She was sure she was being watched, so she decided to take the higher ground and get a better view. Meckenzie stepped out on the balcony and walked over to stand in the shadow of one of the large plants flanking the ends of the balcony. From there Meckenzie could see the trees, the pathway, and well into the park. She scanned the area looking for anyone suspicious.

After scanning the area for a few minutes, Meckenzie determined it must be the creepiness of the stories they had heard today that had her thinking someone was watching her. She couldn't see the Trefoil Arch from here. Meckenzie wondered who Isabel was meeting. All these years and there mother had just been one magic box away. All these years she could have been asking her mother important questions.

Meckenzie was sure that Taggart would be okay after all of this, he was strong. Kellan, on the other hand, was sensitive despite her muscular build. She took so many things personally. It was possible that Kellan would never trust their mother, or Isabel, for that matter, ever again. Kellan could hold a grudge.

Meckenzie remembered one game of hide and seek the trips had been playing when they were younger. Taggart was it and Meckenzie and Kellan had run off to hide. Taggart found Meckenzie first and they decided to leave Kellan hidden and went and had a snack. When Kellan finally gave up, Taggart and Meckenzie were swimming in the pool. She hadn't spoken to them for nearly two days, which was quiet a fete for a ten year old. Meckenzie knew that the betrayal Kellan was feeling was a real emotion. Their mother had been trying to protect them, but it did not make the hurt any less. It was a gaping hole in their lives where a mother's love should have been.

At that moment Meckenzie spotted Isabel coming out of the park. She watched Isabel as she walked cautiously to the cross walk, watching behind her for anyone following. Isabel crossed the street and continued walking down the side street not to the front door of the house. Meckenzie began scanning the park for any suspicious movements. Meckenzie saw a large guy about her age emerge from the trees that she had been watching. His hair had the reflective darkness of a raven's feathers, it was long enough to cover his face. From Meckenzie's viewpoint on the second floor balcony, he seemed to be well over six feet tall and must have weighed more than 200 pounds. He rushed across the street, not waiting for traffic, and down the side street that Isabel had taken.

Meckenzie ran upstairs and grabbed her phone and her backpack that contained a cane of pepper spray. As she was headed downstairs, she passed Taggart in his sitting area. "Someone is following Isabel out of the park." She shouted as she sped down the stairs.

Taggart leapt off the couch and ran after Meckenzie down the stairs.

"What do you think you are going to do? Isabel is smart enough to keep herself out of trouble. Don't go getting yourself into some kind of trouble because you think it is your destiny to rescue the world." Taggart said the last part with spite.

Meckenzie wheeled around, ready for a fight. "Come or don't come, but don't lecture me. Isabel has been the closest thing we have had to a mother figure for a big part of our life and I will not let her get hurt protecting us."

Taggart followed her down the steps, already several steps behind Meckenzie. They headed toward the side street that Meckenzie had seen the rather large man follow Isabel. As they worked their way down the street, they looked inside the windows and doors of shops looking for some sign of Isabel.

"What did the guy look like?" Taggart said as they neared the end of the block.

"He was over six foot tall, 200 or more pounds, and dark shoulder length hair. He was wearing dark clothes, like a trench coat. I don't know anything else. He was a big fella."

As they got to the end of the block, Meckenzie saw the mystery man further down the street. Meckenzie began to run with Taggart trailing behind. She got about twenty steps behind the guy, when he suddenly turned around and stared right at her.

His crystal blue eyes seemed out of place amongst his strong features and dark hair, they seemed so pure. He had a scar from his right ear to the middle of his cheek that made him look a seasoned warrior. He was built like a tall boulder, pure muscle rippled under his dirty disheveled clothes. He seemed to be covered in a thin layer of dust that did not look out of place on him. It was like it was his second skin. His eyes searched Meckenzie's for some kind of recognition.

Taggart grabbed Meckenzie's hand and pulled her inside the coffee shop across the street. He weaved them through the crowd towards the back where a table with two chairs open faced the door. Meckenzie protested by trying to pull away from him.

"We have to avoid him figuring out who we are. If he is Fae, he might be looking for us through Isabel. We know he doesn't have her, because he is by himself." Taggart looked pleadingly into Meckenzie's eyes with his last statement.

Meckenzie knew he was right but there were so many questions she had, and she knew this man had answers. She could see in his eyes that he was looking for them. There had been a spark of recognition in the stranger's eyes as he had looked at Meckenzie, but he had made no move towards her, no move to hurt her.

Taggart stood up just as the mystery man looked in the door. "I'll get us some coffee. Pull out your phone and pretend to make a phone call."

Meckenzie did as Taggart had instructed her. She pulled out her phone, but instead of pretending, she called Kellan. As she held the phone to her ear, she once again made eye contact with the large stranger. He looked at her, once again recognition sparked in his eyes, but he moved on and didn't enter the coffee shop.

"Kellan"

"Yeah, are you in the house somewhere?"

"No, someone was following Isabel out of the park, so I took off to follow him and Taggart came with me. We are at the World Coffee around the corner. Can you check to see if Isabel has made it back to the house yet?"

"Sure, I'm in my room so let me run down stairs."

"You want us to bring you back a coffee or something?"

Kellan laughed, "You run off chasing some strange guy who is following Isabel and now you're taking my coffee order. You really are something you know."

"No reason to be impolite. Plus we are trying to look indiscrete, the strange guy spotted us following him and we ducked into the coffee shop to look inconspicuous."

"I don't see Isabel anywhere." Kellan said. "Isabel? You here?"

Meckenzie waited for Kellan to finish looking for Isabel. She hoped she would come home so that they could just grab their coffees and head back to the house. She could hear Kellan opening doors and shouting for Isabel.

"She's not here. You want me to come to you guys and we can search for her?"

"I think we will take our coffees and stroll back to the house the long way. Thanks Kellan."

"No prob."

As Meckenzie was hanging up the phone with Kellan, Taggart returned to the table with two coffees. "I called Kellan and had her see if Isabel had made it back to the house."

"Any luck?"

"She isn't there. I think we should take our coffees and go for a casual stroll back to the house. Maybe going down the way he was facing and then doubling back to the house in a couple of blocks."

Taggart and Meckenzie headed out of the coffee shop. They headed southwest for a couple of blocks then doubled back in front of the Natural History Museum. Meckenzie spotted Isabel sitting in front of the Museum looking intently at some brochures. She met Meckenzie's eyes and made the slightest head shake indicating that they should not acknowledge her.

Meckenzie grabbed Taggart's attention, "We should head home."

Taggart looked confused, "Isn't that what we are doing."

"Yes, but I spotted Isabel. Don't look. She indicated that we should just head home."

As they entered the front door, Kellan was waiting for them by the window.

"I've been watching for you guys. No sign of Isabel."

"She's sitting in front of the Museum." Meckenzie replied.

"So what exactly happened," Kellan asked.

"Isabel went to meet the courier that would be delivering the messages to mom. She headed off into the park and I thought I saw something in the trees, so I ran upstairs to Dad's balcony to watch. As she was leaving the park, some large guy followed her from the trees right across from the house. They both headed down the side street. Taggart and I followed them, then ran into big scary guy across from Coffee World."

Taggart interjected, "He was kinda scary."

"Like what kind of scary? Creepy, drag you into the park and take advantage of you scary? Mug you in the side street scary? Or trying to take over the world kinda scary?" Kellan seemed more amused with her wit than actually interested in an answer.

"He was just scary. It's hard to explain. He was huge first of all and dirty. He seemed to be looking for Isabel. When he spotted us he followed us to the coffee shop, but didn't come in after us." Meckenzie remembered the dirt that layered his clothes, it was so curious. Like years of dust had been building up on him and he had never actually thought that cleaning it off was a good idea.

Taggart headed for the kitchen. "Let's have some lunch and wait for Isabel."

"That's a plan." Kellan and Meckenzie said at the same time.

CHAPTER 8

It was two hours later before Isabel made it back to the house. She had walked through the park and stopped and had lunch. She gathered the trips in the garden to have a talk about that morning's events. Everyone was on edge and their father hadn't been heard from since his exit during this morning's initial conversation.

The tension was hanging over the room like a fog rolling in from the ocean. Meckenzie couldn't help but feel an overwhelming desire to hide in her room and sleep, but she knew that sleep, no matter how tempting, would bring no relief.

Isabel started slowly, "I appreciate your concern for me Meckenzie. It was very brave of you to try to come save me. But you must understand, there is nothing that would hurt me more than for you to be discovered here. I cannot say this enough, you have to be careful. And running out into the street to follow someone who is following me is beyond careless."

Meckenzie opened her mouth to protest, but Taggart placed his hand on her.

"I think Isabel has a point. You put yourself in harm's way. That guy was huge and he saw you. If we hadn't ducked into the coffee shop and put on a heck of a ruse, I think he would have figured it out. That is if he hasn't already."

"He saw you?" Isabel questioned.

"Yes," Taggart responded. "He turned and looked right at Meckenzie, so I grabbed her hand and pulled her into Coffee World. We got some coffee and hung out for a minute. Then we headed further away from the house and doubled back. That's when Meckenzie saw you in front of the Museum."

Meckenzie thought about telling all of them how his eyes had met her own and that there had been a spark of recognition. She was sure that the stranger knew who she was, but she didn't know why he had not tried to harm her in some way. After a moments contemplation, Meckenzie decided not to share that information with the group, it would only worry them more.

"I think we have to do some protection spells for the house and you guys. I need to get a few things from upstairs, but you stay here. I'll come back and we'll try some things. I also want you to describe him to me, I never saw him. I just felt his presence."

Isabel ran up the stairs and left the trips to contemplate the upcoming spell casting.

Kellan was the first to speak. "What do you think this is going to consist of? We aren't going to have to kill a live chicken and drink it's blood are we?"

"Chicken?" Taggart was laughing so hard that was all he could manage to say.

"I think it is a reasonable question. I don't want any part of killing some animal so that we can be safe. I am not about to get all witchy because Isabel says we should." Kellan protested with a hurt look on her face.

"Kellan, I think it will probably be herbs and chanting. She did a calming spell on me earlier and all she did was chant some weird words and stare at me."

"I'm not sure I'm any more comfortable with that. I have some serious reservations about everything that is going on. I am not sure I want any part of this." Kellan responded. She seemed to be lost in some thought process as she stared at the water bubbling in the garden fountain. "I really would just like everything to go back to normal. I love you both, but I'm not sure I'm willing to put my life on the line for people I don't know."

"I'm not sure we are going to have a choice. If everything that we are being told is true then we have people coming after us and they don't seem like the type of people who would just let us disappear into the world. The guy from earlier was huge and he looked like he could hurt someone without even trying. Plus he had some battle scars that looked like he may have already hurt someone." Taggart stumbled through this statement trying to get Kellan to snap back to reality. "I know that we had lives planned. I'll never be a doctor now. I don't think that is really fair, but I don't think I have a choice."

Kellan burst out, "A choice! We have a choice. We can just send Isabel away and just ignore it all. I don't think they will come for us if we don't have Isabel here drawing attention to us and she is the one that went into the park and exposed us. She is the one who wants to do magic and the one that wants to take us back. Dad would support us. He would protect us. We can just disappear into our lives. I could go play ball. You could go to Harvard. Meckenzie could..." Kellan paused. "What is it that you would do Meckenzie if we didn't have to go rescue a world of fairies?"

"I don't know." Meckenzie responded. "I think I've been drifting through my life because this is what I'm supposed to do. I won't lose some future I haven't planned. I don't want you guys to have to give up your plans, but I don't think I can do this on my own. I think we have to do it all together."

Kellan began to speak when Isabel started back down the stairs. She paused knowing what she would say would only met argument from both of her siblings and this woman who was here to protect them. She just couldn't imagine that any of this was really the way life was supposed to turn out for her. Kellan needed more proof.

Isabel looked at the group with fascination. "With all this tension and quiet, it would give a girl the impression that you guys were talking about me."

"What do you expect? We are being asked to believe a story that is written in a fairy tale book. We are being asked to give up our lives for people we don't know. Did you think we would just all sign up and go to our deaths for you because you say you're our great-great aunt or whatever?" Kellan's anger was turning her complexion a curious shade of crimson. She seemed to be growing larger, her body was expanding. It was like she was one of those balloons in the Macy's Thanksgiving parade.

Isabel looked at Kellan and giggled. This only instigated Kellan's anger more. She didn't know what was happening to her.

"Kellan, look at me. Breath. Your experiencing something called *ar fheabhas fás colainn*. It roughly translates to super body growth. Your anger has triggered it, so you have to relax. Let Taggart and Meckenzie hold your hands, we are going to calm you. Everyone hold hands."

Meckenzie and Taggart took Kellan's hands which were already twice their natural size.

"Now you two join hands and we are going to repeat the *ciúnaigh* spell I used earlier. So everyone close your eyes."

Kellan looked horrified as she stood there at well over seven feet tall. Tears began to roll down her cheeks. She was losing some of her anger as fear took over. She seemed to have stopped growing.

"Now repeat after me. Ciúnaigh reacht. Ciúnaigh stuaim. And then repeat it. Ciúnaigh reacht. Ciúnaigh stuaim."

Isabel started circling the triplets as she spoke these words aloud. Taggart and Meckenzie picked up the chant, finding the right resonance and annunciation. Finally Kellan joined in and it felt as if a low voltage of electricity was flowing through their bodies in a circle.

Then with a jolt, Kellan began to shrink back down to her normal size. She slowly returned to her normal self and the group dropped their hands. Everyone was exhausted.

Isabel was excited. She didn't seem exhausted, she seemed rejuvenated.

"That was fantastic. You guys are so much more powerful than I thought. Kellan you seem to have a very special gift. I've only heard of one fairy that could ever *ar fheabhas fás colainn*, King Treigold. You are truly the progeny of the King."

"So all you have to do is get me really angry like the Hulk." Kellan said in a huff. "Kellan grow big." She said mockingly. "I guess I should be glad I didn't turn green."

Taggart laughed, "You were a little red in the face though."

"I'm glad I could amuse you." Kellan laughed, though tears still stained her cheeks.

The mood seemed to lighten. Meckenzie wondered if the spell had worked on all of their moods. She had a sense of well-being that everything was just alright.

Isabel sat on the wall of the fountain and watched the triplets closely. They had done something amazing. They had cast a spell so effective that it had returned Kellan to her normal state without taking hours. It would have taken Isabel and several other fairies hours to effect any change in Kellan. The power in these three was so great that they could perform great feats, if she could just get them focused and on the right track.

"You three are very powerful. That spell should not have worked so fast. It is a sign of your power that it only took minutes. I believe with a little training you will be great and powerful Fae rulers."

The trips looked at her confused. Rulers? Were they intended to rule Aquinas?

"Rulers?" Meckenzie was confused.

"Of course, you are the heir's to the throne. Your mother rules Aquinas now. You will obviously rule the kingdom, you are the Trefoil. With your power you will free all the kingdoms and unite them again to be ruled peacefully." Isabel was obviously as happy as a kitten. She seemed to not see the problem with this scenario. In order for them to rule, they had to leave their home and they had to fight a war. They had to win, yet none of them had been trained to fight or trained to rule.

Isabel stood and began organizing the materials that she had brought downstairs with her.

"We will start by casting a protection spell for the house. It will work like a smoke detector. When someone enters the house that means you harm it will sound a warning buzz. Anyone with enough Fae blood will be able to feel the buzz, so we will need to warn your father about them." Isabel started piling some shiny black stones in front of the trips. "We will need to place these throughout the house next to doors and ground floor windows. But first we have to cast the spell on them."

Meckenzie picked up one of the shiny black stones that Isabel had placed in front of her. They were round, smooth, and black. She thought they might be obsidian.

"Is this obsidian?"

Isabel smiled, "No, they are the hearts of gnomes. Gnomes are the guardians of the passages between lands. It is considered an honor among the gnomes to have you heart taken after death. If the heart is pure, it is the best stone for protection."

Meckenzie dropped the stone. It landed on the floor with a ping like it was hollow.

Isabel cried out, "Careful! They are very rare. We would be at a loss if we broke one."

Taggart picked up the gnome heart and placed it on the top of the stack of hearts.

"Taggart, place the hearts in three triangles with their points touching, it should look somewhat like a clover. Meckenzie take this powder and draw a circle around the hearts. Kellan, drink this tea; you are probably drained from the change and the spell casting. Don't worry it's just herbal, no chicken blood." Isabel was trying to lighten the mood; she didn't know how accurate her comment was to Kellan's fears.

"Okay, the three of you will stand at the base of a triangle outside the circle. I will speak the words with you, but you will be performing the spell. So like before you'll need to join hands and close your eyes and speak the words clearly. The inflection is important, so listen carefully."

The trips took their positions and joined hands. They closed their eyes as Isabel began to speak.

"Cosain culdin. Cosain colainn. Cosain intinn. Cosain anan. Daingnigh croi seo. Okay, when it is working the hearts will glow red for a moment. You should be able to feel it. Like a humming in your body. Okay, ready."

They all nodded. They were all a bit scared. Meckenzie was curious as to how they would know the hearts were glowing red, seeing as how their eyes were closed.

Isabel began the spell again, "Cosain culdin. Cosain colainn. Cosain intinn. Cosain anan. Daingnigh croi seo. Cosain culdin. Cosain colainn. Cosain intinn. Cosain anan. Daingnigh croi seo."

The trips began to recite the words over and over again in the same cadence as Isabel had taught them. The buzzing began in their hands, slowly working its way up their arms. It was like the hum of electricity coming from the power lines. It gradual worked its way into their chests. Spreading down to their feet, and finally working its way into their heads. As they continued their chant, the world seemed to fade away. The only thing in existence was the three of them, the humming and the words they were speaking which seemed to hang in the air around them.

Just when Meckenzie began to think that the spell wasn't working, there was a faint red light that was growing in the center of her mind, it began to take shape. It was the triangles of hearts that Taggart had built. Each stone became clearer, glowing red like an ember from a fire. The glow throbbing in time with the cadence of their voices.

As if some internal alarm had informed them that the spell was complete they finished the last word of the spell and opened their eyes.

"Did it work?" Kellan asked.

"You tell me, what did you see?" Isabel answered.

"For me, at least, I saw the hearts appear as they are here, but glowing red. They keep time with our words, then they glowed bright red and solid for a moment and we stopped." Meckenzie responded.

"What did you feel?" Isabel asked

"It was like a buzzing of electricity. It started in my hands and worked its way up my arms. Then, it filled my chest and traveled down my legs with the buzzing sensation. Finally, it filled my head and that is when the hearts appeared in my mind." Taggart chimed in.

"Then it is complete. How do you feel?"

"Tired." All three responded at the same time.

"Then let's place them around the house. We'll do it together so that you know where they should be. We will start by leaving one here in the garden, over here near the wall." Isabel placed one of the hearts in the ivy that grew up the wall that faced the street.

"Then we will need to put one near the front door. They do better if they are near soil, so preferably in a potted plant. We will need to move a plant into the elevator and place one there. Though I doubt an intruder would use the elevator, it is better to be safe than sorry. We'll place one on every floor."

They set off on their task of setting the protection hearts throughout the house. Ending their task on the top floor next to the door that led to the roof patio. Meckenzie realized that it would be better if Isabel stayed with them from now on. She knew she should talk to her father before moving Isabel into the house, but it seemed like an emergency. They did have the spare room on the top floor and with all that was going on, the more eyes the better.

Just as she was about to ask Isabel to stay, Taggart looked at her.

"Did you say something?" He asked. He knew that she had not spoken out loud, but he had definitely heard her.

"No." Meckenzie replied.

"I heard it too." Kellan said.

Isabel looked at the three of them. "What were you thinking Meckenzie?"

"I was thinking that you should stay here, in this room. That it was better to have you here with all that was going on. That the more eyes we have here the better."

"That is what I heard," said Kellan.

Taggart interjected, "Me too."

"Let's try something." Isabel walked over to Meckenzie. "Face me, and think of a number between one and five. Put up the number of fingers so I can see them. Then try to send the number to Kellan and Taggart."

Meckenzie faced Isabel and thought of a number. She held up two fingers and concentrated on sending the number to her siblings.

"Two." They said together.

"Good. Try it again." Isabel said.

Meckenzie held up a fist.

"Zero." They both responded.

"Okay, I think you might have a couple of talents. Though it is possible that you share a bond that allows you to communicate with each other."

Meckenzie remembered hearing Kellan's voice this morning while she was laying hurt in the gym. She had forgotten all about it and she hadn't told anyone that she had heard Kellan. Could Kellan have been calling out with her mind?

"I heard Kellan this morning in my room. I heard her call my name, and I went looking for her. That is when I found her in the gym with the broken arm."

Isabel smiled, she seemed to be enjoying this day more than the trips. Every hour revealed something amazing.

"Let's try it with Taggart. Turn around and we will do numbers again. But this time we will use one through ten."

Taggart turned around and put up seven fingers. He then projected the number in his head.

This time only Meckenzie responded. "Seven."

Kellan looked confused. "I didn't hear anything."

"Let's try it again." Isabel said.

Taggart held up one finger and waited.

This time Meckenzie paused to see if Kellan would get it. Maybe she had just been too fast.

Kellan began to laugh, "One, but it was Meckenzie's voice I heard not Taggart's."

"So it seems that Meckenzie can send and receive messages. Since you three performed the spell earlier, she may be tied into your brains. So it is really easy for her to hear. I think we have all had enough excitement for today. I'm going to go get my things from my apartment, I'll be back in an hour and then I'll make protection charms for the three of you. Don't leave the house and try to get some rest, eat something. You'll need to cast the spell on the charms after I complete them."

Isabel headed downstairs and left the siblings to their own devices. Meckenzie walked into the spare room to check the sheets and towels. The sheets would probably need to be changed. No one had slept in the spare room in a very long time.

"I'll get some sheets. You are really loud in my head right now." Taggart shouted as he headed down the stairs.

Kellan joined Meckenzie in the guest room and sat down in the chair.

"This is really happening isn't it."

"Yes it is. I think we just have to accept it."

"Well at least you got something cool as a power. I turn into a she-hulk."

Meckenzie's eyes grew sad as she replied, "I'll trade my dream for your she-hulk any day."

CHAPTER 9

When their father returned home, he found his children and Isabel preparing dinner. There was little evidence of all the events that had happened that day. Everyone seemed to be in a very good mood.

Taggart was setting the table, and though no one had openly discussed it, he set five settings. Isabel had not previously taken her meals with the family, but since she would be staying as a guest, the trips had decided to treat her as one. Lawrence Desmond noticed immediately the number of place settings, but did not say a word.

Meckenzie and Kellan began bringing in dinner and took their places at the table. When Isabel started into the room with the chicken she had roasted, she was surprised to see Taggart holding a chair out for her.

"Sit here beside me Isabel." Taggart said.

Isabel smiled at him and took her place at the table.

"Let's make a deal not to talk about anything fairy related at dinner this evening." Lawrence said.

They all nodded their heads in agreement and began serving themselves.

"How was your day dad?" Meckenzie asked.

"It was very busy. I have a couple of big deals coming up, so I've been preparing for those. I have also decided to take a couple of days off for your birthday and I thought I might be able to help with the preparations. We also have to make a trip to the bank, though I did say we wouldn't discuss that at dinner."

"I was thinking we could change the fabric on the patio furniture. It might be nice to match it with the color scheme we have chosen for the party." Taggart stated.

Meckenzie giggled, "Maybe Adam can help you find someone to reupholster the cushions. He might also be able to show you some fabric swatches that would match what he is going to use."

"Who is Adam?" Their father asked.

"He is the designer that Doreen is using for the party. He was here yesterday with her so he could sketch the design for the ballroom set up." Meckenzie replied. "He took quiet a fancy to Taggart."

Lawrence Desmond blushed at this statement. He cleared his throat as if he was going to talk, when Taggart spoke up to save him the trouble of addressing the issue that his son might have taken a fancy to Adam as well.

"Meckenzie is just trying to start something because she thought he was cute. So I had to save him from her admiring looks." Taggart started to laugh.

"Oh Taggart if only you were into boys, Adam would be such a catch." Kellan threw in her two cents worth at this point and the whole table was laughing before dinner was finished. No fights, no spells, and no fairy talk.

As Isabel began clearing the dishes from the table, Meckenzie took the lead on speaking to their father about the day's events.

"Dad, I think we need to talk to you about today. Do you want to do that now?"

"Let's go up to the study."

The three siblings followed their father up the stairs and into the study. Meckenzie silently communicated with her brother and sister.

"I think we should start with the fact that we sent letters to mom. Then the guy in the park. Then the spell that is protecting the house. Then we should tell him that Isabel is going to stay with us."

Taggart and Kellan both nodded in agreement.

Their father sat in one of the wingback chairs and the trips took the couch.

"Well, what has happened?" Lawrence asked.

"First, after we and Isabel talked, she decided that there was reason enough to warn mom that we might already have been spotted by some of the Fae. So she sent her a message via a courier that can travel between the worlds. She allowed us the option of sending a message along with hers. Taggart and I sent one, but Kellan decided against it." Meckenzie paused to judge her father's response. He remained calm and unemotional, so she continued.

"Then when Isabel went to meet the courier in the park, she felt like she was being watched. She had given us strict orders to stay in the house so that we wouldn't be spotted with her. I was watching from your balcony when I saw Isabel come out of the park and a guy was following her."

Meckenzie paused again to judge her father's reaction.

"I guess I acted a little reckless, because I grabbed my phone and pepper spray and went to follow them. Taggart caught me coming down the stairs and came with me. We had lost them, but as we turned the corner a couple of blocks away, we ran into the guy. He saw me, but I don't think he knew anything was up. Taggart pulled me into World Coffee and we got some coffee and hung out for a few minutes. Then we continued on away from the house and doubled back a few blocks away. On our way back we saw Isabel hanging out in front of the Natural History Museum. She indicated from a distance that we should head home and not acknowledge her. So that is what we did."

This time Lawrence Desmond could not hold his tongue. "That was very careless of you. I am very glad you made it back okay, but you are both still teenagers. You could have been hurt, or killed. Neither of you is trained to protect yourself. I don't want to lose you before I have to."

"That is why when Isabel got back, she thought we should cast a protection spell on the house. So we did. You might see some little black stones in various locations. They are part of the spell." Taggart interjected.

"Spells? What is a spell going to do? I think I would feel better if I hired someone to protect you three."

"That might help, but the spells that Isabel taught us really do work. We did a calming spell this afternoon to help Kellan. Also, I think it would be hard for one person to guard all three of us, our schedules are so different. There is just so much going on, how are we going to explain to a security person that we are possibly being followed by fairies." Taggart was being very level headed with his arguments. Meckenzie thought it might be better if he informed their father of Isabel's staying.

I think Taggart should tell dad about Isabel staying. Meckenzie projected to her siblings.

Taggart took the lead again, "Also, we invited Isabel to stay here in the guest quarters. She has the most knowledge about what we are possibly looking for. She also said she could sense the guy this afternoon. So maybe Isabel would be able to sense if someone was watching us. She is making some protection charms for us. I'm not sure how they work, but I'm sure they will help with our safety. Isabel is going to train us over the next few months, so we need her close. Also, all of us will carry pepper spray and our cell phones. I think it is best if we just return to school tomorrow and try to live as normal as possible."

Their father sat silently for a moment. Then he stood up and went to his desk. As he shuffled some papers around he seemed to be thinking about what his children had said.

"I will agree to Isabel staying here. I will also hire a security guy to follow you to school and home, if possible leave together. I know that Kellan has workouts after school. So as long as you call the guy when you are getting ready to leave, I think it will be fine. I will call the security company tonight, so expect him here tomorrow. Also, no more running in the park, you can use the treadmill in the gym instead."

They all agreed. Their father seemed to be dealing with all the day's events really well. Meckenzie sent a thought to her siblings.

I think we should not tell him about Kellan's new talent. I also think that we should avoid telling him about my new mind trick.

Taggart and Kellan nodded again, this was coming in pretty handy. The three of them could communicate if necessary without anyone knowing. Meckenzie wished she had come into this talent earlier. She might have done better in school for one. Meckenzie was an above average student, but she could have been way above average.

The three siblings left their father's study and went to find Isabel. She was still in the kitchen cleaning the dinner mess. Meckenzie and Kellan began helping her clean up. Taggart found a pen and paper. He thought it might be important to write down some of the stuff they had learned today. He wanted to remember the spells and learn as much about all of their new talents as possible.

Taggart really did feel like they were on the brink of doing something amazing. If he could just resolve himself to the fact that his lifelong dream of being a doctor was about to be shattered into a million pieces. He would still be a healer, but he had just always imagined being able to hang that diploma from Harvard on his wall.

"I'd like to take some notes about the spells and our gifts." He said to Isabel.

She turned to him and smiled. "I thought you might say that, so I brought a book from Aquinas that I had in my apartment. It has other spells and description of gifts that people had in the past. I think you'll find almost everything you are looking for in it. I just ask that you not try any spells before talking to me about them. I don't want something to go awry."

"I think I can handle that. So should we start on the protection charms?"

"Sure, meet me in the garden?" Isabel said.

Kellan asked, "Is there a reason we always meet in the garden?"

"Yes, spells like the Fae have created work better among nature. Especially if you are surrounded by all four elements of the Fae nature, Earth, Air, Fire, and Water. So that is why we sit in the garden, with the soil, the open air, the fire from a candle, and the water from the fountain."

With that explanation Isabel went to grab her bag from beside the front door and they all headed to the garden yet again.

Isabel pulled a candle from her bag and lit it, sitting it in the middle of the open space by the fountain. She then pulled three leather bracelets out of her bag. She handed one to each of the trips. They were intricately woven leather with a clear crystal set in behind two pieces in the center of the bracelet.

"Tie them on your right wrist, so the stone is against your skin. Then stand around the candle and join hands. We will use the same spell from earlier. It will work in a similar way. You will feel the buzzing of the spell work its way through you, then in your mind's eye you will see the clear crystal. It will then burn bright and change color."

"What color?" Kellan asked.

"That depends, it is never the same. The crystal represents your spirit and your spirits are different. Each of your gifts represents a different color. I will say that the crystals that are in the Trefoil charms were clear until the original Trefoil transferred their powers into them. They are now red, blue and green. I imagine that the same thing will happen with your bracelets."

They took their positions and joined hands. Isabel began chanting the spell again and the trips joined in. Soon the buzzing was working its way through their bodies. They soon saw the crystals in their minds eye. The bright flash of light that exploded from the vision made them all flinch a little, then it was over.

Each of them flipped the leather over to see the color the stone had turned.

"It seems that your stones have taken on the colors of the Trefoil. Be sure and keep the stone against your skin, it will help fuel the protection charm and keep the stones color out of sight if anyone should see you with them on. I'm sure that when you receive the Trefoil necklaces that they will match the stones in your bracelets. Now, I think we should all retire for the evening.

You guys will be going back to school tomorrow and we have the arrival of the security guard your father hired."

"How did you know that?" Meckenzie asked.

"You are transmitting quite loudly right now. I think it is because we have done so much spell casting today and because of our familial link. I'll start teaching you shielding techniques soon. We will have to start individual training soon. All of you will need different training, though some spell casting training will be needed. We'll talk about it tomorrow after school."

With that, Isabel left and headed up to her room. The triplets all sat down in the garden. No one spoke for a long time; everyone was caught up in their own thoughts.

Meckenzie was trying to not transmit her thoughts to her siblings. Kellan was thinking about working out. It had been a long day and she needed some endorphins to keep her mind clear. Taggart wanted to study the book Isabel had given him, but he thought his sisters might want to talk, so he had not left to go up to his room yet.

"Can you hear me in your head?" Meckenzie asked.

"Not since before the spell." Taggart responded.

"I'm trying not to transmit; I think it might be weird if at school tomorrow someone hears me, since I'm not entirely sure how this works."

"I think I need to swim, or run, or something. Anyone want to come?" Kellan asked.

"Nope." Taggart responded, "I'm going to take the book Isabel gave me and head up to my room to study it."

"I'm going to try to sleep. I haven't' had much sleep this week." Meckenzie felt tired, but she still had tons of energy running through her body from the spell casting.

"Maybe if we do the calming spell, you'll be able to sleep." Taggart said excitedly.

"We could try." Kellan added.

They all joined hands and began the words to the calming spell that Taggart found in the book.

"Ciunaigh reacht. Ciunaigh stuaim." The triplets began chanting and soon the buzzing feeling took over them again.

Meckenzie began to feel an overwhelming sense of calm. She felt peaceful and tired. She knew she would sleep well tonight.

They all stopped chanting at the same time. All three of them smiled and dropped their hands. There was nothing else to be said; they all felt the calming effect of the spell, so they went their separate ways for the night.

CHAPTER 10

The next day Meckenzie awoke feeling refreshed. She was happy to report to her siblings that she had not been revisited by her dream and she had slept the whole night through. The calming spell they had performed last night had carried through to her sleep.

The three decided to walk to school together, since they were going to have to keep an eye out for anyone following them. They were met at the front door by a young military looking guy who must be their new bodyguard. Meckenzie stumbled out the door, her eyes never leaving the gorgeous man standing in front of her. He caught her as she tripped, his strong arms holding her up so she didn't tumble down the front steps and out into the street. He smiled and introduced himself as Jones, his eyes sparkled their grey color mesmerizing Meckenzie. He was tall and fit, but not incredibly bulky, like he was a swimmer. Meckenzie thought about asking for his first name, but he had introduced himself as Jones. Not Mister Jones, not Mike Jones, just Jones.

Meckenzie giggled at the idea of this man's mother calling him Jones. He didn't seem to mind the giggling and probably assumed that the giddy little teenager was feeling a little teenage lust, which wasn't entirely false. That initiated Meckenzie's giggles to escalate. Taggart elbowed her and smiled. She must have been transmitting because even Kellan had an evil grin on her face.

They spent part their walk to school testing their mental communication abilities. Meckenzie acted as the conduit and the three were able to have full conversations without saying a word. Isabel had mentioned that doing this too much would probably cause Meckenzie to become tired and worn down, so they should limit their experimentation to when they were at home, but they thought a little pre-school practicing would be ok.

As they sat down in their chairs for first period, Meckenzie decided to communicate her uneasiness about Ty. He had not arrived to class yet, but she had a feeling that he was somehow linked to all of this.

I don't like the new guy, Ty. I think he may be involved in this all somehow. Meckenzie said mentally to her siblings.

He is a little creepy, but do you really think he is involved. How can we test it without giving ourselves away? Taggart thought.

I'm not sure, but maybe we should all keep an eye on him. We should probably not communicate mentally unless absolutely necessary. Meckenzie knew that if he was involved, he would be looking for hints. The trips had not mastered hiding the facial expressions involved in conversation, so when they were speaking mentally, sometimes they had facial expressions that did not fit the particular situation they were in.

Just as Meckenzie was setting up mental road blocks in her head, like Isabel had showed her how to do over breakfast, Tynan walked into class. Immediately, there was a buzzing sound that was pushing against Meckenzie's mind. She had felt a similar buzzing when they had performed spells, but this buzzing seemed more aggressive. Meckenzie touched Taggart's hand and made a quick eye dart to the door. Taggart looked up and saw Tynan staring back at him. Taggart moved his chair closer to Meckenzie so that he could touch her with his knee under the table. He hoped that this would help her to keep from experiencing whatever she was experiencing, because her eyes looked wild and angry.

With the touch, Meckenzie began to relax and the buzzing dissipated. She was sure now that Ty was pushing against her mind somehow. If only she could find a way to test it. She considered for a moment reaching out her mental hand and pushing against his mind to see what he was thinking.

Meckenzie thought this might tip him off to who she was, so she decided against it. There had to be a way to determine what was going on with Ty and the buzzing that always occurred when he was in the room.

Ty made his way across the room like a snake slithering through the grass towards its prey. Meckenzie couldn't help but feel the urge to run. She did the opposite however, and smiled at Ty as he sat down at their table.

"Good morning." Ty said.

"Good morning." The trips responded in unison.

"We missed you yesterday. I was tempted to think that you didn't like me and were going to switch classes." Ty smiled, "I like your bracelets, I don't believe I saw them before."

Meckenzie knew now that this was his way of testing them, "Oh you like these, we got them at a street fair last year. Some woman who sold crystals and sacks full of herbs to ward off all kinds of things sold them to us. She said they were each for something different. Mine is for knowledge, Kellan's is for strength, and Taggart's is for money. I think that is what she said. Right Taggart?"

Taggart was dumbfounded with the exchange he was seeing. Meckenzie seemed to be trying to charm Tynan into believing everything was not as it was. Taggart knew that it would take more than a story about a witchy street fair sales woman, but he played along.

"Yeah I think so, though I could have sworn mine was for knowledge and yours was for money," he laughed as he said the last part.

Tynan gave a wry grin as he responded, "I think they are actually protection bracelets, my aunt used to make something similar to them for an internet website she ran. People will buy anything off the computer these days."

Kellan, who had remained silent during the exchange added, "I saw where someone was selling their appendix that the doctor had removed on eBay. Who would possibly want someone else's rotten appendix?"

Just then the teacher began class. Meckenzie couldn't see any way around discussing the exchange at this moment. She decided to see if she could create a mental block around her thoughts and place them into the heads of her siblings.

I'm going to try doing this mental telepathy thing by placing the thoughts specifically in your heads and no one else's. Taggart, keep an eye on Ty. And when you respond, try putting the thought in a box that is just for me. Has Tynan reacted? Meckenzie knew this was risky, but there had to be some advantage to them being the Trefoil.

Taggart looked up at the teacher, trying to watch both the front of the class and Tynan who was to his left. *I don't think he can hear you. What was the bracelet story about?*

I wanted him to think that there might be some logical explanation as to why we had some kind of magical bracelets on. I didn't think telling him the truth was what we should do. Do you think he believes us?

No. I think he is trying to figure us out right now. He keeps looking at you through the corner of his eye. I would almost venture that he will try to ask you out on a date. I think he wants to get inside your head. Kellan added.

I can't date him. I'm not even sure I could pretend to go on a single date with him. What do I do?

Just then the teacher called Taggart's name. Meckenzie searched the heads of other students and the teacher to find the question, and then placed it into Taggart's mind. He either was paying attention or it went more smoothly than planned, because he never missed a beat. Taggart answered the question without hesitation.

Thanks, Taggart looked down at his book and flipped the page. *I don't think I have ever not answered a question in this class. I'm sure Mr. Humphries would have had a field day with it if I had not had the answer. I think we should talk at lunch. I don't want to push the chance that someone will figure us out. This was awfully risky of you Meckenzie*

Meckenzie began to protest, but she agreed and the rest of class went smoothly. Several times Meckenzie caught Ty staring at her. He always had a devilish grin on his face. Meckenzie wondered if she was imagining the grin. Maybe she was imagining that he was somehow out to get her. She was a little paranoid lately, with good reason, but still a little paranoid. She decided to ask Isabel what she should do if this boy asked her out. Would the advantage of putting herself in danger be worth the reward of any information she might get from going on a date with him? If he was a Fae spy, then it would make sense that he would know what her mother looked like, and since Meckenzie looked so much like her mother, it was reasonable to think he saw the resemblance. This was a war, and if they were going to bring the war to her, then she would have to respond by gathering as much information as possible. The best way to do that would be for her to appear unknowledgeable and go out with him. Maybe he would let something slip. Meckenzie believed that if things were planned well enough, then she could probably handle the situation. She was pretty sure that if he asked her out, she would go.

Meckenzie laughed out loud at the idea that her first date might actually be with someone who ultimately wanted her dead, everyone in the class turned towards her, so she blushed and looked down at her book. Meckenzie had never really wanted to date. It was not that she hadn't been asked, or that she didn't have an interest in boys, she had always just wanted to get through high school and college without the distraction of some romance that might not last pulling her down. Meckenzie knew eventually someday, love would push down her walls, she just didn't think it would be some high school boy only interested in a little action. It would be someone like Jones the bodyguard, with his grey eyes and strong arms; she blushed at her school girl crush.

The rest of the morning dragged on and it was a relief when the lunch bell rang, Kellan and Meckenzie quickly found Taggart and headed off to lunch together. Most often they ate separately with friends, or in Taggart's case, on his way to the lab or studying somewhere quiet. They decided to head across the street to a sandwich shop that was probably only in business because of the school. It was always busy at lunch, but Taggart had enough foresight to text their order in a half hour early, so their food was ready when they got there. They picked up their order and headed for a small park-like area beside the school. They were able to find a bench that was unoccupied to have their lunch and discuss things. Meckenzie scanned the area to see if anyone they knew was hanging around or listening.

"I feel like we talk more now than we ever did before," Kellan stated while opening her sandwich.

"I hope that through all of this we get closer and not father apart. It would be easy for all of this to get the better of us and lose sight of the fact that we are brother and sisters. I like that we are talking more." Taggart added.

Both of her siblings looked at Meckenzie expecting an addition to their comments. She bit into her sandwich and thought to herself that she wasn't sure they would all come out of this. The foreboding feeling she had all morning was getting stronger. Meckenzie wondered if they could tell something wasn't right. She knew that she needed to stay positive, but something was telling her that there was something about to happen that would change them all.

"I think something is up with Ty. He freaks me out. I don't know if it is just normal boy stuff, or if it is something else, but I don't like him." Meckenzie felt like saying more, she just couldn't put her finger on what it is she wanted to say. She knew he was really interested in the three of them, but Ty was also new at school and maybe he was just looking for friends. He also seemed to come with a buzzing noise that constantly went off in Meckenzie's head whenever he was around. She knew from the little experience that she had that this was associated with magic. Meckenzie felt the buzzing directed out of her whenever they had performed the spells that Isabel had taught them.

Kellan kind of giggled. "You have always kept your distance from boys Meckenzie. Maybe he just has a crush on you and you don't know how to respond."

"I don't know. She does get those buzzing headaches when he is around, that can't be normal. Today when he came into class, our connection was enough that I could feel the buzzing, not in my head, but like you were letting me feel it through our connection." Taggart added.

"You could feel it?"

"Just enough to know that something wasn't right. Then you touched me and it subsided. That is why I shifted toward you so we could touch and you could concentrate. I thought if Ty was doing it, then he might be aware of our connection and be able to tap into it while we communicated silently."

Kellan looked at the two of them with disbelief.

"I don't want to become this conspiracy theory person." Kellan stated. "I just want to live as normal as possible for as long as possible. If I had my way, I would ignore the whole thing and go to college and live my life. I really can't do this right now."

Kellan was getting angry. Meckenzie thought that Kellan had dealt with her feelings of denial, but it seemed that Kellan was just trying to go with the flow. Well that didn't seem to be working right now.

Taggart reached out to touch Kellan's hand, but Kellan jumped up from the bench. "I have to go. I'm going to work out after school, let that freaky security guy know. He has been standing over by the side of the building watching us this whole time. I just can't deal with this, I need to be alone."

With that, Kellan stormed off toward the school. She had always had a temper. Of the three of them, Kellan had always been the one to have the least amount of patience with the other two. It was a good thing that Taggart had an overabundance of patience and Meckenzie was blessed with an overabundance of love. They always seemed to forgive Kellan of her temper, and she especially liked to direct it at them from time to time.

Once when they were kids, she had accused Meckenzie of being too weak. She had locked Meckenzie in a closet by pushing a table in front of the door. Kellan had then said she wouldn't let her out that Meckenzie had to push the door open on her own. Taggart tried to convince Kellan to move the table. He had even tried to move it himself, but Kellan had been stronger than both of them even then. She had pinned him to the ground and sat on his chest. It had been Isabel who had finally come along and removed Kellan from Taggart's chest and opened the closet door.

Isabel had punished Kellan by sending her to her room for the rest of the afternoon. Meckenzie hadn't cried at all, that was until she snuck into Kellan's room and told her she still loved her. Kellan's response had been that she didn't care and she could never love anyone as weak as Meckenzie. Meckenzie had snuck off and cried in her own room so Kellan couldn't see her tears. Then the next day Kellan acted as if nothing had happened. Meckenzie just went along with it because she loved Kellan too much to ever hold it against her.

Kellan had always pushed her siblings away. Meckenzie had always thought that it was her way of seeking individuality in a situation where people always thought of them as triplets. So this situation was no different, they were once again triplets in a situation where they were expected to act as a unit and not as individuals. It would take a lot of love and patience to get Kellan through this.

"I think we are going to have to be extra patient with Kellan. She is going to resist this at every turn. I think that we should do something special for her. Maybe we can convert part of the gym into a boxing ring and convince Dad to hire someone to come in and teach us self-defense. I think Kellan would eat that up. She would love the physicality of it."

Taggart agreed. They finished their lunches in silence. Meckenzie could feel that Taggart wanted to sneak off to study or work in the lab. Taggart was nothing if not predictable. She felt like keeping him with her for comfort. He relaxed her so much, especially knowing that somewhere on the campus Ty was lurking.

Finally Meckenzie broke the silence, "I can tell you want to go study, so why don't you go ahead and go. I'll go to the library; I want to find a book for that English paper we have to write."

"That's not due for six weeks, are you getting studious on me?" Taggart asked.

"No, I just don't want to be wandering around here with the chance that I might run into Ty. So I'm going to go hide in the library. I figure not too many people will be in there and it will be quiet. I think I wore myself out from the telepathy this morning."

"Are you practicing shielding your thoughts? That could be causing you to get worn down too."

"Yes, I'm trying not to broadcast my thoughts, but I don't know how well I'm doing though. Have you been able to hear me?"

"No." Taggart responded.

"Well it must be working." Meckenzie hoped no one was hearing her thoughts, but she still couldn't be sure. "When do you plan on going home today, should I wait for you or should I find the hot security guy and head out by myself?"

"I'll leave with you; I can come in early tomorrow. I kind of want to get home and read the book Isabel gave me some more. I found a section on healing spells and potions and I want to ask her some questions."

"Ok, I'll meet you on the steps then." With that they both headed back towards the school to finish the second half of their day. Meckenzie headed for the small library that the school had. It was meager because the students had access to the New York Public Library system and most kids did the majority of their research on-line now.

Meckenzie was looking for a literary classic that would be easy enough to get through, but would have enough material that she could write a term paper on it. She had just begun to read through the first few pages of *The Bell Jar* by Sylvia Plath when the buzzing started. Meckenzie immediately began looking for Ty. She worked diligently in her mind building a wall between her thoughts and the outside world. She knew that Ty must have spotted her and thought that he would sneak into her mind while she was unaware of his presence. Ty had no way of knowing she could feel him when he was near her.

After several minutes of mental wall building, the buzzing began to dull. She must be keeping him out. Meckenzie continued to fortify her mental wall, which consisted of her visualizing a wall around her thoughts, and soon the buzzing stopped completely. She thought that she would find Ty instead of running from him. Maybe she needed to do a little recon on this guy.

Meckenzie found Ty standing two rows away in the non-fiction section. He had pulled a book off the shelf on Biochemistry. Meckenzie decided to approach this situation like a flirty teen. She wasn't really schooled in it, so she hoped it worked.

"I bet if you look in the front of that book, you'll see my brother's name on the check-out card." Meckenzie knew she was off to a rough start, but it was the only thing that came to her mind.

Ty turned and smiled, something was very off about his smile. It always seemed like he was getting ready to eat her, like she was some tasty delicacy that he would consume. Meckenzie felt her will faltering, but she knew she needed to know more about this guy.

"Huh, his name is in the front of the book." Ty said as he closed the book. "You always hide out in the library on your lunch hour?"

Meckenzie giggled not to convincingly, "No, I was just picking up a book for my English term paper. I hate reading so much that I have to give myself enough time to plough through it." This was a total fabrication; Meckenzie loved to read, and had actually already read *The Bell Jar.* She had chosen this approach because she had heard that guys don't like smart girls. Not that Meckenzie really wanted this guy to like her, or the real her at least, he was free to like the flirty teenage dimbot that she was creating in her mind to flirt with him.

"I'm glad you came over here. I was hoping to run into you." Ty was staring into her eyes in a way that made her think he was trying to burrow into her mind. Meckenzie smiled and continued to keep her mental wall up. "I was hoping you might be interested in going out sometime, on a date. I'd like to get to know you." He smiled that grin again and reached out to touch Meckenzie's arm.

Initially she wanted to run as far away as she could get, but Meckenzie knew that this would defeat the purpose of her coming over here in the first place. She knew she needed to learn more about this guy, one way or another. Even though the thought of him touching her made Meckenzie sick to her stomach, she didn't move away from him.

"I'd love to, though you will have to come by the house and meet my father first. I am not allowed to go out with anyone that my father has not met. When would you like to go? So I can arrange a meeting."

"I was hoping since tomorrow is Thursday night that I'd be able to meet your father tomorrow so we could go out Friday night. I thought we could go get some dinner and maybe have a walk in the park, a chance to really talk."

"That sounds nice. I'll talk to my father tonight." As Meckenzie finished the sentence the bell rang. She smiled and headed off to class, happy to be away from Ty.

Just three hours to go and she could go home and discuss this with Isabel and her father. Meckenzie wasn't sure she really wanted to go on this date. Maybe her father would insist on sending the security guy with them; she would feel so much safer then. That should have been her first clue that something was definitely wrong with this plan.

CHAPTER 11

Meckenzie was sitting in study hall, her last class of the day, working on her homework when she heard Kellan calling her name. She looked around the classroom but there was no Kellan in sight. Meckenzie thought she might have imagined it. Then the thought crossed her mind that Kellan might be calling her mentally. She knew that Kellan was in her athletics class. Kellan would be working out or practicing in the gym.

"Meckenzie I need you."

That time there was no doubting that Kellan was talking to Meckenzie telepathically. She was surprised that it was working at such a distance. She was going to try to call back to her, when a girl that Meckenzie recognized but didn't really know came into the room and began talking to the teacher and pointing at Meckenzie.

Mrs. Thompson, Meckenzie's study hall teacher called to her, "Meckenzie, your needed in the gym."

"Yes ma'am." Meckenzie made her way to the front of the class to follow the girl to the gym. "Is something wrong with Kellan?"

"Yes. I don't know what though. We were running basketball drills and Sarah set a screen on Kellan that knocked her down. It was kind of a cheap shot, but I heard that Jake, Sarah's boyfriend has a crush on Kellan. So anyways, Kellan got mad and then she started shaking. Before we knew what was going on, she had locked herself in the equipment room. She just kept yelling to get you and Taggart."

"Do we need to get Taggart? He is probably in the science lab."

"No, Sarah felt bad so she went to get Taggart. Though I think she may have a crush on him. That brother of yours is super cute. Is he seeing anyone?"

Meckenzie could not remember this girl's name, but she was sure that Taggart wasn't interested. "Umm, I think he is seeing someone from another school. He is kind of private about his romantic life."

"Oh, that's too bad. I was sure he had to be seeing someone. With all the girls that are interested, he could have his pick of almost any girl in the school. He is going to Harvard right?"

Meckenzie just wanted to get to the gym and find out what was wrong with Kellan. This girl was super chatty and Meckenzie wasn't sure if she wanted her to date Taggart if he was available and willing

"Yes, he is going to Harvard. He is excited and we are all very proud of him."

Finally they were at the gym. Meckenzie ran across the gym to the equipment closet where Taggart was standing with the coach. He seemed to be trying to explain that Kellan was not feeling well lately and may just need some time.

"I think if you just allow us to talk to her, we can probably get her out of the closet. She really has been feeling poorly. Maybe you could get us some water and a towel. Kellan stomach has been really queasy lately." Taggart was saying to the coach.

"I'll send one of the trainers over with some water and some towels." The coach walked back to practice and left Meckenzie and Taggart alone.

"Do you know what's wrong?" Meckenzie asked.

"I think she may have gotten mad and had one of her growing incidents. Let's go find out."

"Kellan, it's me and Taggart, let us in."

Kellan opened the door. Meckenzie slipped in and was astounded at how big Kellan was. She had to be eight feet tall and was at least three feet wide at the shoulders. Her clothes had been ripped apart, but she had managed to strategically place what was left so as not to be completely naked.

Taggart stood outside the door and waited for the water and towels. The door was mostly closed, so that no one would be able to see the exact nature of Kellan's "illness".

"Oh Kellan, are you okay?"

"Yeah, except I'm freaking huge. I almost didn't make it into the closet before I exploded into she-hulk. I don't know what we are going to do. Do you think we can do the spell?"

"I don't know, I don't remember all of it. Maybe we can try to do it without the funky words." Meckenzie was sure that they could, she knew that they had a power to get this thing done, they had to. She knew that they couldn't get Kellan home like this, she was too big.

Taggart entered the closet with some bottles of water and some towels. He immediately started laughing. Kellan was getting more irritated by Taggart's laughter and you could see the anger affecting her physically.

"You think it is funny." Kellan said with rage.

"No it's not funny, it's amusing. Amusing that your body reflects who you are on the inside." Taggart said with a smile.

"What I'm a she-hulk? A huge monster?"

"No, you're larger than life and your natural body can't hold all of your personality. So it creates this body that can hold all that you are." Lovingly Taggart added, "I think you are amazing. I just find it amusing. There will be a time in life where you will appreciate all that you are, I know I do."

Kellan couldn't help but feel a little better. Taggart had a charm that was so much part of his personality that it didn't come off as fake, or condescending. He just really believed what he was saying.

"Well I think we should concentrate on getting her back to normal size so we can get her home." Meckenzie decided to get the three back on track. "Do you remember the spell that we performed last time to get her back to normal?"

Taggart shook his head, "No, but I think we can do this without the spell. I've been reading the spell books and I think I've determined that is not so much the words, but the intention and the power. I think if say 'Be calm, be still' it should work."

Kellan was not looking very trusting, "Should work? What do we do if doesn't work? I mean how can we remedy this situation if it doesn't work."

"Let's just try it." Meckenzie added.

The three of them joined hands and began to chant quietly.

"Be calm. Be still. Be calm. Be Still." Over and over again they chanted with no results. The chanting grew louder and more intense as they went on. Meckenzie began slowly to feel a buzzing start in her hands. She felt it flow through the connection she had with her siblings. Power flowing through her body and out of her mind into the ethereal. Still, there was no effect on Kellan.

Kellan interrupted the chanting, "I don't think this is working."

"Maybe we should try different words." Meckenzie said.

"Kellan, are you really concentrating? You have to believe this is going to work. We can't do it without you believing in your power. I know that it is hard right now. You are really frustrated, I would be too. We just need you to be totally with us on this." Taggart implored Kellan to concentrate.

"I could feel the buzzing. I just don't know why it didn't work." Meckenzie added.

"Hold on, I'm going to go get something. Give me five minutes." Taggart slipped out the door and left Meckenzie and Kellan in the equipment room.

"Kellan, I know you aren't happy right now. I wish I could make this all better for you. I know you just want everything to go back to normal, but we don't have that option. I hope you can find happiness in what we are and what we have to do. I want that for all of us. I think Taggart will be fine; he seems to adjust very well to any situation. I just worry about you."

Kellan let out of sigh, "You don't have to worry about me Meckenzie, your not my mother. Remember she ran away from us, and didn't tell us anything about what was going on till it was already here. Yes, I want everything to go back to normal and I don't want any of this. I want to live my life, not some life that everyone thinks I'm predestined to live. I am not a hero, I am just me. Why can't you understand that? Why can't we just be normal?"

Kellan's large shoulders began to heave as tears rolled down her checks. Meckenzie felt helpless, she knew she couldn't comfort Kellan. Meckenzie had always tried to protect Kellan. It was such a funny thought now, with Kellan being so big, to think that she would need any protection.

"What do you think Taggart's up to?" Meckenzie subtly tried to change the subject as much as the subject could be changed.

"I don't know." Kellan said through tears. "I hope he thinks of something soon. I'm getting cold."

"We are going to have to get you some more clothes before you can come out of here, you've ruined your work out clothes. We will have to ask Isabel how this is going to work if you are to use this power. You can't be destroying your clothes every time you get big."

"I have no intention of using this." Kellan said dismissively.

"Then you will need to figure out how to control it." Meckenzie was trying not to become frustrated with Kellan's petulance. It was hard to not grab Kellan by the shoulders and shake some sense into her. Though it would be quiet impossible for Meckenzie to reach Kellan's shoulders right now. The idea made Meckenzie laugh out loud.

"What?" Kellan asked.

"I just had an image of me trying to shake some sense into you. I'm not sure that I could have ever done it, with you being almost eight feet tall it would be impossible. It is a funny thought though."

Kellan began to laugh. "I can only imagine you climbing up on the equipment box over there and trying to reach my shoulders." She began to laugh harder and the sadness went away from her eyes.

Just then, Taggart slipped back into the room. He had retrieved what looked like a sheet and his backpack.

"Okay, I think we should wrap Kellan in the sheet and we will wrap our arms around her as best we can and perform the spell that way. Maybe with my healing touch and your mental abilities we will be able to amplify the spell and make it work."

"Why the sheet?" Kellan said.

"Well I figured with the clothing issue, you wouldn't want us hugging you. So here's a sheet to wrap you in. I also got my backpack, because my phone is in there and if this doesn't work, we will call Isabel."

Kellan took the sheet and wrapped it around her body like a sarong. She tried to look confident by smiling, but the smile didn't quiet reassure anyone.

Meckenzie and Taggart stepped in and placed their arms around Kellan. They tried to place their bodies against Kellan's so all the energy would flow from them into Kellan. It was a long shot, but it was really worth trying anything at this point. Meckenzie was sure that if this didn't work, someone was going to have to go get Isabel.

"Let's try saying 'Be calm, be still' again." Taggart said from the other side of Kellan.

"Okay." Meckenzie and Kellan responded together.

Once again the three siblings began chanting, "Be calm, be still." This time Meckenzie closed her eyes and imagined Kellan in her natural state. She saw in her mind's eye Kellan shrinking back down to normal size. Meckenzie felt the buzzing begin again in her hands and flow through her body. She focused her energy and tried to push it out of her mind into Kellan's body. Without opening her eyes, Meckenzie could feel Kellan changing before her. Kellan's body began to move away from Meckenzie's as if she were stepping backwards. Taggart pulled Meckenzie closer, forcing her body to continue touching Kellan's. Meckenzie focused again on visualizing Kellan's body gradually returning to its natural form. Meckenzie felt the power flowing between the three of them, she felt it working.

Kellan was the first to break the chanting, "You guys can stop now."

Meckenzie opened her eyes and standing before her was her sister, normal. They had done it! She didn't know if the change in positions had accomplished this, or if it had been her visualization. Maybe Taggart's touch had been the key, or maybe it had been a combination of many things that they had not had going for them the first time around.

Whatever the circumstances, the results were amazing. They had managed to return Kellan to her natural state without the spell from the book or Isabel's supervision. Meckenzie felt amazing. She wanted to run home and tell Isabel right away. First though, she should get Kellan some clothes.

"I'll get your clothes from the locker room." Meckenzie made her way to the door and let herself out into the gym, immediately all the girls turned to look at her.

"She's doing better. Just something she ate at lunch I think. I'm going to get her clothes and let her change." She didn't ask for permission, Meckenzie just headed to the locker room and went to where she knew Kellan's locker was. She removed all of Kellan's clothes and placed them in her bag. Meckenzie felt a power flowing through her still. She reached out her mind and searched for Kellan.

"I have your clothes and your backpack, is there anything else you need?"

"Meckenzie that freaks me out a little. How do you telepathically talk to me from so far away?" Kellan had an edge to her voice as if she was ready to scream.

"I think I'm still super charged from the bit of magic that we performed. I thought it would be easier to ask you what I needed to get out of your locker rather than forgetting something. Now your clothes and your backpack, is that all you need?"

"Yes. Thank you." Kellan's voice seemed to be returning to normal. Taggart had a calming effect and it was probably working on Kellan right now.

As Meckenzie grabbed Kellan's stuff and headed back to the equipment closet, the bell rang to signal the end of the day. Meckenzie slipped in and handed Kellan her clothes. Then she pushed Taggart out the door so that Kellan could change.

"How do you feel?" Meckenzie was concerned that Kellan was going to try to go back out there and work out, so she added, "I told your coach that you had something that didn't sit well for lunch."

"Thanks, I don't want Sarah thinking that the hit she put on me affected me in any way." Kellan said, trying to keep up her tough woman persona.

"But it did affect you?" Meckenzie questioned.

"Yes, but Sarah doesn't need to know that. She thinks that I'm interested in Jake. I could really care less about Jake and Sarah for that matter. We have enough stuff going on in our lives. Frankly,I don't need some boy in my life that I'm just going to have to leave. I'm not sure I'd be interested in him if we weren't going away, anyway." Kellan chuckled at her last sentence.

"Well, let's get you home. I'm sure Isabel will be interested in what happened today."

Kellan looked at Meckenzie with disgust and said, "I really don't care what Isabel thinks. She knew where mom was this whole time and never told us." Kellan looked as if she were going to cry again. Meckenzie could feel her heart breaking for Kellan. She knew Kellan would never fully forgive their mother, or Isabel for that matter, for the deception.

"You know she couldn't tell us. It would have put our lives in danger for us to know before now. I mean our lives are in danger now, so it doesn't really matter. I wish that mom had been able to tell us where she was going before she left too, but that is not what happened, so we have to find a way to deal with it." Meckenzie walked over to Kellan and put her arms around her. "I love you and promise to never go away without telling you where and why, that is all I can promise."

Kellan smiled, "I love you too, even if you are a sappy sister. I appreciate all you are doing for me. I know I can be moody and not easy to deal with. I really hope you always have this patience, or that I grow out of these moods."

Meckenzie laughed, "I wouldn't hope for growing. You never know what that will get you."

Kellan grabbed Meckenzie in a wrestling hold, "Don't tell me you are trying to take Taggart's place as the comedian. I don't think you are strong enough, or fast enough, to make those jokes." Kellan laughed as she lifted Meckenzie off the ground in a bear hug.

This was the Kellan that Meckenzie remembered from childhood. Always using her strength and agility to get the better of Meckenzie. Meckenzie had always just let her; it was easier to let her win than to fight. Plus, Kellan had a temper and if Meckenzie had ever won, there would be hell to pay.

"Let's get you home." Meckenzie said to wave the white flag of surrender. Kellan let go and picked up her stuff. They headed out of the equipment room together. Taggart was waiting patiently beside the door.

"I need to get my stuff. I'll meet you by the front doors." Taggart said as he led them out of the gym. He was trying to ignore the fact that all eyes were on them as they exited, all three of them were trying to ignore that fact.

"I have to get my stuff from study hall and swing by my locker, you want to come with me Kellan, or meet us at the front door?" Meckenzie knew that giving her a choice would make her feel like she had some free will back. Kellan was very much all about her free will.

"I'll go with you. It will just be easier." There was still a look of desperation in Kellan's eyes from knowing that she had very little control over her body. It was going to be a long hard road to get Kellan to fell like she had control. Meckenzie knew that more than likely, Kellan would never have full control of her emotions. Kellan's emotions fluctuated like the weather. She could be hot one minute and completely cold the next. There were few temperate days in Kellan's life. Meckenzie hoped that Isabel had some idea of how to teach Kellan how to control either this power, or her emotions better.

They parted ways with Taggart and headed back to the room where Meckenzie had study hall. As they were walking down the hall towards the room, Meckenzie felt like she was being watched. Her senses were going off like a car alarm on the New York streets. She stopped short of her destination and did a slow 360 degree turn in the hall hoping to catch sight of whoever was causing this alarm to go off inside her head. Meckenzie didn't see anyone, or anything, unusual. Kellan stared at Meckenzie, waiting for her to share whatever it was that was going on.

"It felt like someone was watching me. It was like an alarm was going off in my head, danger, danger."

Kellan slowly turned in very much the same way that Meckenzie had just done. She stopped when she was facing a classroom on the left hand side of the hall.

"Did you see someone?" Meckenzie asked.

"No, but I have a feeling." As Kellan said this, she started walking towards the classroom. She slowly pulled back the door. Meckenzie couldn't see around Kellan into the classroom. She hoped there was no danger waiting for them in that room. Kellan stepped into the room with one hand out in front of her in a defensive stance. As she did this, Meckenzie slid in beside her. Kellan dropped her hand to her side and sighed. Standing there in the center of the room, like a deer caught in headlights, was Jake Cummings, the source of this afternoons illegal basketball screen. Kellan turned around abruptly and marched out of the room. Meckenzie followed, knowing that Kellan was not in the mood for chit chat.

Meckenzie retrieved her books from study hall and her locker. They met Taggart at the front door along with the handsome bodyguard that was waiting patiently for the three of them. Jones greeted them, Meckenzie giggled again, as he smiled at her. The trips started the walk home, and Jones followed at a polite pace behind them. He must have worked with high school kids before because he seemed to have the disappearing into the crowd down bit to a fine art. Jones was there and aware, but in no way was he in their way. Maybe their dad was right about having him around, he could definitely come in handy if anyone tried approach the triplets, and Meckenzie thought he was very easy on the eyes. Bodyguards were a common enough occurrence at their school. For a short time there had been a couple of children of foreign diplomats at the school. Some of them from countries that had been fighting wars for most of their lives. I guess that though no one knew it that was the triplet's situation as well. The land that their mom was from, and now protecting, had been at war for hundreds maybe even thousands of years. Life was changing fast and Meckenzie knew that not evolving with it usually meant becoming obsolete. Needless to say, she hoped she could evolve.

CHAPTER 12

When the three siblings arrived home it was clear that Isabel had been at work. A large yoga looking mat was rolled up against one wall and there were several boxes scattered throughout the entryway. Meckenzie could only assume that these were the tools that Isabel intended to use to train them in combat and defensive skills. Kellan actually started to get excited as she inspected the boxes.

"This is all martial arts gear." She said as she looked inside one of the boxes and pulled out what looked like a red breast plate made of foam. "I wonder when we get to start learning."

Kellan's excitement was not contagious, in fact Meckenzie felt slightly sick at her stomach. She had never been much of a fighter. She preferred to talk herself out of most fights. Or Meckenzie would just let the other person win and wait till the fight subsided. It was her opinion that there was nothing so important that violence would solve the problem. Meckenzie knew she would have to learn to defend herself, because she was now headed into a scenario where the person coming after her would want her dead, and not just humiliated.

As Kellan dug into the third box, Isabel came into the entry and smiled really big.

"Good your home, I could use some young folks to carry boxes downstairs."

"I need to change clothes, but I think we should actually tell you about our day first." Meckenzie said as Isabel eyed her curiously. "We had some excitement and I got asked out on a date."

"What?" Both of her siblings and Isabel responded simultaneously.

"Oh yeah, with Kellan's 'the incredibly growing woman' routine, I forgot to tell you that Ty found me in the library and asked me out. I told him that he would have to meet my father and that I couldn't go out with him until he did."

"Do you think that is a good idea? I mean this guy makes your head buzz like Kim Kardashin's phone on vibrate. He may have plans if he is from the enemy." Taggart was being his naturally protective self and trying to keep Meckenzie out of harm's way.

"I thought it would be a good way to get some information. I was hoping that by bringing him by the house, Isabel might be able to scope him out and tell us what she thought. I didn't know if there was a better way to have Isabel get a look at him. I know it could be dangerous if we actually went out, but I thought we would deal with that scenario when the time came." Meckenzie felt a little defensive, she knew it wasn't a well thought out plan, but it was a plan none the less.

"Well, it would be good to bring him by the house. I am not sure if I should actually meet him; he may recognize me or have some information that I am supposed to be here, protection you three. Maybe we can find a way for me to see him, without him seeing me." Isabel said.

"I could set up some web cams around the house and we could run them to a computer that you could watch." Taggart was actually getting excited at the prospect of getting to do some spy work. "I'm sure that we could get the stuff this evening and get it all set up before he came by tomorrow. I'll go find a store nearby that I can get all the stuff. Maybe the security guy knows of a place, I think he is outside somewhere."

Taggart headed out the front door to find the Jones. He was so excited that he completely forgot about helping get the sparring equipment downstairs.

"So what else happened at school today?" Isabel redirected the conversation back to the trip's day.

Kellan looked a little worried about how Isabel would react to the next bit of news. She stepped away from the conversation to lean against the wall. Kellan seemed to be trying her best to blend in as a piece of furniture, but Isabel was all too aware of her trepidation.

"So what happened with Kellan?" Isabel astutely surmised.

"Well, she had a little growing spell in gym class." Meckenzie tried to make this as easy as possible for Kellan to endure. "She got knocked around a bit by another girl on her basketball team. Her anger sparked a growing spurt, but she was able to make it to the equipment closet without anyone seeing what had happened. The coach had some students come find Taggart and myself. We were able after a couple of attempts to return her to normal size, though her workout clothes were not as lucky."

Isabel was smiling, she seemed extremely pleased and not mad at all. She actually seemed to be laughing. Meckenzie thought maybe Isabel had not understood what she had just said. Either that or Isabel had finally lost it from having to deal with the three of them for all these years.

"I knew that there was always a possibility that Kellan's little talent would erupt at an inopportune time. That is why I thought it important to work on Kellan's patience. I would normally suggest a lot of meditation and yoga for you Kellan, but I know we really don't have the time to get you in that state of mind. So I'm very pleased that the three of you were able to solve this problem without me. It also means that you guys picked up the spell pretty quickly." Isabel was absolutely glowing with pride.

"Well," Meckenzie began, "we actually didn't remember the spell. We used 'Be calm, be still.' It didn't work at first, so we hugged her and did it again. With the touching we were able to amplify the spell and make it work. At least that is what we assumed. We always had Taggart's phone as a backup."

"Backup?"

"Yeah, if we couldn't get it to work we were going to call you to get help."

"I'm glad you guys tried it on your own first. It shows great ingenuity and power that you were able to get Kellan changed back without the proper words to the spell." Isabel seemed to be very pleased with the whole situation. "Kellan, I think you had real peace of mind to run for the equipment closet. It isn't your fault that you changed. Your powers are very much tied into your emotions and until we can get you guys trained in how to focus your emotions, it is quite possible that you might have this problem from time to time."

Kellan looked relieved and frustrated at the same time. Her face seem to be contorting every second into a new emotion. "I don't know if I can handle this." She said looking dejected. "I cannot live with this being an everyday occurrence. I can't handle changing every time I stub my toe or get knocked down in gym class. I just want to be normal." Kellan began crying. She crumbled against the wall, unable to hold the weight of the emotions that had been buried within her throughout this whole ordeal.

"Kellan," Meckenzie reached out to her sister hoping to help her work through this emotion. "I am sorry you have to go through this. I know how you feel."

"You don't know how I feel. Your powers don't turn you into a monster. Your powers are hidden. They aren't out there for the whole world to see. It's not like your head swells up when you are talking with us mentally. None of you understand. I am a freak." Kellan pulled herself up and pushed through Isabel and Meckenzie. "Just leave me alone. You have no idea what it feels like to be the she-hulk, and don't pretend you do. I just want to be normal." Kellan ran up the stairs to her room. Meckenzie's heart was breaking with the pain that Kellan was experiencing. She knew that she didn't know what Kellan felt like. She would have given anything to be able to take away Kellan's pain or to make her feel normal. Meckenzie also knew that there was no possibility of their lives being normal again.

Just then Taggart stepped in the door smiling from ear to ear.

"The security guy is going to take care of everything. Jones made a call to one of his pals who does surveillance and he is going to bring a basic system over in an hour and set it up. I figure we can get dad on board since it is basically just extra security. He is going to bring over a DVR, some cameras and a viewing monitor. Jones can set the whole system up this evening. Then we can talk to Dad about upgrading the cameras or whatever." Just then Taggart noticed the dejected look on Meckenzie's face. He realized that Kellan was missing from the room and knew that something must be up. "What happened?"

Isabel quickly stepped in to avoid having Meckenzie have to relive the whole situation. "Meckenzie why don't you go up and change, we should start some defense training before I have to prepare dinner."

Meckenzie turned to head up the stairs and heard Isabel begin to talk to Taggart about Kellan. Meckenzie really didn't want to relive Kellan's outburst, but she knew she would have to at some point. It was important that she mend Kellan's feelings.

Though Meckenzie didn't have the same problems as Kellan, she knew what Kellan was feeling. She knew that every moment was a possible time bomb of emotions that could explode Kellan's body into a gigantic state. She knew that Kellan lived very much by her emotions. Kellan being the youngest had always been slightly more emotionally charged than her siblings. Meckenzie had always been the sympathetic one, Taggart the level headed one, and Kellan the emotional dynamo.

As Meckenzie came up the stairs to her floor, she could hear Kellan throwing stuff around in her room. Meckenzie was going to check on her, but it seemed that it might be best to leave her alone for now. So Meckenzie quickly changed and headed back down stairs.

When she got back to the entry way to help move the boxes, Taggart had already loaded most of them onto the elevator.

"So, what are we going to do about Kellan?" Taggart said without making eye contact with Meckenzie.

"I don't know, I don't think I can do anything. She seems to be maddest at me. It's like Kellan blames me for everything that is going on."

"I think it's because you look the most like Mom. It's easy to blame you, because she wants to blame Mom." Taggart sat the last box into the elevator and hit the button to send it down stairs leaving Meckenzie standing alone on the ground floor.

Meckenzie wasn't exactly sure what to make of Taggart's statement that she looked the most like Mom and therefore Kellan was blaming her for everything. She wasn't sure how she felt about him dropping that bomb on her and then heading off in the elevator without giving her the opportunity for rebuttal.

Meckenzie headed to the kitchen to grab some bottles of water. Maybe Taggart was trying to give her some time to think over what he had said. She had always been told that she looked like her mother. For the most part she considered it a compliment because her mother was very beautiful. The resemblance to her mother would become a problem though if other Fae spotted her in public. Meckenzie didn't want to be the easiest target because of her looks. Taggart hadn't meant it as an insult; he had simply been stating his theory to the Kellan dilemma.

It was sad for Meckenzie to think of her sister as a dilemma; that seemed so cold and heartless to her. Meckenzie loved Kellan and she only wanted the best for her. She wanted her to be happy. The only problem was there were extenuating circumstances that were going to make it difficult for Kellan to be happy. So now Meckenzie had to figure out how to get Kellan to deal with those circumstances and do what was best for everyone, not what was best for Kellan necessarily.

As she headed downstairs, Meckenzie still didn't feel like she had any real idea how to make this better. She was sure that Taggart was probably right though. Kellan probably did blame Mom for all of this. And if it was true that Meckenzie reminded Kellan of their mother, then Meckenzie couldn't make this better for Kellan. She would just have to stand back and let the others work it out. Maybe it was time for Meckenzie to stop trying to make Kellan's life easy. Maybe it was time that Meckenzie focus on herself for a change. There were so many things going on in their lives that Meckenzie hadn't been really focusing on how this would affect her. She had been worried too much about how it would affect everyone else instead.

If she were meant to rule Aquanis someday, she would have to always take into consideration what was best for everyone around her. So why not take some time to focus on her for a while. Meckenzie needed to start acting like the queen she would someday have to be. She would have to take control with confidence and leadership, Meckenzie would have to make decisions.

She reached the gym with a new attitude. She would focus on making herself the best she could be with her new powers. The best she could be with defending herself, the best queen she could be. Then maybe she would try to help Kellan with her problems.

Taggart was already unloading boxes. Isabel had cleared a corner of the gym where all of the self-defense equipment was being unloaded. Meckenzie grabbed a box out of the elevator and headed that direction. With her new attitude she was really looking forward to learning some self-defense moves. Meckenzie was never much for physical activity other than running. She enjoyed a good muscle burning, heart pounding run, but really never got into any other sport.

"So what kind of moves are you going to teach us Isabel?" Meckenzie asked.

"I thought we would start with some basic self-defense. It's going to be beneficial to you to know how to fend off a physical attack, as a lot of the Fae don't have powers still. It will only be your generation that has their powers back. With the three of you, there is less than a hundred Fae with powers that we know of." Isabel began to unroll the mat as she dropped that last little tidbit of knowledge.

"Really, one hundred of us. I thought the number would be much lower." Taggart questioned.

"It would be if the fairies hadn't started breeding. Several families aware that the binding of powers would be over with this generation, began having multiple children. We as a species are not one for huge families. We tend to live a long time, so usually a couple will only have one child, unless there are multiple births such as you three. But in the last 20 years, people have been having two or three children."

Meckenzie's curiosity was peaked. "Are there often multiple births among the fairy people?"

"It does happen, there are many sets of twins and triplets in your family tree. It seems that some families, such as in humans, are more prone to multiple births. The closer you are to royalty in our world, the better chance of a multiple birth. They are considered the highest blessing given by the Morrigan."

"Morrigan, like King Arthur?" Taggart asked.

"Actually, that is a more recent fictional literary reference. The Morrigan is the embodiment of the goddess of the Fae. She blesses one family with the birth of a triplet set of female children who are the chosen ones to lead the religious temples. Every generation has a Morrigan. They, much like you three, are blessed with a three-fold power structure; that of the mind, body and soul. They are renamed upon their sixteenth birthday to reflect their powers. Dian, the sister of soul, is our goddess of healing. Brigid, the sister of body, is our goddess of battle. Morgan, the sister of mind, is our goddess of peace. They have been without powers for many years, but still function as our Morrigan. From my understanding, the new Morrigan is taking power right now and should be ruling the temple when you return to Aquanis."

"What have they been doing all these years without powers? Wouldn't their powers be the way that they are named?" Taggart's curiosity had been peeked and he was very interested in learning as much as he could about this particular part of his ancestry.

"The Morrigan have another way that their powers manifest themselves. It is another way we know that they are the Morrigan. They each have a different hair color. It is an oddity that triplet sisters would be born with each a unique hair color. Dian's hair is blond, Brigid's hair is red, and Morgan's hair is black. Some of the earlier human legends are born because one of the Morrigan, Morgan, crossed into the human world during the time of the Celts and visited one of their tribes. They wrote her into their legends."

"Will we meet them? Where do they live? How many have there been?" Taggart's mind was in overdrive. He wanted to know everything there was to know about the Morrigan.

Isabel laughed. "Yes you will meet them. They will perform your coronation. I have a book about them. I'll loan it to you, it has their history and some stories about certain Morrigan from the past. Now, we have enough equipment unloaded to start some basic sparring. I think we should start on the defensive training. Meckenzie, try calling out to Kellan and ask her to join us."

Meckenzie was not excited about the prospect of her first conversation with Kellan being a mental one. She had hoped that she would have time later to sit down with Kellan and just have a sisterly conversation, no talk of powers, no talk of ruling a kingdom, just some nice sisterly conversation.

"Kellan, Isabel would like for you to join us and learn some defense moves. You might get a chance to hit me. We are in the gym." Meckenzie didn't wait for a response; she didn't necessarily want to hear what Kellan had to say.

Isabel threw some sparring pads at Taggart and what looked like unfinished boxing gloves to Meckenzie.

"What are these for?" Meckenzie wasn't sure she could hit anyone, let alone Taggart, but she had an inkling that Isabel was expecting her to do just that.

"You put them on your hands. They allow you to hit without hurting your knuckles but still have the flexibility to use your hands to deflect as you might have to in hand to hand combat." Taggart answered with far more awareness than Meckenzie expected.

"How do you know all this?"

"I am not just a pretty face." Taggart smiled back at Meckenzie as he strapped on the defensive pads.

"Okay we are going to try some light combat, no actual punch throwing. Though we will simulate in slow motion the proper way to throw a punch. Here, both of you need to put in mouthpieces just in case something goes wrong, I don't want either of you losing a tooth." Isabel seemed amused at her last comment, but Meckenzie was more racked with fear than she had expected.

Meckenzie slid the mouthpiece into her mouth. This is really not what she expected. She had been expecting self-defense classes like she had seen on TV where the women learned to step on their attackers toes and knee them in the groin. Meckenzie had not expected to be throwing actual punches. She was not in any way a violent person. Meckenzie had never thrown a punch in all of her life. In all the fights she had ever been in, and all of them had been with Kellan, she had always run away, hid, or taken a defensive position. Taking the punches was never her first choice, but she didn't fight back so sometimes it was the necessary one.

As Meckenzie and Taggart were taking their positions opposite each other, Kellan came down the stairs to join them. Isabel didn't skip a beat with her instruction; she simply nodded towards the equipment and Kellan. They began their training learning the proper way to throw a body punch. With Kellan and Meckenzie standing on either side of Taggart, they slowly began punching him in his abdominal pads as he circled between them. Isabel would bring Meckenzie's elbow in when she would begin to let her arms get to loose. Kellan had a real talent for picking up the basics of fighting. She had always been better at physical activity than her siblings. Soon, Isabel was instructing Kellan on how to throw different punches and asking Taggart to try to maneuver out of Kellan's way. Meckenzie stepped back and watched as Kellan mastered punch after punch. Taggart had begun to breathe heavily and was looking worse for the wear, as Kellan's punches began falling with more and more strength.

Just as Isabel had shouted out new instructions for Kellan's punch combination, their father descended the stairs calling out their names. This momentary distraction caused Taggart to drop his arms just as Kellan connected with his lower jaw. The force of her punch spun him around. With a thud, Taggart hit the mat, his mouth piece landing a few feet away.

"Taggart!" Meckenzie screamed and ran to his motionless body on the mat. As she looked up at Kellan, a slight smile of satisfaction faded from Kellan's face and morphed into a look of horror.

"Taggart can you hear me." Meckenzie dropped to her knees and tried to roll Taggart's lifeless body over. Isabel knelt down on his other side and helped Meckenzie roll him face up.

Their father rushed across the gym. "What were you thinking Isabel? Kellan could have killed him." As he felt Taggart's pulse, he knew that Taggart was only unconscious. "You said that Kellan was getting stronger and faster than the Meckenzie and Taggart, she should not be fighting with them.

"We were doing fine till you distracted him. He'll be fine, he just got his bell rung." Just as Isabel finished her sentence, Taggart began to open his eyes.

Unexpectedly, he smiled. "Next time I get the gloves and Kellan gets the pads."

Kellan let out a snort, "See he's fine. No harm no foul."

"I'm fine, let me sit up." Taggart pushed himself up on his elbows and reached out a hand in Kellan's direction. Kellan held out her hand and pulled Taggart up in one smooth pull. Kellan seemed to be without emotion regarding the entire situation. She simply stepped back and started taking off her gloves.

"Hey Dad," Taggart had decided a change of subject was the best solution for the situation, "I thought it might be a good idea to have some cameras installed around the house for security. I talked to Jones the security guy you hired, and he called one of his friends who sets up surveillance cameras for security companies. He is going to come by tonight and install some cameras and a recording system."

"What happened to my family that we need security cameras and self-defense training?" Lawrence Desmond said to no one in particular.

"Well, for one, Meckenzie has a date." Taggart threw Meckenzie under the bus on that one. He smiled at her and stepped off to the side to take off his pads, knowing that their father would not be particularly happy about the date.

"No!" Lawrence said to Meckenzie. "There is too much going on right now. Why would you want to date? Why is it that everytime I come down here someone is hurt or bleeding or unconscious?"

"Okay." Meckenzie agreed. "There is really too much going on right now anyway. I just thought it would be nice to have some normal teenage activity in my life. I'll call him and tell him that he doesn't need to come by and meet you."

Meckenzie looked at her siblings and silently sent them a message. *"Don't say a word about who he might be."*

Kellan didn't even acknowledge the communication; she simply turned and headed up the stairs. Taggart still had his back to the group taking off his pads, but Meckenzie detected a slight raise in his shoulders indicating that he might be laughing. Isabel just stood and watched the exchange. Meckenzie could tell that she was interested in the outcome, but not willing to interject any of her concerns.

"Well, I guess if he came by to meet me I could consider letting you go out on a date. You would have to take the security guy with you. And I have final say as to whether you can go." Lawrence Desmond simply wanted to have some control over his family again. He knew that there was little possibility of that happening, so he would take a little control over his daughter's love life for now.

"Thank you Daddy." Meckenzie stood up on her tip toes and kissed his cheek.

"What's for dinner this evening?" It seemed the men in this family thought that a change of subject would be the best way to get life back to normal.

"I've prepared lasagna that just needs to be reheated. I'll go do that now and prepare a salad." Isabel headed upstairs with their father leaving Meckenzie and Taggart alone.

"Do you think she did it on purpose?" Taggart asked.

"I think she was mad enough. The look on her face after you went down was somewhat akin to satisfaction. I am not sure if she meant to do it, but I'm sure she enjoyed it." Meckenzie hated thinking of her sister in this way. She knew that Kellan was mad and that when her temper got the best of her she could be cruel.

"How are we going to fix this?"

"I'm not sure we can." Meckenzie responded knowing that Taggart wouldn't like a problem that he couldn't solve. Taggart had always been the problem solver. Give him something that he could find the answer to and he was at his happiest.

"What do you think we should do?" He asked Meckenzie. This wasn't really a situation that she was ready for. He tended to be the man with the plan. Meckenzie was always willing to go along as best as she could to help, but she was never one for devising the plans. She thought back to her knew attitude towards life, and decided it was time for her to start making the plans.

"Well, I think Kellan needs something to focus on. She seems to enjoy and excel at the self-defense and combat training. Maybe we just let her beat the crap out of us a few times. Maybe Isabel has some ideas of how to train her so that she can get some of this negative energy out."

"I sure hope so. I don't think I can take too many more of her uppercuts. I felt that one all the way down to my toes." He was laughing as he rubbed his jaw, but there was a slight amount of concern in his eyes.

"Do you think she will do something desperate?" Meckenzie asked.

"Like what?"

"I don't know. I just know that she is not thinking clearly right now and it could get her in trouble. I am afraid Kellan will go after someone. I mean I can just see her taking a swing at someone and with her new found strength, I'm not sure that it wouldn't be fatal."

"Well, we just need to not tick her off."

"Easier said than done." Meckenzie really felt a concern for Kellan. She was so angry that she wasn't thinking clearly. Throughout their lives Kellan had not been very forgiving or very level headed. It seemed that she was somewhat like the Hulk.

"I'm going to go get a shower and get ready for dinner." Taggart said as he headed for the stairs.

"Good idea." Meckenzie followed him. As they reached the ground floor they overheard their father speaking with someone in the foyer.

"Must be the surveillance guy." Taggart said and headed in that direction.

Meckenzie would let Taggart take care of the surveillance stuff, she had no clue as to what to expect or what to ask for in that department. Though she wouldn't have minded getting another look at Jones, he seemed to sneak into her mind all day. She headed up to her room to get a shower and to think about what to do about Kellan. Meckenzie wasn't sure there was any solution right now.

CHAPTER 13

When Meckenzie had gotten out of the shower, she could think of nothing that she would like more than to climb into bed and hide for the rest of the night. She decided she would settle for lying down for a few moments and thinking about all that had happened today. It seemed that every day since they had found out about their Fae heritage had been some kind of drama. Her days for wishing for excitement were over, she didn't think she would ever have to do that again.

Kellan was her biggest concern right now. She couldn't get the idea out of her head that Kellan was going to do something drastic. Meckenzie knew she couldn't stop it. Kellan had never really let anyone stop her from doing anything. That is what made her such an incredible athlete. So that was one problem Meckenzie would just have to put on the back burner for now.

Ty was another problem entirely. She was starting to regret her decision to go out with him. She knew that this was their best hope for getting some kind of information about him; she just didn't know if she was ready for what that my entail. Meckenzie wasn't really good spy material. She had never been good at telling lies. She wasn't good at being sneaky and she was a horrible fighter. Her only hope is that they would get enough information simply from him showing up at the house. This is when Meckenzie could really use Kellan's advice on what she should do.

Meckenzie's mind drifted to the story of the Morrigan that Isabel had been telling them in the gym. She had not thought of the Fae having a religion.

Her family, as a whole, had never really been religious. They had celebrated Christmas and Easter, but never really gone to church. Meckenzie wondered what the teachings of the Morrigan were. How long were they expected to rule the temples? As she thought through what Isabel had told them, she began to drift off to sleep.

Suddenly Meckenzie realized she was sitting in front of her mirror. There before her the mirror was shimmering silver and changing shape. What was going on? She had just been lying in bed, how did she get here? Then right before her eyes appeared a girl about her age with pitch black hair and deep blue eyes.

The girl stared back at Meckenzie in amazement; she seemed as surprised as Meckenzie to be sitting here in front of the mirror. Meckenzie reached out and touched the mirror's cold surface. She felt the hardness of it under her fingertips, the coldness of the glass. The girl on the other side of the mirror was doing the same. Meckenzie brought her hand back up to touch her face. She felt the warmth and softness of her skin, she felt real. She still did not understand what was going on.

Just then the girl opened her mouth and spoke, "What does this mean?"

Meckenzie was surprised to find that the girl was addressing the question to her. She wasn't sure what was going on. She had no idea what this was supposed to mean. All of her visions had been silent. Meckenzie had never spoken to anyone in them.

"I don't know." She responded. "I thought this was a dream. Who are you?"

"I'm Morgan of the Morrigan and you are Queen Deidra's daughter. You look so much like her."

"You know my mother. Is this real?"

"I spoke to your mother only moments ago. She told us the story of your birth, the story of her escape to New York."

Could it really be that she was speaking to someone who knew her Mother, someone who was real and alive at this time in another place?

"You are really in Aquanis. You really know my mother. How are we communicating?" Meckenzie asked.

"I don't know. I've never done this before. What is your name? Your mother told us your names, but I don't know which one you are."

Meckenzie wasn't sure if this was a trick. She thought that this could be the enemy trying to get information. How would they know if she was really Deidra's daughter though?

"I am Meckenzie. I expected the Morrigan to be older. How old are you?"

"I am sixteen. Today was our naming day. Today is my first day as Morgan and our first day as the Morrigan. I have been training for this day since I was born. My sisters and I have been in the temple since we were but weeks old."

Whether it was a trick or not, Meckenzie decided to go along with the conversation and get as much information as possible. If this was a trick, then Isabel would be able to send a message to her mother and find out the truth. A thought hit Meckenzie at that moment about Morgan's last statement. She had grown up in a temple without her parents. She had grown up without a mother.

"So you grew up without a mother too?"

"My mother is the Goddess Morrigan. She has imbued me with my powers and given me her life essence to guide my people through life. I have never been without my mother. My birth mother was but a vessel to bring me into the world with my sisters."

Meckenzie realized that Morgan was repeating something that she had been taught her whole life. Sadness overwhelmed Meckenzie that this girl had never known her real mother, that she had spent her whole life in the service of a Goddess. Meckenzie's heart was breaking for Morgan. She wanted to reach out and give this girl a hug.

"There must be a reason the Goddess is allowing us to talk in this dream state. Is there something that you want to tell your mother? Is there some news from your side that needs to be relayed?" Morgan said interrupting Meckenzie's thought process.

"I can think of nothing that has happened that is that important. I mean we have all gotten our powers. We are struggling to control them. Isabel is trying to teach us as much as she can." Meckenzie had no idea what she might need to relay. She had almost completely dismissed the idea that this was some kind of trick.

"What powers do you possess? Your mother might be interested in knowing what you have been blessed with." Morgan asked.

Meckenzie went back to the idea that this was a trick. If it was, this was just the sort of information that the enemy would want to have. She had to make a decision as to whether she was going to trust the vision, or hide her sibling's talents. She decided that she would trust the vision. Their powers would be discovered eventually anyways.

"Well, I have visions. I can also communicate telepathically especially with my siblings, but I have been able to communicate with Isabel as well. Taggart, my brother, is a healer. He healed Kellan's broken arm already. It was very disgusting and quite miraculous. Kellan, my sister, is strong, fast and agile. She also can grow in size. She got angry today and grew to eight feet tall. She calls herself She-Hulk."

"She-Hulk? What is that, a nickname?" Morgan asked confused.

Meckenzie forgot that she was communicating with someone who wasn't in the human world. This girl looked so much like a normal human teenager. It was hard to imagine that she was one third of the Morrigan.

"No, she thinks she is some kind of monster. The Hulk is a fictional character that grows really large and turns green when he is angry. Do you have powers too?"

"Yes, I'm the only one of my three sisters whose powers have manifested. I have had one vision, a vision of you running in the park."

"Of me?" Meckenzie asked.

"Yes, I think it was a way to let your mom tell us about you. You are a very big secret here. No one but my sisters and two of your mom's advisors know of your existence."

"Do you think we will be able to do this again?" Meckenzie was interested in whether she would be able to get messages to her mom. This would be so much quicker and easier than the currier system that Isabel was using. Though she had no idea how it was actually working.

"I don't know. I don't actually know how we are doing it now. I mean I only learned of your existence this afternoon and I was thinking about the three of you as I lay down for my nap." Morgan said.

Meckenzie realized this must be the key. She had remembered thinking about the conversation in the gym regarding the Morrigan right before she must have drifted off.

"I was thinking about you before I fell asleep. We found out about the Morrigan this afternoon. My brother is very interested in your history and asked lots of questions. Isabel was telling us about you and as I was lying down before dinner, I was thinking about the things she had told us. Maybe that is the key. Maybe we have to be thinking about each other when we are about to go to sleep."

"Let's test it out. I'll try to contact you tomorrow night."

Meckenzie hoped that Isabel had an idea as to whether this was really Morgan of the Morrigan. She really wanted this to work out. She really wanted this to be an opportunity to use her powers to communicate with her mother.

"Okay. Do you know how we get out of this?"

"I guess we just have to wake up." No sooner had Morgan spoke the words was Meckenzie awake in her bed. She sat up quickly to orientate herself. She looked at the clock and realized only about fifteen minutes had passed since she had gotten out of the shower. Meckenzie jumped up and threw on some clothes. She had to talk to Isabel.

Isabel was in the kitchen making a salad. The look on Meckenzie's face must have worried her because she sat down the knife she was using to cut the vegetables and came around the island.

"Sit. What is it?" Isabel asked.

"I was upstairs taking a shower and when I was done, I decided to lie down for a minute and get my thoughts straight. I thought about Kellan, and then the date with Ty. Then I started to the think of the Morrigan and I must have drifted off to sleep. All of a sudden I was having what I assumed was a dream, it was of a young girl with black hair and blue eyes sitting on the other side of my dressing table mirror. We had a conversation and she said she was Morgan of the Morrigan." Meckenzie paused trying to decide what to say next.

"What did she say?" Isabel interjected.

Meckenzie recapped the whole conversation with Isabel trying not to leave out any detail. She wanted to make sure that she had the whole conversation so that they could determine whether it was a real vision or something else.

Isabel seemed perplexed. "I've never heard of fairies communicating between the worlds in a dream state. I'm not even sure it is possible, though your powers may be stronger because they have been dormant for so long. It may be that both you three and the Morrigan will have powers greater than any we have seen before. If you both have similar powers then it would make sense that you would be able to communicate telepathically. I have just never heard of this kind of inter-world communication."

"Should we send a message to mom? I mean I don't think that we could get an answer by tomorrow, but maybe we could set up some code words or something that could be given when the vision starts." Meckenzie really wanted this to be part of her new powers. She wanted to be able to help out in this way.

"That's a good idea. I'll call for a currier and deliver a message to your mom that will give a specific phrase to be said at the beginning of the conversation so that you will know that your mother has giving the okay for this form of communication."

Isabel went off to make a phone call. Meckenzie decided to stay busy by finishing the salad for dinner. So much was going on; she was having a hard time wrapping her head around it. She couldn't wait for tomorrow night.

M C Moore

CHAPTER 14

The rest of that evening was fairly normal. The family had dinner together. Taggart and their father evaluated all of the surveillance equipment that had been installed. Meckenzie finished her homework and was able to catch a little TV. Kellan had been quiet most of the evening, but she hadn't been overly glum, or started any fights.

Isabel took Kellan aside after dinner for what Meckenzie could only assume was a pep talk. Kellan had come back upstairs smiling and laughing with Isabel. Meckenzie hoped that this was a turning point for Kellan. With their birthday less than four weeks away, the trips needed to do as much training as possible and still maintain their school work. The end of the school year was just around the corner, and it was hard to say what would happen after their graduation.

Meckenzie headed to bed, wishing she was supposed to meet Morgan in her dreams this evening. She would love to ask her more questions. There was so much she wanted to know about Aquanis, her mother, and the Morrigan. Meckenzie hadn't told Kellan about her vision this evening. She really hadn't talked to Kellan about anything. Taggart was so distracted with all the spy stuff going on, that Meckenzie never really even saw him except at dinner. She didn't think that she should bring up her inter-world communication at the dinner table. Her father was one more revelation away from a heart attack.

Meckenzie decided that it would be best to clear her head of all thoughts as she fell asleep. She didn't want to accidently end up talking to Morgan or even worse to Ty in her dreams.

The next morning came without any dream interruptions. Meckenzie had slept terrifically and was ready for her day. She was not ready to face Ty and tell him that her father had agreed to meet him at seven this evening for a face to face. Over breakfast Meckenzie was given the run down over how the evening should go from Taggart and Isabel. It seemed that there was a monitor set up in her father's office, as well as in the kitchen. Plus, and this was what Taggart seemed to love the most, they had tied the DVR system into the theater system on the third floor. So you could view any camera on the big screen. Taggart had spent part of last night watching the cameras. Since there was one over the front door, you could get a pretty clear shot of the street and the park.

Kellan failed to make an appearance at breakfast, but Isabel said she had grabbed something before heading off to school to work out. Jones the security guy had walked her in about an hour ago. So Taggart and Meckenzie headed off to school together after breakfast. The security guy nodded at them as they exited the door and dropped in behind them as they began their walk. Meckenzie couldn't help but sneak a peek over her shoulder to see what he was wearing today. He was still in a suit, and today his tie matched the grey color of his eyes.

"Have you talked to Kellan?" Taggart asked.

"No. I really haven't seen her, I figured she just needed some space. I'm not sure what is going on. I mean yesterday when we were in the equipment closet; she and I had a nice heart to heart talk. When we got home, she was like a totally different person. I think her mood swings are getting worse. Maybe it is a side effect of her powers, like my headaches and your growing weak after healing someone."

"Kellan has always been moody, maybe she is just frustrated and its coming off as really moody. I wouldn't call her moody to her face though, she might go all She-Hulk on you." Taggart laughed.

"I think you are the one that needs to worry. She did knock you out yesterday and you were the one that laughed at her in the equipment closet."

"Yeah, I should probably lay off of her huh?"

"I think so, unless you want to eat your meals through a straw." Meckenzie actually cracked herself up with that one.

They reached first period and Kellan was already in her seat. She seemed to be concentrating on her book and didn't even look up when her siblings sat down.

"How goes it lil sis?" Taggart ventured to break the ice.

"Good." Kellan replied, but never looked up.

Kellan was going to be a pain to deal with today, Meckenzie could already tell. If this was any indication as to how well the talk with Isabel went, Meckenzie could not figure out for the life of her what they had been laughing about. Meckenzie decided that she would not let Kellan's mood affect her day. She was already going to have to deal with giving Ty the "good" news. She really was dreading his entrance this morning.

As if Meckenzie had beckoned him with her thoughts, Ty smugly strolled into class. He smiled as he met Meckenzie's eyes and headed straight for her. Kellan, as if sensing Meckenzie's discomfort, moved to the end of the table vacating the seat between them for Ty.

As he slid into his newly appointed seat, he gave Kellan a pat on the back and turned to face Meckenzie.

"So how was the conversation with your dad? Are we good to go for my meeting him tonight?"

Meckenzie shifted uneasily in her chair to face Ty. "Yes, he said you should come over around seven, if that was okay with your parents."

"Yeah, my parents are never really home, so it won't be a problem. I'm very excited about tomorrow night. Is there some particular kind of food that you enjoy?" Ty licked his lips as he said this. To Meckenzie it brought to mind someone getting ready to consume a big meal. She hoped she wasn't the big meal that Ty was hoping to consume.

She still didn't feel too good about this date. Meckenzie knew that there was information that needed to be gathered. The situation with Ty was weird at best. His proximity to her always brought on the headaches and buzzing that was slightly driving her mad. Meckenzie hoped that it wouldn't happen all throughout their date. The buzzing would make it almost impossible for her to concentrate.

"I like Thai food a lot but I am also fond of Indian food. I had Italian last night, so I probably won't want that. You pick something, I'm sure I love it." Meckenzie was trying her hand at flirting. She coyly smiled at Ty, letting her eyes move down to her hands were she was tracing an outline of nothing in particular on her jeans.

Meckenzie didn't know if it was working, but she heard Taggart giggle a little behind her. She was sure Taggart was getting great amusement out of the situation. Any instance that made Meckenzie uneasy was always a great pleasure to Taggart. She could only imagine the amount of teasing she would take from him later in the day.

Just then the bell rang and Mr. Humphries started class. Meckenzie turned her focus to the front of the room; she just wanted this class to be over. It used to be her favorite class of the day. It was the only class that the trips had together and usually they enjoyed sitting in the back of the room, just being. But now with Kellan in such a foul mood and Ty taking up residence at their table, there was a black cloud hanging over the table.

Meckenzie felt like she had never focused so much in her life. She threw herself into today's lecture, taking clear notes, participating whenever possible, and reading along in the book with Mr. Humphries. As soon as the bell rang, Meckenzie was ready to go. She left class barely acknowledging Kellan, giving a brief goodbye to Ty, and punching Taggart in the shoulder as she raced past him to the door.

Meckenzie spent the rest of her classes focused in much the same manner. She learned after about the third class that the day seemed to fly when she threw herself into her school work. Meckenzie had always been able to get

A's with only half listening. If she finished out the school year this way, she might even make the honor roll.

As Meckenzie headed down the steps after school, she caught sight of Jones, the body guard, who waited to walk the siblings home. Meckenzie had not thought to ask Taggart or Kellan if they would be leaving as soon as school was out. She hoped they had communicated this information to the guard.

Meckenzie walked right up to him, which was not the normal way of communicating with him. Normally she just nodded and headed towards the house, knowing he would follow.

"Did my sister and brother indicate whether they were staying late?" Meckenzie asked with a matter of fact attitude.

"Your sister said she would be working out late when I walked her in this morning. Your brother found me a little while ago and said he would be in the lab until 4:30."

"Can I ask you a question?" Meckenzie wanted to get some information from this guy. She thought he might have some helpful tips on determining if someone was being honest or trying to pull the wool over her eyes. She assumed Jones had been military at some point. He had that look about him. Jones was about 6'2" probably weighed about 180 pounds, he looked ready for anything. His arms were not only muscular, but very tan, which indicated that he probably spent a lot of time outside. His brown hair was cut close to his head and he always had sunglasses handy. She assumed it was so he could look wherever he wanted without anyone knowing he was looking at them.

"I guess," Jones responded, "within reason."

"Okay, well I'll ask and then you can answer if you want. Let's say there's this guy and you haven't known him for very long. He seems okay, polite, clean cut, and attractive. No real defects on the outside."

"Ma'am, I'm going to stop you. If you are asking me a dating question, I'm not the person to ask. I've been married and divorced, and have not had a lot of luck with picking ladies who were not after something other than my wallet." He laughed at his own joke. Meckenzie thought for a second, because it was sort of a dating question. She was going on a date with him, but it was really more of a 'Can I trust this guy enough to not think he is going to kidnap or kill me question?'

"Okay, it is sort of a dating question; it is sort of a personal security question."

"Continue then."

"Well, this guy asked me out on a date. I think he might be up to something no good. Maybe even a safety risk. How can I find out?" Meckenzie ended her question with a shrug of her shoulders. She was really wanting to find out what this guy would do.

"I'd run a background check. Anyone can run them now with the internet. If he is in High School, I'd check out where he says he's from and see if he is really from there. Google him. Anyone with a history has a history on the internet."

"Can you show me how to run a background check?"

"Sure, you wanna do it now since I have an hour before I have to come back and get your brother."

"That would be great if you don't mind. I'm Meckenzie by the way; I don't think I ever got your first name." Meckenzie had been wondering since yesterday when he introduced himself what his first name was. She still had the image of his mother calling him Jones in her mind.

"Jeff Jones." He held out his hand as he said his totally all American name.

"Really, Jeff Jones. It seems so, I don't know. It just doesn't seem like it fits you." Meckenzie giggled. "I expected Butch or Duke, something rough and tough."

"What Jeff isn't rough enough for you? I mean it is really Jeffrey. Does that make it better?"

Meckenzie was actually laughing now. "Jeffrey fits even less."

They started walking towards the house with Meckenzie laughing and saying Jeffrey every few minutes. Every time she would say it she would laugh a little more. She had created an image for super scary security guy, and the name Jeffrey didn't really fit the image. She hoped she wasn't offending him by laughing at his name. She caught him smiling out of the corner of her eye and knew that he was okay with her laughing.

When they got to the house, Meckenzie headed up to her dad's office so they could use his computer. Meckenzie's laptop was in her room and though it could be moved anywhere in the house, she thought it better to do this in her dad's office so any information she found she could leave it up for her dad to see.

As Meckenzie sat down to start her first attempt at spy work, Jeff took off his sunglasses and pulled up a chair beside her. She was mesmerized by his grey eyes. Meckenzie found herself staring at him blankly wishing she could reach out and touch his hair or his face. Jeff smiled a dazzling smile that sent shivers down her spin. Meckenzie snapped herself back to reality; this was not what she was here for.

Jeff thought it might be better for her to start with Google since this was the easiest. So Meckenzie typed in Tynan Rabe in the search engine and let it do its work. There were several results, but none where Tynan and Rabe were the individual's full name. She then used Ty Rabe and came up with a director at Hewlett Packard and some guy in Massachusetts who was too old to be the Ty in her class. After clicking several links, Jeff suggested that they search for his school record. Unfortunately, Meckenzie didn't know where he went to school prior to moving here.

That had hit a road block, because Meckenzie also didn't have enough information to run a background check either.

"He's coming over tonight to meet my dad. Do you think you could give my dad a list of questions that would help us be able to run a background check?"

"Maybe. I mean if we have his birthday and his name, I can probably find something out. Do you think you should go out with this guy if you're having this much of a bad feeling about him?" Jeff said.

"No, but we need to find out who he is, it's a long story. I don't know what my dad told you about what's going on, but I am just feeling extra cautious lately." Meckenzie paused wondering how much her dad had actually told Jeff. "Okay, let's say hypothetically that we are long lost royalty from a war torn country. Let's say the faction of this war that is against the royalty has decided to seek them out and kill them or something in that nature. So, we find out only this week that we are long lost royalty, the same day this kid shows up in my class. Then he asks me out within days of moving to the school. Coincidence? I just want to protect my family and it seems like finding out who this guy is, whether by the internet or by going on a date with him is something that would help."

"Hypothetically, the date sounds like a horrible idea. If you just want information there are other ways of getting it. If you are determined to go on this date though, maybe I should go on it with you. We could tell him that your father has a big business deal going on and he thought it best to protect you."

Meckenzie had actually already considered the possibility of Jeff coming with her on her date. "I think we should just run it by my father when he gets home. It might be worth it for you to be here tonight when Ty comes over to meet my dad."

"I can pull some of the stills off the video equipment and call in a favor or two. We might be able to find something out before you actually have to go out with him." Jeff seemed more than a little concerned at this point.

"May I ask you a personal question?" Meckenzie was starting to really like Jeff. She didn't want to put him in danger. She really wanted to know how much experience he had.

"Maybe, ask and we'll see if I can answer it." Jeff smiled.

"How long have you been doing this?" Meckenzie started small.

"Two years." Sadness flashed into Jeff's eyes. It was as if something horrible had happened and it was buried behind those beautiful eyes. "I served in the Marines for six years. I was deployed overseas; I can't really tell you where. Let's just say after six years, I determined that I would rather be protecting people before the danger occurred. So a friend of mine had that gotten out a year before me got a job with a security firm here in New York. He wrote me a few times and told me I should come join him. The pay was excellent and the damage was minimal. Mostly we just do security for movie stars and the such when they come to town or have to go somewhere."

"Really, so have you met anyone really famous?" Meckenzie decided a light change of subject was in order.

"Yes, but I can't discuss our client list. Let's just say I have shown up in the background of many tabloid photos." Jeff laughed at this. He had a good laugh, a strong laugh that came from deep inside. Meckenzie had to be careful, she was very attracted to her body guard and he was at least ten years older than her.

"Well, I should probably do my homework, or work out. Hopefully you'll be able to help us out tonight, and thank you Jeff for all your help this afternoon." Meckenzie excused herself and headed downstairs to find Isabel. She knew that nothing could ever come of her crush, so she would just put it out of her mind.

Isabel was setting up a training dummy in the gym. She didn't even turn around as Meckenzie came down the stairs, she just laughed.

"Your emotions will either help you or hurt you, but for sure, they amplify your thought transmission."

Meckenzie blushed. She had been thinking about the way Jeff's shirt hugged his chest and arms, and how strong he must be, plus what a wonderful smile he had.

"What's on the agenda today?" She said.

"Well, so no one gets hurt, I thought we might take a few hits at the dummy. I think for you this will be easier for training purposes. I think for Kellan, it will make sure she doesn't accidently kill someone."

"Oh, Ty is coming over tonight to meet dad. I was hoping that you and Jeff could get a look at him. Jeff's going to run a background check on him."

"Jeff?" Isabel questioned, already knowing the answer.

"Yes, the body guard that dad hired. I asked him how we could find out about Ty and determine if he is who he says he is."

"Not a bad idea. You know if he means you any ill will, the gnome hearts will let us know as soon as he enters the house."

Meckenzie had almost forgotten about the magical alarm system that had been armed around all the entrances to their home. She hoped all the precautions she was taking would lead her to some answers regarding the effect Ty had on her.

Meckenzie decided to throw herself into her workout and started putting on her gear. She would learn as much as she could about fighting. Frankly, anything would be more than her current knowledge.

Isabel showed Meckenzie how to get the most power from her punches by using her body. She also taught her how to do a leg sweep and to break free from someone if they caught her from behind. Isabel was an excellent trainer; she was patient and had a ton of knowledge about the subject. Meckenzie could only imagine that somewhere in Aquanis there was a facility training fairies in hand to hand combat.

"Actually," Isabel interrupted her thought, "there are several training facilities in Aquanis. One for hand to hand combat, one for magical combat, one for weapons combat, and one for espionage. At least those are the ones I was trained at. We should actually work on you protecting your thoughts while trying to fight. It seems the more concentrated you get on one subject, the more your thoughts seem to transmit. Try building the wall around your thoughts again, then think about one thing very hard. I will see if I can pick it out of your brain."

Meckenzie starting putting up her mental wall. She decided she would think about her mother and the conversation she was going to have with Morgan tonight. It would be nice to hear news from her mother. To know what was going on. She was very excited. As she went through her punches she tried to determine what she might want to ask of her mother. What questions did she have? Almost everything she came up with didn't seem relevant to the battles at hand.

"Good." Isabel interrupted her thought process. "I can't hear anything."

"Did you send word to my mom about the conversation with Morgan?" Meckenzie had been so excited about the possibility of talking to Morgan again, that she hadn't even thought that she might not get to.

"Yes. We haven't received any word back from them. So in this instance, no news is good news. I gave a password that Morgan should give you at the beginning of the conversation that tells you that it is alright to talk with her. We should go through a list of things that it might be important for them to know."

Meckenzie had gotten distracted by her thoughts and the conversation with Isabel, so when she threw her last punch and it ricocheted off the dummy and the glove came back and hit her in the mouth, she was completely surprised. It was also unfortunate that Meckenzie had not put in her mouth piece, because the force of the glove off the dummy had cut her lip on her teeth. She tasted the cooper taste of blood as it started to pour out of her lip.

"Oh." Isabel hurried to Meckenzie and began inspecting her mouth. "You got yourself pretty good. I think you should go wash your mouth out in the bathroom and get some ice on it before it begins to swell."

Isabel started unlacing Meckenzie's gloves. Just then Taggart came down the stairs and headed over to where Meckenzie was now pretty bloody.

"Oh crap." Taggart exclaimed. "Did the dummy beat you up?"

"No, I can do that all on my own." Meckenzie laughed at herself.

"Well as long as you got some punches in on someone." Taggart was never going to let Meckenzie live this one down. She was a bit embarrassed by the whole thing, but she wouldn't let that deter her from throwing herself right back into training.

"Meckenzie can you check the chicken I have in the oven when you go up? Make sure it isn't getting too dry. Just be sure to wash up before you go handling the food." Isabel was trying to rescue Meckenzie from Taggart's mockery, because Isabel then threw a pair of gloves at Taggart and tossed him his mouth piece. "It's your turn big boy. Let's see what you got."

Meckenzie left the gym and headed upstairs to take care of her busted lip. It had already begun to throb with pain, so she decided to hit the pain reliever drawer their dad had in the kitchen. With a pack of frozen peas and a couple of ibuprofen, Meckenzie checked on dinner and then headed up to her room. She decided to knock out her homework and jump in the shower before dinner. It was going to be a long night and she didn't want any loose ends that needed to be tied up.

CHAPTER 15

Dinner went pretty smoothly. Kellan was still quiet, but at least she wasn't outwardly angry at anyone. They briefly discussed Ty's impeding visit and their father stated his objections once more. Meckenzie informed everyone that Jeff would be participating in the viewing so that he could gather information to run a background check. It was then determined that everyone would watch Ty's arrival and interview with their father, in the media room upstairs. The TV up there was much larger and there was enough room for everyone to sit comfortably.

Taggart was super excited about getting to try out the equipment and after dinner he went and found Jeff so they could go through the cameras that they might need. Isabel and Meckenzie did the dishes while Kellan disappeared to the gym. Their father took his position in his study, where Meckenzie would ultimately take Ty for his interview.

Everything seemed to on track when the doorbell rang at seven o'clock announcing Ty's arrival. Meckenzie took in a deep breath and headed for the door. She still felt so unprepared for this, like she was headed into a lion's den for everyone else's entertainment. She put on a big smile and opened the door. There Ty stood smiling back at her. Meckenzie felt a slight buzzing begin in the back of her head. She quickly concentrated on her mental walls.

"Hello Ty. It's nice of you to come over. Won't you come in?" Meckenzie couldn't believe her own ability to act as if nothing was amiss. She stepped back and held out an arm indicating that Ty should step into the foyer. She braced herself for the magical alarm to sound, but nothing happened. Meckenzie wondered if the gnome's hearts were even working, because she really had no doubt in her mind that this boy was up to no good.

As Ty stepped past her, he reached out and grabbed her hand to pull her in for a hug. As he touched her, the buzzing inside Meckenzie's head intensified and was accompanied by several flashes of what she could only assume were thoughts going through his head. Meckenzie really couldn't make out anything, she was just getting words. As Ty pulled her in for a hug, she braced herself for whatever would happen next. To her surprise, his lips dipped down and touched hers, sending electricity throughout her body. Her breath caught in her chest, she became light headed.

That's when it happened; Meckenzie was plunged into his brain. She could see clearly Ty and two other people standing in the park. A girl and boy with his dark hair and crystal blue eyes. They were talking in a huddle, glancing every so often at Meckenzie's house. Meckenzie couldn't hear their words, but she could understand the intent. Ty was going to find out once and for all if these were the Trefoil triplets. She could feel the malevolence of his thoughts. The connection broke as he pulled away.

For a moment, Meckenzie had lost all sense of where she was, she swayed a little like she might faint. Ty reached out and took her arm trying to steady her, but all this did was reinstitute the connection that had been made by that intimate kiss. Meckenzie stepped back and leaned up against the wall trying to regain her composure.

"I'm fine," She said. "I just got a little dizzy there. You have quite the effect on women don't you."

Ty laughed, though not all together a trusting laugh. He looked at her trying to discern what had just happened. The look on his face said he wasn't sure that it was the kiss that had caused her dizziness. Though that was partially true, Meckenzie was going to swear that it was the kiss until she could speak to Isabel.

"My father is waiting for us in the study." She led the way out of the entry and started towards the stairs.

"You have a lovely home, might I have a tour?" Ty asked.

"I'm sure we will have time after you meet my dad. We don't want to keep him waiting; I believe he still has some business to attend to this evening." Meckenzie was hoping this could go as quickly as possible. She didn't really want to give him the tour, but maybe she could get Taggart to come down and go with them. Meckenzie heard Taggart's laugh upstairs and wondered if she had been transmitting to him just now.

Her father was on the phone at his desk when they came in. He indicated that they should take a seat in the sitting area, so Meckenzie directed Ty to a seat. The office was open to the night and the air was helping to clear Meckenzie thoughts. She was still contemplating the image she had witnessed in Ty's head during that kiss. Maybe Ty was planning on taking her tonight. Meckenzie knew that there were enough people here to make sure that didn't happen, but she really had felt such hatred in his thoughts that she couldn't imagine what else he was planning. Unless Ty meant to kill them all and the meeting was just a way for him to gain entry into the house.

Meckenzie began to panic; she felt a knot growing in her stomach. She didn't want to do this anymore, she just wanted to go to bed so she could dream and talk to Morgan. Just as Meckenzie was about to completely freak out and ask Ty to leave, her father got off the phone.

"Hey kids, sorry about that, but when duty calls you best take the phone call." Her father smiled and made his way over to the sitting area. "Now, what is this I hear about you wanting take my daughter out on a date?"

"Yes sir, I would be most honored if I was allowed to take Meckenzie out tomorrow night. I have a simple evening planned. Dinner close by, then I thought some coffee at the shop around the corner, home by ten." Ty was quite charming when he wanted to be, but Meckenzie wasn't falling for it. She had felt the malevolence in his thoughts. Meckenzie knew that there would be no being home by ten.

"Well, I'd like to know a little more about you if that's okay. Where did you move from? What do you parents do?"

"My parents are both in the export/import business. My mother focuses mainly on antiquities and art. My father has a wide range of materials that he imports. They have always lived in New York; I was at a boarding school in

Connecticut for most of my life. I was set to graduate from there this fall, but my younger brother was in an accident there and my parents brought us both home. It was kind of a bummer. I had to leave my friends and it was the only school I've ever known. The one good thing that has come of the move is meeting Meckenzie."

"What did you say your parent's names were?" Lawrence Desmond asked, going through the list of questions that Jeff had written up for this evening's interview.

"I didn't sir, but they are Fredrick and Lillian Rabe." Ty smiled, he must have felt like he was doing well. Meckenzie just smiled and followed the conversation. She didn't feel like she could have spoken if she were asked to. She was still experiencing the buzzing that had been happening ever since Ty's arrival.

"So what are your plans after high school?"

"Well, I will probably go to Brown, my father went there. I was planning on studying business administration, and then probably going into business with my dad. He will be ready in about five or six years to start taking some time off. My mother is always trying to get him to go on a vacation that doesn't involve stopping over somewhere to visit a business contact, or to view a product." Ty was giving answers to every question that would have calmed the woes of most parents. In fact it looked like Meckenzie's father was falling for it as well. She just hoped that upstairs someone was doing everything they could to check out Ty's story.

"Well, I don't see any reason why you two can't go out tomorrow night. You'll have to take the security guard that is in charge of Meckenzie's safety, but other than that, I hope the two of you have a nice time." Meckenzie was floored by her father's response. She thought there had to be more questions that needed to be answered. There had to be something that could be done to keep her from having to go out with Ty. Meckenzie realized she could have just said no, but what kind of help would she be if she didn't try to find out everything she could to help her family.

"I guess I'll give Ty a tour of the house now. Then I have some homework left to do before the evening is over." Meckenzie walked over to her dad.

She leaned down and kissed him gently on the cheek. She wasn't sure why she did this, maybe as a way of letting her know she loved him in case something happened in the next few minutes.

As Meckenzie was leading Ty out of the study, Taggart came running down the stairs. He had a smile on his face and looked like he was ready to give her a hard time.

"Hey Ty, how are you doing?" Taggart stuck out his hand to shake Ty's. Ty looked a little thrown off by this gesture. He stuck his hand out and Taggart gave him a hearty hand shake. "What are you guys up to?"

"Meckenzie was about to give me a tour of the house." Ty responded.

"Oh she is no good at giving the tour; she forgets all the great details of how our grandmother built the house. Let me show you around." Taggart took up the lead and explained the upstairs were our private living quarters and that it was a strict rule of our dads that no guys were allowed past the third floor. He showed off the spiral staircase and pointed out the dome at the top. He led Ty around the ground floor pointing out the hand carved features and the intricate tile work in the kitchen. He led Ty down to the garden level and explained that how our grandmother had entertained the elite of New York here. Taggart also mentioned how the trips would be having a birthday party there in a few weeks.

Taggart showed off the gym and the swimming pool, all to Meckenzie's pleasure of not having to deal with it all. Just when Meckenzie thought she couldn't take another moment of having to smile and pretend nice with Ty, Taggart led them back up the stairs and out to the entry way.

"Well, I know you must be getting back to your homework Meckenzie." Ty said. "I'll pick you up tomorrow night at seven."

Meckenzie nodded, "Yes that would be nice. See you then."

With that Ty was out of the house and Meckenzie was able to collapse right there in the entry way. Taggart leaned over her to check her pulse. She was fine, she had just been holding in all the anger and anguish she had felt from the moment Ty walked in the house.

"I'm fine, just help me up." Meckenzie reached out her hand for a little assistance. Taggart pulled her up and put his arm around her shoulders in case she decided to take another spill onto the floor.

"So what the heck happened?" Taggart asked.

"I really only want to tell the story once, can we get Isabel first? I'll meet you in the garden." Meckenzie headed off to the garden and let Taggart locate and retrieve Isabel. It seemed like everyday something happened that required a family meeting. Meckenzie had always wished for adventure in her life. That's why she and Kellan had made up all those stories about their mother. She just knew that there was adventure there somewhere if she looked hard enough. This might be one of those instances where you should be careful what you wish for because you just might get it. Meckenzie just wanted one day to collect her thoughts and be a normal teenager, but she was sure that those days were long gone and far behind her.

Taggart, Isabel, Kellan, and to Meckenzie's surprise, Jeff came out to the garden. Meckenzie couldn't imagine that Jeff was here for the magical meeting. Maybe it was just to get the low down on what was determined from the conversation that had happened between Ty and her father.

"I think I have enough to do a background check. Though I would say that all the searching that I did while he was here indicated that he was telling the truth about his parents at least." Jeff started the conversation off with the pieces of information that he had. "Though I will say it isn't very hard to set up a background like that. I mean he may or may not be the son of the people he indicated were his parents. I will do some more background research and get back to you in the morning. I think I'll excuse myself if there is nothing else you need from me."

Meckenzie really didn't want him to leave, but she couldn't think of anything to keep him there. She liked him being around, she felt safer.

"Thanks Jeff for all your work on this. It may just be me being overly cautious."

Jeff smiled that million dollar smile, "There is no such thing as overly cautious. There is cautious, and there is that behavior that gets people in trouble."

Taggart laughed, "Isn't the saying, 'There is cautious and there is dead.'"

Kellan hit Taggart in the shoulder indicating that he was being a jerk. He just laughed even harder.

"Well, I was hoping to avoid the word dead. I assume we are trying to avoid death by all of this. And I'm sure your sister really doesn't want to think like that." Jeff was still protecting Meckenzie. Maybe he felt something too. Meckenzie pushed that thought out of her head remembering how easily she had transmitted to Isabel this afternoon.

Jeff excused himself and everyone else took seats in the garden. It had been a long night for Meckenzie and she still had to go to sleep and talk to Morgan. She really was excited about that part of her day though. Meckenzie knew she would be communicating with her mother tonight, even if she was talking to Morgan.

"So what about that kiss?" Kellan spoke her first words to Meckenzie in days. Were Kellan's words meant to hurt her a little bit? Everyone was bound to have seen her reaction to the kiss and know that it was not a positive one.

"You know you have been nothing but mean and rude for the last two days Kellan. If you don't have anything to contribute maybe you should just go away. I don't have the energy, or even the patience to deal with you right now." Meckenzie went off on Kellan like she had never done before in her life. Meckenzie had always been the patient one, taking the hits, taking the jabs, and taking Kellan's foul mood and just loving her no matter what, but Kellan had pushed her too far this time.

"I wouldn't be here if Isabel hadn't insisted that I be. I have no urge to participate in any discussions about fairies or a fairy war. I just want my life back." Kellan had begun yelling. "This is stupid. I want you all to know now that I'm not going to Aquanis, I am staying here. I'm going to college. You can all go run off and fight a war. Get yourselves killed. I'm not going."

"Kellan, just relax. No one is going anywhere right now. We are just trying to keep ourselves safe. You are going to have to learn how to deal with your powers just like the rest of us. If you don't, you are going to have a hard time having a college basketball career. It wouldn't be good for you to go exploding into a giant on the court. For now, just put your anger aside." Taggart's words fell on deaf ears. Kellan was having no part of it.

As she stood up to leave, Isabel stood up too. She started mumbling something under her breath. Gradually she got louder and louder. Isabel was pointing her hands and words at Kellan. Isabel was casting a spell, a spell that none of them had heard before. A spell was causing Kellan to have the most frightened look come across her face. Kellan couldn't move.

Isabel stopped her spell. She slowly made her way to Kellan and gently pushed her back into her chair.

"Now I want you to listen to me. You kind of have to listen to me because you can't talk or move right now. It's only temporary, but you need to hear something. You don't have any control over your life anymore. It's unfortunate that it has happened this way, but it is what you have to deal with. It's more than anyone should be asked to deal with, especially a child such as you. You have been given these gifts to help all of Fae kind. They are a great responsibility. The idea that you can control them in the human world is a frivolous one. Kellan, you have too much of a temper. You are a spoiled child and thus you will listen to me. You will go to Aquanis. You will fight this war, and you will stop harassing your sister, it is counterproductive. So if you will calm down and stay here and listen to what we have to discuss I will let you go. If this is something you think you can do then blink twice. If it is not, I will keep you like this while we continue our conversation. So what do you think?"

Kellan didn't do anything at first. She stared hatefully at Isabel. Kellan's temper was going to be the end of her. Meckenzie had always thought it would benefit her, but now Kellan appeared to have met her match. Isabel was not backing down this time. Isabel turned to go back to her seat.

"Okay, since your sister seems to be attentive, let's talk about this boy." Isabel redirected the conversation back to Ty. "I think he is Fae. I felt it when he walked in the house. He is powerful too. I am pretty sure that he is here for you three. I can't say I know who he is, but he is definitely Fae."

"Really Meckenzie what was up with the kiss?" Taggart asked again. "You almost passed out afterword."

"I had a vision. The buzzing started when he walked in the door. Then he touched me and it intensified. When he kissed me, I saw him in the park talking to two other people. They were looking at the house and I felt such malevolence that when he stopped kissing me, I almost fainted."

"Did you hear anything that they were saying?" Isabel asked.

"No, it was just some gesturing and then a brief flash of the house and the deep feeling of hatred. I was sure he was going to try and kidnap me tonight, or worse, kill us all." Meckenzie shivered at the last statement. She really hadn't allowed herself anytime to work through that moment in the foyer, she had just marched on to the rest of her evenings tasks.

All of sudden, Isabel looked at Kellan. She had been sitting paralyzed and mute, but now she was starting to move a little bit. Isabel stood up and began casting another spell. Meckenzie couldn't tell if it was the same one or not, but Kellan once again looked like something was wrong. Kellan was scared, that much Meckenzie could tell.

When Isabel finished her spell, Kellan was completely mobile again. Her eyes darted from Isabel to Meckenzie and Taggart sitting across from her.

"I'm glad that everyone thought it was okay that she paralyzed me." Kellan was almost in tears.

"Look Kellan, you just needed a time out. I won't do it again if you promise to cooperate with us." Isabel pleaded with Kellan to understand reason. Meckenzie couldn't say she would have reacted any different if someone had cast the spell on her.

"I think we have all had a long day." Meckenzie interjected. "I still have to go have my little dream conversation with Morgan."

Both Taggart and Kellan whipped their heads around to look at Meckenzie.

"Morgan?" Taggart asked. "What are you talking about?"

"Well, yesterday, I came upon a new gift so to speak. I can communicate with Morgan; she is part of the Morrigan. She and I are set to have another conversation tonight. It is a way that we can communicate with Mom without having to use the courier."

"Great, Meckenzie gets another cool power, and I'm still she-hulk." Kellan was openly crying now. "I'm going to bed."

With that Kellan stormed off. Meckenzie thought it was probably for the best since everything seemed to set Kellan off.

"What do we do about her?" Taggart asked.

"I don't know." Meckenzie felt hopeless.

"Give her some more time. I'm sure it will get easier the further along we get." Isabel tried to stay positive too, but there was a look in her eyes that said she wasn't sure either.

"Do you mind if I watch you sleep?" Taggart said out of the blue.

"What?" Meckenzie looked at him dumbfounded.

"Yeah, I want to see what happens when you do this dream communication. See if your body does anything out of the ordinary."

"It might not be a bad idea to have someone in the room with you." Isabel added.

"Okay, but let me get ready for bed and then I'll come get you." Meckenzie felt weird having someone watch her sleep, but she knew that Taggart's curiosity would only be abated by watching her sleep.

They all headed off in their separate directions. Meckenzie was so tired from her day, she didn't know if she would even be able to do this. Well, only one way to find out she thought.

CHAPTER 16

As Meckenzie showered away her day, she thought back to only a week ago when she had just been struggling with sleeping due to her reoccurring dream. In hindsight, Meckenzie saw that , she was so lost then, without any idea as to what it all meant. Over the course of the few short days, she had gotten more information than her mind knew what to do with.

She brushed out her hair, staring at her reflection. Meckenzie felt she looked like a different person. There was some knowledge in her eyes that said she had lived, or maybe it was just the exhaustion she saw around her eyes. Meckenzie had only this evening gotten her first kiss from a boy and it seemed to be the worst experience of her life. Meckenzie knew that the revolting feeling she had received in the vision, that had accompanied the kiss, was going to be how she remembered her first kiss for the rest of her life. It was really disappointing. Meckenzie had always imagined her first kiss would be something wonderful. Some magic moment in time that stopped her heart and gave her butterflies. While her heart had stopped, it was not from the kiss, it had been from the vision. The vision of Ty staking out her house with two other people and the feeling of hatred was so strange it had made her feel nauseous.

Meckenzie laughed as she realized that all things she had wanted from her first kiss had happened with her kiss with Ty. Heart stopped. Check. Funny feeling in her stomach. Check. Dizzy, breathlessness after. Check. Yet there was something glaringly missing. The attraction.

Meckenzie got dressed for bed and made her way out to the sitting area that she and Kellan shared. She hadn't expected to find Kellan sitting there waiting for her. Meckenzie hoped that Kellan wasn't going to start anything. Meckenzie had just cleared her mind with a shower and was ready to relax into a dream state so she could talk to Morgan. The last thing she needed was to have Kellan start something right before bed.

"Look," Kellan started off very timidly. It wasn't really in Kellan's nature to be timid. "I know that none of this is your fault. I know you didn't start this. I just can't understand why you are so okay with it. Why do you just go along with everything that Isabel says?"

"Kellan, I'm not really in the mood for this. I am tired and I have to do this thing. I don't know why I'm just okay with it. I never really thought about not being okay with it. I am just trying to make it through the day. It would help if you would lay off of me for a while. You are right I didn't cause this, but if you keep coming after me and Taggart the way you are, you might not have anyone left to help you get through it." Meckenzie had really had enough of Kellan's whiny attitude. She wasn't in the mood and she wasn't going to take it anymore.

Kellan didn't even look at Meckenzie as she got up and went back into her room. Meckenzie thought she heard Kellan start to cry, but she didn't really have time to deal with it at this point.

Meckenzie decided she didn't want to go running all over the house looking for Taggart, so she sent out a mental message to him. *If you're ready, I'm so tired I can barely stay awake. Come up to my room.* She didn't even wait for a response; she just headed back into her room and got into bed.

Taggart was up the stairs in a minute flat. He had the biggest smile on his face. He really was taking this better than the rest of them. Meckenzie just felt tired all the time, but Taggart always seemed to be happy. Actually, excited was a better way to describe his attitude about this whole situation. He was just so curious about everything, that he got excited anytime anything new happened.

"Okay, so how does this work?" Taggart asked.

"I'm not all together sure. Last time, I just fell asleep while thinking about the Morrigan. So this time I'm going to try and fall asleep thinking about Morgan specifically. I think it's best if we turn off the light, but leave the bathroom light on, so you're not in totally darkness."

Taggart turned on the light in the bathroom and moved a chair next to the door. He then walked over and turned off the light to the room. Meckenzie waited for him to settle in, then she closed her eyes and started thinking about Morgan. It was going to be hard not to think about her mom during this. She really wanted to talk to her, but she was happy she at least had Morgan to communicate with.

Meckenzie was running through the questions that she wanted to ask Morgan and the next thing she knew she was sitting in front of the mirror again staring at her. It was so surreal to see this girl staring back at her. This girl, Morgan, who was now expected to enlighten and lead a people through her Goddess.

"Hello Morgan. Do you have a password for me?"

"Yes, your mother said that we would be using a password from now on. That was a great idea by the way. The password is Dr. Seuss. Who is this Dr. Seuss? Your mother just laughed and said it was someone from your childhood."

Meckenzie knew that her mother would remember that Dr. Seuss was her favorite author when she was a child. She still had many Dr. Seuss books on her bookshelf.

"He was a children's author, my favorite as a child. Do you have any other news from my mother?"

"She believes that there are several spies in New York City looking for you. She thinks that you and your siblings should be really careful. She is hoping that she can find out in the next few days who some of them are. She doesn't have any names yet."

"Ask her if Ty Rabe is familiar to her. He started at our school a few days ago and has taken an interest in me. I'm not sure if that is his real name, but that is all I have. I am supposed to go out on a date with him tomorrow night. It is sort of a fact finding mission."

"Meckenzie, do you think it is wise to go out with someone that may or may not be out to get you? I will talk to your mom. I'm supposed to tell you to retrieve the necklace from the bank. She said you would know what I mean."

"Yes of course. We have been meaning to do that, but with all that has been going on, we got sidetracked. Isabel wanted her to know that the thing she sent got here and is working out great. I don't know what that means, but she said mom would."

"Okay, I'll remember that. She wanted to know how each of you is doing."

"I'm doing well. Just trying to get the hang of my gifts and learning all of this new information about myself and my family's history. I think Taggart is doing the best. He finds everything very curious. He was always the inquisitive one of the three of us. He is reading any book that Isabel gives him. He also is trying to keep the peace with Kellan. Kellan is taking it horribly. She blames everyone for what is going on. She just wants her normal life is what she says. I would say that is out of reach. She loses her temper and grows almost twice her size. She doesn't seem to want to deal with anything. Her only recourse is to lash out at Taggart and me. She knocked Taggart out while we were doing defensive training. Kellan has gotten so strong that one good punch and she might be able to kill someone."

"Your mom was also wondering how your father was?"

"Did she really ask about my dad?"

"Yes. She seemed really worried. She told me I had to be very secretive about it, because she doesn't want anyone finding out who he is and using him against her, or you guys."

"He seems to be growing grayer by the second. He has taken it really well, considering. I think he always knew something was up. It helps that he just wants what is best for us and wants to protect us. He may change his mind when it comes time for us to go to Aquanis. Do you know if he can come with us?"

"I don't know, but I'll ask. Is there anything else that we need to discuss?"

"I just want mom to know I love her. I miss her. I hope to see her soon. I think we should wait a couple of days before contacting each other again. So how bout in three days we will try this again?"

"Okay, same password or do we need a new one?" Morgan asked.

"How about we try a new one. Any suggestions?"

"We can use my name before I became Morgan, Alia."

"Okay. See you in three days." With that Meckenzie thought wake up, and she was suddenly awake lying in her bed. It was dark except for the light in the bathroom that silhouetted Taggart sitting in a chair staring at the bed.

"Hey." Meckenzie said.

"That was interesting. You talk in your sleep when you do that. So I got one side of the conversation. Thanks by the way, for thinking that I handle this best of the three of us. I don't necessarily think I do. I just try to keep smiling, keep positive. I happened to bring a notepad, so I took notes of your conversation in case you forgot anything."

"Thanks. I still can't believe I can do this. I am really worn out though. So if you don't mind, I'd like to go to sleep now."

Taggart started to make his way to the door. "Do you think Kellan will come around?"

"I don't know. I kind of told her off earlier. I told her if she kept coming after us like she was, she might not have anyone left in her life. I know it was harsh, but I'm just so tired of her whining about this. I expected her to take it better I guess. She is always so tough, so strong. I just can't understand what is causing her to be so angry all the time."

"Really? You can't figure out why our willful temperamental sister is angry about everything that is going on. You have these fantastic powers. Powers that you are using on a daily basis. Powers that allow you to communicate in a roundabout way with mom and Kellan has some speed, strength and agility.

I would think she feels cheated. Not to mention she feels like she turns into a monster every time she does that growing thing."

"I never thought of it like that. I thought her gifts suited her. Kellan has always been athletic."

"Yes, but now she is thinking has she always been athletic, or have the powers always allowed her to be good at sports? She is just confused and scared. We have to be even more supportive of her now." Taggart was always the level headed one. He had such a genuine heart and love for his sisters. He had never complained about being the only boy when they would play as kids. He had just gone with the flow even when they had made him play girl games.

"Okay, I'll try to be better. I really do have to go to sleep. I have had a long day." Meckenzie could think of nothing sweeter than sleep. Taggart flipped off the bathroom light and made his way out of her room.

Meckenzie rolled over in her bed and closed her eyes praying for a dreamless sleep. She just wanted to wake up in the morning and be well rested for yet another trying day that lay ahead. She knew she would need all her energy to get through the school day and the date with Ty. Meckenzie thought of Jeff coming on the date with her and she smiled as she drifted off to sleep.

CHAPTER 17

Meckenzie's sleep was anything but restful. She had dreamt of people trying to get her from the shadows. She had dreamt of Ty trying to kill her with a silver knife. Meckenzie had not dreamt of Jeff sweeping her off her feet and rescuing her. A morning run was what she needed, so she headed down to the gym to get one in before school. As Meckenzie reached the gym she heard Kellan's music playing. Kellan was lifting weights and didn't even acknowledge Meckenzie as she boarded the treadmill and put in her earphones for her iPod.

For the first mile, Meckenzie was having problems finding a rhythm. She had so much on her mind that she was easily distracted and wasn't allowing herself to feel the endorphins that were being produced. As Meckenzie headed into the second mile, one of her favorite Foster the People songs came on her iPod. She got so caught up in singing the song that she blocked out everything in her mind and the surrounding gym. The burn in her legs was spreading throughout her body and she felt a rejuvenation happening. Meckenzie lost herself in the music and the run and by the end of the fifth mile she was ready for her day.

As Meckenzie headed upstairs to shower, she grabbed an apple and a granola bar from the kitchen. Isabel was there preparing breakfast for whoever would take time to eat it. She was humming to herself, as she often did, and was surprised when Meckenzie spoke.

"Good morning"

"My goodness girl, you are quiet this morning. You nearly made me drop the eggs. How was your conversation with the Morrigan?" Isabel said as she started scrambling some eggs.

"It was okay. Taggart took notes, it seems I talk out loud as I am talking to Morgan. So he was able to record my side of the conversation. I thought we would talk about it after school. I need to get a shower and get ready."

"Sure. I'll meet you in the gym after school. I want to teach you a couple of last minute spells for your date tonight."

Meckenzie groaned. "I was trying not to think about that."

"Well, you are going to see the boy in an hour. I think you have to think about it at some point." Isabel said laughing at Meckenzie.

"Not for another hour." Meckenzie said as she ran for the stairs. She had every intention of getting in the shower with her workout high. No date was going to affect her mood this morning, at least not until first period.

She was still in an exceptional mood when she stepped out the front door to head to school. Her mood was only made better by the presence of Jeff waiting for her on the front steps.

"Good morning." Meckenzie said with a smile. "How are you today?"

"You are in a great mood. Looking forward to your date I suppose?" Jeff said in a questioning manner. He didn't seem happy, though he had smiled a little bit when Meckenzie had first come out of the door. Meckenzie thought she might have imagined it. It would be totally like her to inflict her feelings for this guy into his emotions.

"Not really, I just had a great workout. I feel good about the day. Positive thinking is what I'm going for." As Meckenzie finished her sentence, she caught the grin on Jeff's face. He had definitely smiled that time.

The walk into school was too quick for Meckenzie. She really enjoyed the peace of mind that just being in Jeff's presence afforded her. She also knew that within minutes, there would be a classroom full of kids and Ty.

"Well, thank you for the escort into school." Meckenzie smiled.

"Anytime milady." Jeff bowed to her which Meckenzie found very odd and yet very flattering. She giggled and ran up the steps so she would make it to class on time.

Just as the bell was ringing she slid into her seat between Ty and Taggart. Kellan was her ever so sullen self at the other end of the table. Meckenzie carried her attitude into class, and was determined to make the most of this day.

"Good morning Ty. Good morning Taggart. Good morning Kellan." Meckenzie smiled at everyone as she said her good mornings. "It is a beautiful day outside, it sucks that we have to be in this classroom."

"I could remedy that for you." Ty said as he leaned closer to Meckenzie. She realized at that moment that the buzzing that so often flooded her head when he was around was mysteriously absent. "We could always skip out and go have an adventure."

"Oh that sounds lovely, but I would hate to get into trouble and miss our date tonight." Meckenzie was really pouring it on thick. Taggart gently kicked her under the table trying to get her attention. Meckenzie decided to ignore him for a moment and continue her new found acting abilities.

"I can't wait." Ty said as he reached out and touched the back of Meckenzie's hand. Just as he touched her, the buzzing started in the back of her head. She was starting to understand that his proximity was important, but his touch was even more important to the intensity of the buzz. Ty took his hand away and the buzzing stopped completely. Maybe the good mood, endorphins, and her mental wall that she had started constructing every morning were working together to make the buzzing stop.

Just then Mr. Humphries started class. Meckenzie could feel Taggart staring at her so she finally made eye contact with him. He seemed to be trying to tell her something, but her mental wall was so well constructed that not even Taggart could get through.

What is it Taggart? It was quite fun to be able to speak with her mind. She could easily focus on Taggart and make sure he was the only one hearing her.

What has gotten into you? You are freaking me out.

I'm just doing my part. I feel good today. There is no buzzing. I think the work out helped this morning. Not to mention I think I'm getting better at focusing my powers. I think if I wanted to I might be able to directly focus on someone and hear what they are thinking.

Don't you think that would be letting them have access to your thoughts too? Taggart seemed really upset by Meckenzie's new attitude.

I think the key is to lock up my thoughts and focus on gleaning thoughts from their head. I don't know why, but I feel like that is what I should do. Meckenzie was starting to think that she was going crazy. She seemed to feel a confidence and knowledge about everything that hadn't been there last night.

Taggart focused back on the front of the class. Meckenzie decided she would try to pick thoughts out of people's brains. She first focused on a girl who was sitting near the front of the class looking out the window. The girl seemed to be anywhere but here. Meckenzie focused her thoughts and imagined she was opening a window into the girls mind. At first it didn't make sense, it was random words that didn't really go together. Meckenzie realized she was picking up other people's thoughts as well, so she made her focus into a tunnel.

With a little concentration, the girls mind opened up to Meckenzie. She was thinking about her boyfriend who was in college. She was thinking about their date last night and how much she had enjoyed the Italian food that they had had. She was sad that she didn't eat more of it, but she also knew she didn't want him to think she was a pig. Meckenzie decided to try someone else's mind.

For her next target, Meckenzie chose the boy that Kellan and her basketball teammate had almost come to blows over. Jake Cummings was sitting one row in front of Meckenzie and one table to the left. He was focused on Mr. Humphries, but as soon as Meckenzie entered his mind she knew that his thoughts were on Kellan. He was devising a plan to be alone with her. Meckenzie actually laughed out loud that this boy had no idea what he was getting himself into. Unfortunately the laugh attracted some attention from other members of the class, so Meckenzie ducked her head and began focusing on her text book. She hadn't broken the connection to Jake's brain though and he was wondering what Kellan's strange sister was laughing about. If only he knew how strange she was, how strange Kellan was for that matter.

Meckenzie decided that she would discontinue her experiment. She really wanted to pry into Ty's thoughts, but something about him said he would know if she were in there. Class time seemed to drag on today. Meckenzie couldn't concentrate on the lesson and was only thinking about working out, practicing her magic, and talking to Isabel about her ability to focus her powers. To her dismay the rest of the day went the same way. She hid from Ty at lunch and was able to finish all of her homework during study hall.

So when Meckenzie left school that day, her weekend was completely hers. She had no school work to take care of and that meant Meckenzie could focus her energy into her Fairy endeavors.

Jeff walked Meckenzie home, but stayed two steps behind her the whole time. Meckenzie couldn't figure out what had changed about their relationship since this morning. She wasn't going to let this get her down though. She had managed to be in a good mood all day long even though the day seemed longer than normal.

Meckenzie paused at the top of the steps for a moment. She had an idea; she would try to read Jeff's thoughts. She turned around as if to say something. He had turned his back to her and was facing the park, not really aware that Meckenzie was looking at him. She reached out with her mind and tried to find her way to his thoughts.

Meckenzie was surprised when the first thing she was able to understand was her name. Jeff was thinking about her. She got excited for a moment, then realized that of course he was thinking about her, he had just walked her home. Then she started to make out more of his thoughts. He was conflicted. He felt an attraction to her, but her age was causing him problems. Meckenzie wasn't yet eighteen. Then she got something that she never expected to find there. Her mother's name jumped out of his mind. Jeff knew her mother.

"You know my mother?" Meckenzie questioned him without thinking that this would indicate that she had been in his mind.

He spun around. The look on his face was disbelief. He couldn't for the life of himself figure out how she had figured it out. Meckenzie was still standing there staring at him, and he had yet to answer. She still had access to his mind though. He was cycling through a half a dozen responses when Meckenzie decided she would handle this on her own.

"Come inside. We should talk to Isabel."

Jeff followed Meckenzie obediently. His mind still was racing around trying to figure out how he was going to fix this. He knew he hadn't said anything out loud, but somehow she knew. Jeff knew the triplets had some powers, though he had been told her power was visions. Could it be that Meckenzie read his mind? Meckenzie hearing this thought laughed as she headed downstairs where she assumed Isabel would be.

Meckenzie thought she might want to warn Isabel, so she projected a thought out to her.

Isabel, I think you should tell me who Jeff really is. I am bringing him downstairs.

As they entered the gym, Isabel was sitting down on the mat they used for training. She didn't even look up. Isabel had settled in for the conversation she suspected they were about to have.

"So the secret is out." Isabel patted the mat beside her indicating that Meckenzie should take a seat. "You weren't too hard on Jeff were you? I mean it really isn't his fault that your mother sent him as soon as she realized someone might be following you. When your father decided to hire someone for security, I convinced him that it was better to hire someone who understood more about what was going on. Jeff has contacts around the city that have been established since your great grandmother's time. He can get information from them. Plus, he has been here before on other business so he knows the city. It just made since to have a Fairy guarding you. So how did you get him to tell you?"

"Jeff didn't tell me, I read it in his mind." Meckenzie stated. It never occurred to her that this wasn't part of her ability to transmit and receive messages through telepathic means.

"So it seems your gifts are far greater than we expected. I imagine that your brother and sister are similarly blessed, they just don't realize it yet. It makes sense that the powers that had been bound for all those years would come back greater than before. The only thing I fear is that the enemy is experiencing a similar surge in powers."

Jeff still stood quietly waiting for the reprimand that he thought he deserved.

"You don't deserve to get into trouble." Meckenzie responded to his thoughts. "It's not your fault I read your mind. I can't seem to get out of your mind right now. I'm sorry. It was an invasion of your privacy and I shouldn't have done it."

"What were you looking for anyways?" Jeff asked.

Meckenzie blushed. She had been looking for a reason why Jeff was giving her the cold shoulder. It had been a purely selfish reason for her to pry into his thoughts. Meckenzie was even more embarrassed by the fact that Isabel knew exactly why she was had done it.

"I don't think it's important why she was there, we just need to make sure that Meckenzie stays out of thoughts that are not meant to be gone through. Right Meckenzie? I think you shouldn't be probing anyone that you feel you can." Isabel was rushing in to save Meckenzie and reprimanding her at the same time. Meckenzie would take the reprimand as long as she didn't have to explain what she had been doing picking Jeff's thoughts.

"Yes ma'am. I don't understand something though. I thought this was just an extension of my abilities to communicate with people telepathically. Is it a totally different power all together?"

"Yes it is. How did you discover that you could do this?" Isabel asked.

"I was sitting in class and just thought I bet I can read people's thoughts. So I started trying to push my way into people's minds and find out what they were thinking. It was all jumbled at first, but then I started to be able to make better sense as to what they were thinking. Some people are easier to read. Jeff wasn't easy at all. I mainly just got words, no clear thoughts."

Meckenzie suddenly realized she had questions about Jeff. She didn't know if she should ask them now while he was here or wait to have the conversation with Isabel. She was still feeling the power that her day had given her so she just went for it.

"Jeff doesn't seem like a very Fairy-like name?"

Jeff laughed, "It's not my real name. It's the name I use when I'm in the human world. My real name is Ardan."

"Ardan, it seems to suit you more than Jeff. Should I continue to call you Jeff?"

"Yes, it is part of my cover. We all have to stay as invisible as possible."

"Do you have gifts?" Meckenzie still had many questions she wanted to ask and she didn't know how long Isabel would let her head down this path.

"I do. I was one of the first of the Fae to receive my gifts."

"Oh, what can you do?" Meckenzie was very excited about the idea of someone else having powers such as their own.

"I'm quite good at combat. I am what you might call bullet proof."

"What does that mean?" Meckenzie's curiosity was peeked. She wanted to know everything she could about Jeff. She was hypnotized by his voice. There was something about him that made her feel all warm and tingly inside. She still wondered if he felt anything for her. It occurred to Meckenzie that he might not be as old as she thought he was.

"Well, my body is very hard, so when someone fires a bullet at me, it just bounces off. The same works for other objects such as knives or swords. I can be hurt by magic and fire, but most everything else is not a problem."

"How old are you?" Meckenzie was pushing the envelope a little with that question. She knew that it was way more personal than she should have really been asking. The need to know if he was too old for her was just out weighing her judgment at this point.

"I'm actually just twenty-three. I have a cover story that puts me at twenty-eight, but I have been traveling back and forth to this world since I was sixteen and it was necessary for me to be older than I actually was. So they started me out at twenty-one."

Meckenzie almost did a backflip of joy. He was only five years older than her. There was a sliver of hope that she might be able to date him, if Jeff actually wanted to date her. Meckenzie knew she was putting the cart before the horse, but she had never really liked a guy before. She just couldn't help but feel a little elated over the possibility that she might be able to date him.

"I think it is time that Meckenzie and I began training. Not to mention the fact that there are two other teenagers unaccounted for." Isabel had reached the limit to which she would allow Meckenzie to investigate. She stood up from the mat and began preparing some kind of mixture that Meckenzie hadn't noticed.

Jeff left the two of them alone and went off to find Taggart and Kellan. Meckenzie couldn't seem to quit thinking about him, she was obsessed. Maybe she should talk to Isabel about it. Meckenzie had never really had a female figure to discuss these things with and Isabel was her great aunt. She decided it could wait till another time. Meckenzie needed to focus on her training now and she did still have the date with Ty tonight.

"I know that you like him, but you need to put it out of your mind for a while. He will have a hard time doing his job if he is only worried about you and not your siblings as well. I will send Jeff away if it becomes a problem." Isabel may have not been able to read Meckenzie's mind, but she sure knew what Meckenzie was thinking.

"So what's on the agenda for this afternoon?"

"I am going to teach you a defensive spell that will allow you to confuse someone long enough to get away if necessary. It is really simple. I need you to drink this tea first. It is a mix that will amplify your powers and allow you to keep a better mental block up while on your date." Isabel handed her a cup of what looked like tea. It smelt of bad eggs and pumpkin spice. Meckenzie almost spit it out when she took her first sip. It tasted worse than it smelled.

"I know it tastes horrible. You should just toss it back like you're taking medicine. It'll probably be less painful that way."

Meckenzie opened her mouth and took a deep breath, which was the wrong thing to do because the smell hit her right before the taste hit her tongue. Meckenzie had to use all her will power not to throw up. After a minute the taste still lingered in her mouth so Isabel offered her a slice of orange to help with the bitterness that was hanging around the back of her tongue.

"Okay. You only need to learn two words on this one. Mearhball sáraigh. It basically means 'confusion violate'."

"Mearhball sáraigh." Meckenzie spoke the words. The language was difficult, it felt funny on her tongue. "How will I direct it?" She asked Isabel.

"Direct what?" Isabel asked throwing Meckenzie into a state of panic. Had her spell casting been so accurate that she had befuddled Isabel simply by speaking the phrase.

"The spell." Meckenzie replied. Isabel just looked at her confused, then she cracked a grin and began to laugh. Meckenzie couldn't understand what was going on.

"I'm just messing with you. It takes a little more concentration than that. First you look at the person in the eyes. Then you say the words. Let's not practice on me though. If it does work, I will need to reverse it."

Meckenzie smiled at Isabel, she was tempted to try and cast the spell on Isabel just to get her back for tricking her. Meckenzie might have done it if Taggart hadn't barreled down the stairs at that moment.

"Shouldn't someone be getting ready for her big date tonight?" Taggart said teasingly.

"Isabel is there a spell that would make Taggart look like me so he could go on the date?" Meckenzie laughed with him. She knew that she was about to get to cast the confusion spell on him, so she would get the last laugh.

"Nope no spell for that, but there is a gift known as trans-configuration that allows someone to project the idea of being someone else into a person's brain. You would believe with all your being what you thought you were seeing."

"Cool. So what are we learning today?" Taggart said.

"You are going to be my guinea pig." Meckenzie laughed knowing what was about to happen. She walked right up to him and looked him deep in the eyes. She smiled as she said, "Mearhball sáraigh."

Within seconds Taggart looked completely lost. He looked around like he had never seen the gym before. He looked at Meckenzie as he had no idea who she was.

"Do you think it worked?" Meckenzie asked.

CHAPTER 18

After Meckenzie cast the spell on Taggart, Isabel kicked her out of the gym. The spell had worked, which had pleased Isabel, but not warning Taggart that it was coming had gotten Meckenzie in hot water. Isabel was frustrated enough that she sent her away without teaching Meckenzie the reversal spell. So now she was getting ready for her date.

Meckenzie decided a long shower and some female primping was in order. She did her nails, which hadn't had any attention in weeks. They sparkled now with a light pink polish that had hints of glitter in it. She took extra care in applying lotion to her whole body. Meckenzie had determined that if she were going to get anything out of this date, it would be that she looked and felt good.

Taking extra special care with hair, Meckenzie curled it into large ringlets. It fell like golden waves around her face, causing her blue eyes to stand out even more. Meckenzie had picked out a summer dress, even though it was spring, and had paired it with a sweater to guard against the cool nights of the city.

When Meckenzie was finished getting ready it was almost seven. So she slipped her phone, some lip gloss, and the can of pepper spray her father had gotten for her, into a clutch purse that matched her dress and headed downstairs. Kellan hadn't made an appearance all afternoon, so Meckenzie was surprised to see her sitting at the bar in the kitchen.

"You look nice." Kellan seemed surprised that Meckenzie would go to this much trouble for her date.

"Well thank you. What are your plans for the evening?"

"Taggart and I have decided to stalk you. He activated the GPS locator on your iPhone so that we can be close, but not so close as to get caught."

"Jeff will be with us, do you really think that is necessary?"

"Taggart thinks so, even if you did use a little magic on him this afternoon." Kellan laughingly replied.

"You should have seen him. He was completely lost. I don't think I have ever seen Taggart so confused in his life. Isabel was way ticked off." Even Meckenzie couldn't help but laugh at her brother's state this afternoon.

Meckenzie heard her father talking as he was descending the stairs. To her surprise, Jeff was getting a last minute debriefing from him. Jeff had a look of patience on his face as their father instructed him not to let Meckenzie out of his sight. Knowing what she knew about Jeff, she was pretty sure that he had done this before and she suspected he was pretty good at it.

When Jeff looked up and saw Meckenzie, he stopped dead in his tracks. It took him a moment to regain his composure, and no one seemed to notice he had even stopped except Meckenzie. She melted when he smiled at her. As tempting as it was, Meckenzie tried not to read his mind. She was pretty sure that all her work primping had paid off. Even though Jeff wasn't her date, she sure enjoyed his reaction.

Her father was not as appreciative of all her hard work getting ready. He immediately shook his head.

"Aren't you going to get cold in that dress?" He had attempted to take the logical route to get her to cover up, but it wasn't going to work. Meckenzie felt too good about herself to go changing into something more reasonable.

"I've got a sweater. Plus we are going to a restaurant, it's not like we are going to be dinning outside."

"You don't know that, he may have picked a place with a patio." Her father's objections were not going to work.

"Dad, I'll be fine. Do I look nice?" Meckenzie did a quick spin around so that the full effect of the outfit was visible. When she returned to face her father and Jeff, she noticed a unfamiliar look flash across Jeff's face.

"You look wonderful darling." Her father realized he was not going to win this battle and leaned in to kiss Meckenzie's forehead.

Just as he was pulling away, the doorbell rang. Kellan volunteered to get the door and her father followed closely behind. Meckenzie and Jeff were left alone in the kitchen for a moment. He looked as if he wanted to say something. The emotions were flying across his face and didn't take Meckenzie's mind reading ability to realize that he didn't want her to go out with Ty tonight.

"Are you sure about doing this? You can back out you know. We can try other means to find out who this guy is."

"It'll be fine. It's just one date and I don't really like him so if something goes wrong, we can just get out of there."

Jeff smiled. "You really look amazing. I wonder how great you would look if you really liked the guy?"

Meckenzie blushed, she couldn't help it. She knew that Isabel had said that she should put Jeff out of her mind, but with him so close by, it was nearly impossible.

"We should go." Jeff reached out and touched her arm. Meckenzie felt a million tiny fires ignite all over her body. It was the most magical and wonderful feeling she had ever experienced. She let Jeff lead her to the front door where Ty was getting twenty questions from her father about their plans for the evening.

"Dad," Meckenzie interjected, "I think we should go."

Ty was looking rather dashing in a suit jacket and t-shirt combo that was very city chic. He had gotten a haircut so that his jet black hair was now falling haphazardly around his face.

"You look amazing tonight." Ty said as he took Meckenzie's hand. "Shall we go?"

"Sure. This is Jeff, my bodyguard. He'll be with us this evening."

Ty didn't even acknowledge Jeff's existence; he simply pulled Meckenzie out the door. Ty laced his fingers into hers, which sent electricity through Meckenzie's body, but it was nothing like the wonderful feeling she had received from Jeff's touch in the kitchen. It was like her body was trying to tell her in every way possible to get away from this guy.

Meckenzie distracted herself from the unpleasantness she felt in Ty's presence with pleasantries. "So where are we going tonight?"

Ty smiled at Meckenzie, "I thought we could go to this Thai restaurant that is a couple of blocks over. I hope you like Thai food."

Meckenzie had remembered telling him that Thai food was one of her favorties, she thought she was going to be sick. Ty really revolted her. She couldn't imagine having dinner with him, but here she was, going to dinner. Meckenzie knew she needed to say something to keep the date moving.

"I'd love to have Thai food with Ty." She said in her wittiest voice. "So tell me about yourself. Tell me about your family."

"Well, I have a brother and a sister. I told you about my parents when I met your dad. There really isn't much more to tell."

"Do your brother and sister go to school with us?" Meckenzie tried to sneak a peek at Jeff who was following closely behind them.

"No, they are both out of school."

"So they are older than you?" Getting information out of Ty was difficult; he seemed reluctant to answer questions with any personal detail.

"Yeah. So tell me about you. Are your parents still together? I would love to meet your mom." Ty smiled innocently at Meckenzie.

"My parents are separated." Meckenzie was trying to think of way to explain her mom's absence. "She is in France. I think we are going there to visit her this summer."

Meckenzie thought that was a good cover story. She had been to Paris when she was fifteen. It was a trip her father had planned, taking them all away for two weeks in the summer. It had been a great trip and Meckenzie had fallen in love with Paris.

"France is beautiful. I love Paris, especially in the evenings with all the lights and people. So how long have they been separated?"

Meckenzie knew that this piece of information was public knowledge. There had to have been some record of it. She knew the school had records stating that their mother was not allowed to pick them up anymore. Meckenzie remembered her father going down to the school and talking to the head master.

"They have been separated for eight years."

"Do you get to see her much?" Ty seemed generally concerned.

"Not as often as I'd like. So let's talk about something a little lighter. What do you like to do in your free time?"

"I like to read. I read a lot actually and I listen to music."

"Do you play sports?"

"No. I'm not the athletic type. I have done some fencing, but I'm only adequate at it. What about you?"

"I don't play competitive sports at all. I like to run. I read too, but not as much as I should. I love music. I like to try and see live music whenever I get the chance. It's nice when they have concerts in the park; I can usually go up to the roof and hear the music."

Meckenzie thought she may have made a mistake telling him there was roof access. She knew that if Ty was truly trying to get in the house, he would have figured it out on his own. She didn't need to make his job any easier though.

Meckenzie was relieved when they finally had reached their destination. Jeff took position outside the door of the restaurant as Meckenzie and Ty stepped inside. Ty spoke to the hostess while Meckenzie ran through possible topics of conversation that would get Ty to open up. Meckenzie thought that it might be important to let Jeff know that she could communicate with him if she needed to, so she sent him a telepathic message.

Jeff, it's Meckenzie, I know this is probably pretty freaky. I just wanted you to know that I can communicate with you through my mind. If I need you, I'll let you know.

Jeff responded, seeming to take all of Meckenzie's freakiness in stride. *Thank you for letting me know. This guy is freaky. I'm pretty sure he is Fae.*

Meckenzie thought about that for a moment, Isabel had said the same thing. Meckenzie knew what she had to do. At some point tonight, she was going to have to try and read Ty's mind. She hoped that he didn't have some kind of powers. If Ty did, he might be able to detect her probing. It would almost be worth it to just tell him she thought he was a fairy. Then at least Meckenzie could gage his reaction. If Ty did harbor all the hatred Meckenzie had felt in her vision when he had kissed her, she was sure that it would show in his face when she surprised him with the knowledge that she knew what he was. Meckenzie's logic got the better of her and she decided against doing a big reveal over dinner.

The hostess showed them to their seat and gave them menus. Meckenzie took a quick look at the menu, but she knew she would more than likely have Pad Thai. It was her favorite Thai dish.

"What sounds good?" Ty asked. "Should we start with some chicken satay?"

"Oh that sounds good. I think I'll have the Pad Thai. What about you?"

"I think I'll have the Kang Dang."

"That is so good. I love curry too. I often get the yellow curry."

The waitress came by and took their orders. While Ty was distracted with the waitress, Meckenzie thought she might try and sneak a peek at his thoughts. As soon as she thought about doing it, Ty turned to her and asked her what she would like to drink. The smile on his face was scary. It could have been her imagination but Meckenzie felt like he knew she was prodding at the edge of his thoughts trying to find a way in.

"I'll just have water." Meckenzie knew she was going to have to get into Ty's mind at some point; maybe just push past her trepidations and dive in. It was a pointless date if she didn't find something out. Ty might realize Meckenzie was in there, but she knew he probably wouldn't cause a scene in the restaurant. Then again if Ty really could feel her in there, then Meckenzie wanted an escape route. She took a moment to scope out the restaurant. Meckenzie located the bathroom so if she needed a break, she could always excuse herself. There was probably an exit through the kitchen. Jeff was by the front door, so that was the safest way to flee. Meckenzie realized that nothing had actually happened; she could just be making herself crazy, but better safe than sorry.

Meckenzie decided to let Jeff know that she might try to read Ty's thoughts. *Jeff, I'm going to try and read Ty's mind.* She waited for the telepathic response from Jeff, but she got no response. *Jeff are you there? Jeff?* Meckenzie began to panic, she couldn't see Jeff by the front door and she wasn't able to reach him mentally.

"You have the weirdest look on your face. What are you thinking about?" Ty was staring at her with that devilish grin of his. Meckenzie had gotten so caught up in her escape route and trying to communicate with Jeff that she had forgotten to put on her happy face.

"I was just thinking about the paper we have to write for our humanities class. I was reading the book I've chosen earlier and something just popped into my head about it. Sorry, I do that sometimes. Get lost in my own thoughts."

Meckenzie decided to just go for it. She cleared her mind and looked directly at Ty. She pushed her mind out to his and tried to push herself in. There was a feeling of dense fog surrounding his thoughts. Nothing was visible, just the feeling that something was there.

Ty had begun talking, but Meckenzie was still pushing at the edge of his brain trying to find her way in. She was tugging, pushing and trying to slash her way into his mind. The harder she worked to see, the foggier the thoughts became. Then like a sock to the stomach she clearly got one word. "NO".

Meckenzie inhaled deeply and felt light headed. Ty had begun laughing, she had missed everything he had said, so she laughed too.

"You really think you can just push your way into my mind?" Ty said. "I can feel you in there, and I have had years building up a defense to people trying to read my mind. I guess the cat's out of the bag though. I was really hoping this was going to be an easy little seduction game. I'd get you to fall in love with me, and then I'd sweep you off without so much as a single ounce of blood being shed."

Meckenzie's mind was still reeling from the attempt to read Ty's thoughts. She couldn't understand exactly what he was saying. Ty knew she was in his mind, Meckenzie shook her head in denial. He had pushed her out so forcefully that it had caused sort of a mental whiplash to occur. Meckenzie felt confused and light headed.

"Oh, it'll take a few minutes for your mind to right itself. Especially since your powers are so new and you haven't gotten used to using them. So I'll just talk for a while. You and your siblings were a little bit harder to find that we had hoped. We have been looking for you for twenty years. Of course I haven't been looking for you personally, but my family has. As soon as your mother ran off all that time ago, we suspected that she was going off to have the Trefoil. We needed to stop her, or destroy you, whichever was easier. Now I have you here, within my grasp. What shall I do with you?"

Meckenzie's eyes widened in the shock of what might possibly happen next; she shook her head again in denial. Ty stopped for a moment, contemplating his next move. Meckenzie had her first clear thought since she started trying to read his mind. She needed to tell Jeff. Meckenzie cleared her thoughts again and reached out to Jeff.

He knows who we are. I tried to read Ty's mind and he felt me in there. He is trying to figure out how to get me out of here without you knowing. What do we do? Meckenzie waited for a reply. Jeff still didn't respond. She turned to the door again, trying to see if he was there and she was just not getting through. Jeff was nowhere to be seen, he was gone.

"Oh, your body guard is distracted right now and I sent someone after your snooping brother and sister. So they aren't coming for you either. Meckenzie you should just get up and come with me."

Ty started to stand up from his chair, so Meckenzie did the only thing that she could think of to do. She drew in a deep breath and looked right into his eyes.

"Mearhball sáraigh." Meckenzie said it quickly and quietly. If it didn't work, she didn't want him to know that she had said it.

Ty sat back down in his chair and looked befuddled. He looked around the restaurant trying to figure out where he was. It had worked! Ty was completely confused, so Meckenzie took that moment to reach into his mind. She needed more information; this dangerous situation couldn't be for nothing.

Ty's mind was open now, but it was very confusing. This might not have been the best idea Meckenzie had. She waded through his confused thoughts, past the useless questioning that had been brought on by the confusion spell, until Meckenzie finally found something that was useful. Ty thought about his brother and sister. So he really did have a brother and sister, and they were here in New York City too. Meckenzie remembered for a moment Ty standing outside the park with a girl and a boy about his age. They had the same dark hair. That had to be them.

Finding pertinent information was harder than Meckenzie thought it would be. She didn't know what she was looking for. Meckenzie stumbled around in his brain for another minute then decided she needed to get out of here before Ty recovered. She contemplated saying the spell again to give her some extra time, but that it might only reverse the spell. Meckenzie still hadn't learned the reversal spell, since Isabel had sent her away earlier without teaching it to her.

"Okay Ty, I'm going to go now. You stay here and enjoy your dinner. I'd like to say I had a nice time, but we both know that would be a lie." Meckenzie stood up and made her way to the door, as she came out onto the street, she didn't know what to do. Jeff was gone. Ty had said that he had sent someone after Kellan and Taggart. Meckenzie fished out her phone and tried calling Taggart's phone. He didn't answer, so she called the house.

Meckenzie started walking towards home as the house phone rang in her ear. Walking past the alley next to the Thai restaurant, something caught her eye. Jeff lay partially behind a dumpster about halfway down the alley not moving.

"Hello." Isabel said as she answered the house phone.

"Isabel, everything is going wrong. I need you to come to the Thai restaurant three blocks west of the house, I'm in the alley. Jeff's hurt." Meckenzie had bent down to inspect Jeff's injuries. Meckenzie checked his pulse, he was still alive. He seemed to be fine, no blood, or signs of a fight. He just seemed to be asleep.

"Where is your date?" Isabel asked.

"Sitting confused inside the restaurant. Ty knows who we are. He said they have been looking for us for twenty years. He has a brother and sister, I think he sent them after Taggart and Kellan."

"You mean coming to the house to get Taggart and Kellan?" Isabel asked.

"No. They followed me out on my date. They are somewhere close by. I don't know where though. And Taggart isn't answering his phone."

"Your brother and sister snuck out of the house to follow you on your date? I ought to just go back home if you guys aren't going to protect yourselves." Isabel raised her voice.

"Focus Isabel. Come to me, then we will find Taggart and Kellan." Meckenzie hung up the phone. She crouched down behind the dumpster and slipped Jeff's head into her lap.

"Come on Jeff. Wake up. What did they do to you? I need you to wake up. Taggart and Kellan are in trouble and I don't know when Ty is going to come out of his confused state. I need you to help me here." Meckenzie felt like crying. Everything had gone so terribly wrong. Jeff was hurt. God only knows where Taggart and Kellan were? Possibly being drug off by Ty's malicious siblings.

Meckenzie decided to reach out to Taggart and Kellan mentally. She had done it in the house before, and they had said they were going to be close by. So it was completely possible that they were in mental distance to receive a telepathic message from her.

As she sat there running her fingers through Jeff's hair, she reached out to Taggart and Kellan.

I don't know if you can hear me. They know who we are. They have sent someone after you. Jeff is hurt in the alley beside the Thai restaurant and Isabel is on her way here. Let me know where you are so we can come find you.

Meckenzie didn't expect any response; she was feeling very alone and very scared in the alley. Meckenzie felt like a failure, she had tried to play spy and now everyone was in trouble or hurt.

Meckenzie Taggart's voice came flooding into her brain like a welcome ray of sunlight. *They found us as we were leaving the house. They herded us into the park. One of them is a firestarter, she burned Kellan. The other is some kind of earth mover. They separated us. I don't know where Kellan is.* Taggart sounded desperate.

Can you make your way out of the park? Meckenzie asked.

And leave Kellan. I can't leave her, I need to find her. This is all my fault. It was my idea to follow you. We just wanted to protect you and now Kellan is hurt and missing.

Taggart you have to stop blaming yourself. Go look for Kellan, but stay safe. I can't lose you two.

Isabel came running down the alley and found Meckenzie holding Jeff's head in her lap and stroking his hair.

"Okay, it looks like a sleeping spell. This should be easy to remove."

Isabel started working her magic and within seconds Jeff started waking up. Meckenzie realized she was still holding his head in her lap. She knew that this was way more intimate than they should be, so she tried to help him sit up.

"What happened?" Jeff was still a little groggy from his magical nap, but he was awake enough to realize he had his head in Meckenzie's lap and would like to stay there for a little while.

"Someone cast a sleeping spell on you. Do you remember who?" Isabel reached out her hand to help Jeff to his feet. He stumbled for a moment, and then righted himself. Jeff took a look around; he seemed to be confused as to where he was.

"I don't remember anything. I mean I remember coming to the restaurant and I remember standing outside the door. Then, there is nothing."

"We don't have time to get to the bottom of this. We need to get to the park where Taggart and Kellan are. I talked to Taggart telepathically and Kellan has been burned by a fire starter. They got separated. There is an earthmover, I don't know what Taggart means by that, but he said it and then said that he and Kellan had gotten separated. He is looking for her now. We have to go help." Meckenzie was frantic to go find Kellan. She didn't want to be standing in this alley anymore. "Plus I don't know when the confusion spell I cast on Ty is going to wear off."

"You cast the spell?" Isabel seemed surprised. "What happened?"

"I tell everyone later, lets' go find Kellan and Taggart." With that Meckenzie headed off toward the park, hoping that Isabel and Jeff were going to follow.

CHAPTER 19

As they entered the park, Meckenzie reached out to Kellan and Taggart through her mind. *Kellan, where are you? Taggart, we are in the park. Where are you?*

Taggart immediately replied. *I am close to the carousel. We got separated by the softball fields. I was circling around the trees trying to see if she headed off that direction.*

Meckenzie relayed the information to Jeff and Isabel so they could head off in that direction. She suggested they circle around the fields like Taggart was doing, that way they could spread out and cover more ground.

They were approaching Umpire Rock, when Meckenzie heard a loud creaking sound. It was the sound of stone on stone. Jeff was coming out of the trees when the ground shifted underneath him and he was thrown back. Meckenzie looked around for the cause of the disturbance. There standing on the top of the rock formation, was the stranger who followed Isabel. It was dark, but Meckenzie was able to make out the stranger's resemblance to Ty. This must be his brother.

"Meckenzie go back into the trees." Isabel shouted from about ten yards away. The earth began to tremble under Meckenzie's feet. It was like trying to get traction on Jell-O, she ran as best she could towards the tree line only to have the ground move with her.

Jeff had recovered his footing; the first thing on his mind was getting Meckenzie out of harm's way. He was barreling towards her, coming much faster than anticipated, so when he hit the area of ground moving under Meckenzie's feet, his balance was compromised and he tackled her to the ground. They flew through the air reaching the tree line and the ground with a thud. Jeff's weight crushed Meckenzie to the ground. She could hear a fight going on in the clearing. The pop and sizzle of electrical energy flying through air must have been coming from Isabel's magic. The grinding and earth moving tremors were coming from Ty's brother.

Jeff got back to his feet and pulled Meckenzie to safety.

"You have to stay here. I need to work around behind him. Call out to Taggart, tell him to stay away. They are after you three and we can't bring you to them." Jeff didn't wait for a response he dashed off into the night.

Meckenzie made her way to the edge of the trees so she could watch what was going on. She knew she needed to contact Taggart, though she couldn't imagine with how close he was that he couldn't hear this fight going on in the middle of Central Park.

Taggart stay away from Umpire Rock. Isabel and Jeff are fighting Ty's brother the earth mover. Where are you?

I'm by the chess and checkers house, where are you? Taggart sounded frantic.

The northwest side of the rock in the tree line. Still no sign of Kellan?

No, I don't know where she could have gone. I don't know where the fire starter is either. I am afraid she is circling the tree line too. Taggart's thoughts were all over the place. She knew that Jeff had said they should stay apart, but she felt like they would be stronger together. Plus, if something happened to Taggart, she would never forgive herself.

Meckenzie started to concoct a plan; she needed to take control of the situation. *Move through the trees to the Northwest of where you are. I'm going to come around and meet you. We need to be together.*

Okay. Keep listening for me and call out for Kellan.

Meckenzie started her way around the tree line keeping the battle that was happening to her right in sight. She spotted Jeff moving in the tree line west of Ty's brother. Jeff was moving quickly toward the top of the rock, but it was not an easy climb. There was no cover for him; the playground was at his back. Isabel must have sensed Jeff moving closer because she redoubled her efforts at slinging magic. The ground moving under Isabel's feet did not seem to affect her balance. Wherever and whoever trained Isabel, they did an excellent job, she fought the battle smart and hard.

Kellan? Come on Kellan where are you? I love you sister. Just let me know where you are so we can come get you.

Kellan was still not responding. Meckenzie thought that she was either out of range, knocked out, or, and she didn't want to think this at all, dead. The thought of Kellan dead made the world turned upside down for Meckenzie, losing Kellan would kill her. Since they were in the womb together they really had been together their whole lives. Meckenzie started to cry as she made her way to where Taggart should be coming to meet her.

Kellan? Please answer me. Taggart, she isn't responding. Meckenzie couldn't lose her composure now, she needed to be strong. They were in a battle and somewhere in this park was a fairy fire-starter looking for her and her brother.

Just as Meckenzie was about to call out to Kellan again, she heard the crunch of leaves and branches in front of her. Just in case it wasn't Taggart she ducked behind the nearest tree. Taggart stumbled into sight, looking about like a crazy person. He looked like he could collapse into a pile of emotion and tears at any moment. Meckenzie felt the same way.

I'm behind the tree in front of you. Meckenzie thought it best to make her presence silently known. Just as Taggart turned towards Meckenzie, a girl stepped out beside him. Her hair was black and long, she was thin of frame. She looked like a model; her height was close to six feet tall. With a flick of wrist, she sent a flame sizzling towards Taggart.

Fall down to the ground now. Meckenzie shouted at Taggart. The warning was a second too late and the flames caught the hood of his sweatshirt. He fell to the ground and quickly rolled over to see where the fire was coming from.

The girl quickly ran towards Taggart, her hands ready to disperse the vengeance that flashed across her face. Meckenzie had to do something, so she ran in the direction of the girl and the fight that was about to ensue.

Meckenzie shouted to distract the fire-starter. "Hey." Meckenzie jumped quickly to her left, as she saw the girls thoughts. The flame sizzled past her and hit the tree she had previously taken refuge behind. Meckenzie had no physical powers that could benefit her in this fight, but she did have the ability to read the girl's mind and know what she was thinking before she did it.

Currently, the girl was wondering where her brother Ty was. She couldn't figure out how Meckenzie had gotten away from him. Meckenzie realized this was a bargaining point. She might be able to get Taggart out of here and find Kellan in the process.

"I'll tell you where Ty is and what I've done to him, but first tell me where Kellan is."

The girl stopped dead in her tracks. She was contemplating whether Meckenzie was bluffing. She wanted nothing more than to kill Meckenzie right then and there. Ty was important to her, but her rage was something else entirely.

"Ty is too smart for you to have pulled something over on him. He has to be around here somewhere." She was questioning Meckenzie trying to get a feel for exactly what, if anything, she could have done. She started shifting to the left, which would bring her to the tree line and within sight of her brother, the earth mover, up on Umpire Rock.

"You seem to be living under the impression that I was alone on that date. You seem to think that we wouldn't have had a plan in case Ty was who we thought he was." The fire-starter moved a little closer to what she assumed was her escape. Meckenzie could hear in her thoughts that she was going to blast Meckenzie, then head for the rock.

"Blasting me will not get Ty back to you. If you want to find him, then you will have to tell me where Kellan is."

"Even if you did do something to him, he would kill me if I told you where she is."

Meckenzie's worst nightmare was confirmed. They had Kellan. They had her, but from the sound of it, she was still alive.

"Is she alive?" Meckenzie and the fire-starter were both moving in a circle, each trying to get closer to their brothers. Meckenzie wanted to keep a safe reaction distance between them. She needed to be able to get out of the way when fire-starter finally made her move.

Meckenzie decided to push harder into the girls mind and see if she could see where Kellan was. Meckenzie saw a bridge. There were like 25 bridges and archways in the park. Meckenzie needed to know which bridge it was. The girl was thinking so many different things that Meckenzie needed to ask a specific question to get her thoughts back to Kellan.

"So you hid her near a bridge?" Meckenzie of her lesson in psychology class that had said that people can't help thinking about something if suggest it to them. So she thought saying the word 'bridge' would spark the thought process necessary to get the location from the girl's mind.

"Get out of my head." The fire-starter screamed as she hurled fire at Meckenzie. Meckenzie had seen it coming and dodged it once again. The verbal cue had worked though, the girl had flashed to the Driprock Arch. It was close by. In fact, the way Taggart had been working around the park, he would have come directly upon the arch if he had headed down the walk from the chess and checkers house.

While all the discussion had been going on between the Ty's sister and Meckenzie, Taggart had managed to get himself up and was working his way around the opposite way of Meckenzie. They would have her trapped between the two of them soon; Meckenzie knew that they needed a way to control her though.

That is when Isabel stepped up behind the girl and said, "Dul a chodladh."

The girl went out like a light, Isabel bent down to make sure she was really out. Taggart made his way to Meckenzie.

"Did you figure out where they took Kellan?"

"Yes, she is somewhere near Driprock Arch. I never actually saw her, but that was where the girl was thinking about when I asked about her hiding Kellan. Isabel where's Jeff?"

"He is securing the other one. I don't know what we are going to do with them? It's not like we can take them back to the house and hold them prisoner."

"We can't do that because Ty will come after them and it could be worse for us then. We need to get them out of the park though." Meckenzie didn't want to sit there discussing it anymore, she wanted to go find Kellan. She sense Taggart was feeling the same thing.

"We are going to find Kellan." Meckenzie said as she started walking away from Isabel.

"No you are not. You are not going off without us, too much is unknown. There could be more of them. This could be a trap to get all three of you together. We are going to wait on Jeff."

Meckenzie thought Isabel was being unreasonable. It was completely possible that Kellan was out there somewhere bleeding, or dying. Meckenzie had to go find her. If something happened to Kellan because they were standing here deciding what to do with the bad guys, Meckenzie would never forgive Isabel.

"Taggart go get Jeff and bring the earthmover back over here. We need to go get Kellan and the only way this is going to work is if we put both of Ty's siblings in one place, so one person can guard them and three of us can go look for Kellan." Meckenzie was taking control of the situation, it was the only way that they were going to be able to go recover Kellan. She searched her cell phone out of her purse. Meckenzie figured that Kellan had her cell phone on her and when they got to the bridge she would just call her and wait until she heard the ringing of the phone.

"You are going to have to go by the Thai restaurant and take the confusion curse off of Ty. Can you do that from a distance?" Meckenzie was now telling Isabel what to do. Maybe she did have a leader buried deep inside of her.

"Yes, I can take it off of him from the street. Why do you want to do that though?" Isabel asked.

"Well, the only way this is going to work is if we make a deal with him. We will give him back his siblings, if they promise to leave and not come back. I mean we beat them here tonight and we weren't even ready. Imagine what we can do now that we know who they are and what they can do. I think Ty will agree just so he can get better prepared. This war is not meant to happen here in the human world. If we are going to fight, then we will do it in Aquanis." Meckenzie didn't even know how she was reasoning all this out; it just seemed to make sense to her.

"We need to get them somewhere other than the park though." Isabel added.

"I know. I just don't know where. I mean I need to talk to him tonight and get this settled, so maybe we find Kellan and get her home. Then you and I pick him up from the Thai restaurant and take him for a drive. If we had two limos, then we could put his brother and sister in one with Jeff, since they are asleep it would be no problem, and you and I could go get Ty in the other car. When it's time to exchange, we just take him to the limo with his siblings and Jeff comes with us."

Meckenzie picked up the phone and called her dad.

"Dad, its Meckenzie. Listen, I need you to be calm. A lot of things have happened tonight and it is not over yet, so we need your help to settle it."

"Meckenzie, what is going on? No one is here and no one is answering their phones."

"I know dad, look, I need you to rent two limos. Send them both to Columbus Circle. We ran into some trouble tonight with Ty, his sister, and brother. We have the ability to negotiate with them to leave us alone, so it is important that we have the limos to do the discussing. Jeff and Isabel are both here so we are as safe as we can be. I just need you to stay at home and not do anything crazy."

"Meckenzie this is very scary. Let me talk to Isabel."

Meckenzie handed Isabel the phone and shrugged her shoulders. She went over to Ty's sister and began trying to lift her up. She had gotten her into a sitting position when Jeff and Taggart came up with Ty's brother.

"He's a big fellow." Taggart looked winded. He had almost been set on fire tonight, so it was understandable.

"We need to go find Kellan. I think Isabel, Taggart and I should go. If she needs healing we'll need Taggart. If a spell has been used we'll need Isabel. And I'm the one who saw the vision. I think Jeff can handle these two sleeping beauties." Meckenzie had taken control again. Isabel was still whispering into the phone to Meckenzie's dad, so she didn't have the chance to argue.

Meckenzie and Taggart started off towards the Driprock Arch. Meckenzie motioned for Isabel to follow. She complied, still on the phone. As they got out to the walkway, Meckenzie reached back and took the phone from Isabel.

"Dad, there isn't any more time for discussion. Call the limo service. They need to be limos, because we need the privacy glass, two of them. We don't have any more time to waste. I love you and we will talk to you soon."

With that Meckenzie hung up the phone. She needed people to start cooperating for this thing to work. She didn't need any arguments, just actions.

Isabel laughed, "You are definitely your mother's daughter. You got that Queen thing down pat too."

"Well, thank you, I think." Meckenzie wasn't really in the mood for any of this. She just wanted to find Kellan.

"So what's the plan Queen?" Taggart was getting some of his humor back. He was trying to lighten the mood.

"Dad's sending two limos. We are going to put Ty's brother and sister in one and send them off with Jeff. Then Isabel and I will go find Ty. He should still be in the vicinity of the Thai restaurant, as I cast a confusion spell on him. We will remove the spell and bargain for them to leave, if we return his brother and sister. That should buy us enough time to train, graduate, and then we will go to Aquanis and resume this little fight."

"What makes you think Ty will honor it? He was going to kill us you know. They said as much when they attacked us earlier." Taggart had brought up a valid point. Meckenzie had no way of assuring that they would cooperate.

"Well, I guess we threaten them with numbers. We can bring in a couple of extra people to guard the house. We can stop going to school so they don't have the advantage of finding us in public. We can take the next few weeks and train. Then after our birthday party, we can leave. I think if we tried to leave now, Dad would have a heart attack."

"You want to drop out of school?" Taggart looked shocked.

"We can test out early. Tell them we have a family emergency. All three of us are way ahead anyway. We aren't going to college now, so what does it really matter?"

Taggart looked heartbroken. He had been working so hard to be school valedictorian. Taggart still had hopes of Harvard on his mind.

"Look, when we finish this thing, you can come back and go to Harvard. They will still take you. We just have to make up a convincing family emergency. I have an idea we can discuss later." They had arrived at the arch and Meckenzie wanted to concentrate on finding Kellan. "I'm going to call her phone, so let's spread out and listen for the ringtone."

Meckenzie made the call and the three of them went in separate directions listening for Kellan's phone. Meckenzie had to call five times before she caught the sound of ringing coming from behind a tree between the arch and the skating rink. It was dark enough that Kellan was hidden in the shadows. Kellan was propped up against the tree, sleeping. her hands and face had been badly burned. Kellan had tried to fight Ty's sister, and it had not gone so well for her.

"Taggart, heal Kellan before we wake her up. She will be in a lot of pain if you don't and it might trigger her to grow." Isabel knelt beside Kellan and motioned Taggart to do the same.

Taggart placed his hands on Kellan's face first. Meckenzie noticed tears in Taggart's eyes and she could read in his mind that he felt responsible. Meckenzie placed her hand on Taggart's back letting him know through her thoughts that she knew it was her fault. She was the one that decided to go on this date to get the information from Ty. Meckenzie could have insisted they stay home.

Taggart began healing Kellan's burned hands. Her face was healed and looked more flawless than before. Any traces of acne were gone along with the burns Kellan had suffered. Taggart took her hands in his own, placing them together. Within seconds Kellan was completely healed. Taggart really did have a miraculous gift.

"Okay, now I'm going to wake her up. Kellan will still be in fight mode, so everyone step back."

Isabel began whispering the words to wake Kellan up. Meckenzie and Taggart took a step back. Kellan began to open her eyes. She blinked twice and then jumped to her feet. Her fists went up and she almost took a swing at Isabel.

"Kellan stop." Meckenzie yelled. "It's Isabel. Kellan look at me."

Meckenzie took a step toward Kellan. Taggart tried to grab her so that she wouldn't get in the way of the swing that Kellan was about to throw, but Meckenzie shook him off and stepped closer. Without hesitation, Kellan spun around and threw a vicious right hook that broke Meckenzie's nose. Meckenzie fell back onto the ground with a thud, blood poured out of her nose down the front of her dress.

"Meckenzie." Kellan realized too late that she had just hit her sister. "Are you okay?"

She dropped to the ground beside Meckenzie. Isabel laughed, as she always did when the triplets didn't listen to her.

"I told you to take a step back. I think eventually you will start listening to me. Taggart do you have enough energy to heal your other sister now?"

Taggart didn't respond, he was already kneeling next to Meckenzie, moving her hands away from her face.

"This is going to hurt a little. I need to move your nose back into position." Taggart was pushing and prodding at Meckenzie's broken nose trying to determine exactly where he needed to move it. "Okay, take a deep breath. On the count of three. One. Two. Three."

Taggart popped Meckenzie's nose back into place. Meckenzie screamed. A million little camera flashes went off in her vision. Taggart kept his hands on her nose for a moment so he could mend it. When Taggart was done, he sat back on the grass beside Meckenzie. He had used all the healing he could use in one night. Meckenzie hoped that he wouldn't be asked to heal anyone again tonight.

"I'm sorry Meckenzie. I thought you were that fire breathing witch that attacked me." Kellan said apologetically.

"It's okay. I deserved it. You wouldn't be out here if it wasn't for me and this stupid date." Meckenzie really did think she deserved being punched in the face. The whole evening was a disaster.

"I hate to break up this pity party, but we still have two sleeping fairies that need to be taken care of." Isabel brought them all back to the situation at hand.

The evening was not over yet. They all made their way back to Jeff, who had called in his own reinforcements. Standing beside Jeff was a red haired gentleman. He had the most intriguing green eyes that seemed to sparkle even in the darkness. He had brought with him a wheel chair. Meckenzie had been worried about getting everyone to the cars without attracting attention. The wheel chair would work fantastic for one of the slumbering fairies, but carrying the other would attract a lot of attention.

Jeff noticed the blood on Meckenzie's dress and immediately ran over to her. He looked her over from head to toe, but could find no wounds.

"What happened?" Jeff said with worry in his voice.

"Kellan happened." Taggart laughingly said.

Kellan punched him in the arm and laughed herself. She was starting to forgive herself for hitting Meckenzie.

"I accidently punched her, broke her nose. I think it improved her looks, but Taggart fixed it anyways."

"So what's the plan?" Jeff asked. "I called my friend Bowen. He has a particular talent that might come in handy for us."

Isabel had been particularly quiet since their return. Meckenzie turned to find her staring at Bowen with rapt attention. It seemed that Bowen was as interested in Isabel as she was in him, they had locked eyes. Everyone began to notice the two of them.

"Bowen." Isabel finally spoke.

"Isabel, how are you?" Bowen moved towards Isabel. A smile touched his face, making his eyes dance more than before. The smile made him look twenty years younger than the his fifty-something year old appearance, or maybe it was Isabel that inspired his youthful look

"I'm good. How long have you been in the city?" Isabel's breathing became heavy. The sweetness of her words reminded Meckenzie of cotton candy, there was something happening under the surface of the pleasantries being exchanged..

"A few months, I've been tracking for the Queen. She has had me looking for these guys." Bowen pointed to the ground where the two Fae rested comfortably. "Though I didn't know that I was looking for Tiernan's progeny."

"What?" Isabel was looking back and forth from Bowen to the two on the ground. "Tiernan's progeny. They're the heirs to the throne of the Raven."

"Yes, it seems, as best as my intel can gather, that the fire clan has a produced a set of triplets that they are claiming are the heirs to the throne in Aquanis. It would be best, in my opinion, if we just killed them now and were done with the whole thing."

"I don't think so." Meckenzie objected. "Killing them here brings a whole lot of questions down on my family. There is not going to be any killing tonight."

Bowen bowed at Meckenzie and smiled. "You are your mother's daughter."

"I keep hearing that, thank you." Meckenzie was ready to get this over with. "We need to get to Columbus Circle with these two. There should be two limos waiting for us there. We will put these two in one limo and Isabel and I will go get Ty in the other limo. We will convince him to leave the city, by bartering with him for his siblings."

"That might be where I come in handy." Bowen said.

"Why is that?" Meckenzie couldn't see how this man who wanted to kill the teenagers could be of any help to convincing them to leave.

"I'm what they call a bedazzler." Bowen said.

"That was what I was going to tell you." Jeff interjected. "Bowen here has the special gift of being able to convince people to do what he wants them to."

"It's in the eyes." Bowen said with a smile.

"They are sparkling." Kellan added the words that Meckenzie was thinking.

Bowen laughed from the soles of his feet. "Yes."

"Okay, so Bowen, Meckenzie and I will go retrieve Ty. Jeff will take the other two and meet us when we call him." Isabel finally pulled her eyes away from Bowen and rejoined the conversation.

"Excuse me. What are we supposed to do?" Taggart added.

"Go home." Isabel and Meckenzie said simultaneously.

"No." Kellan objected. "We will go with Jeff. If something happens and they wake up, he'll need some help. Plus, I am not going to be pushed out of this. This is our fight too."

"I agree with Kellan." Taggart looked at Meckenzie. "If something happens, it would be better for there to be more of us."

"Fine." Meckenzie didn't want to argue about it. "This has taken too long already. Let's get them to the cars.

They put the earthmover in the wheel chair so Kellan could push him to Columbus Circle. Bowen and Jeff lifted the fire-starter up and draped her arms around their shoulders. They carried her as if she were drunk and had passed out. That was the cover story that Bowen had determined would be the easiest to sell.

Meckenzie felt like they were heading off into the night to make a deal with the devil himself.

CHAPTER 20

They got everyone into their appropriate cars with no problems. New Yorkers were good at ignoring what was going on around them, so no one actually asked about the passed out girl Jeff and Bowen were carrying.

Meckenzie, Isabel and Bowen hopped into their limo and headed toward the Thai restaurant where Meckenzie had left Ty. Isabel and Bowen sat staring at each other in silence. Meckenzie could only imagine what had happened in the past to cause this reaction in Isabel. Isabel always so calm and collected seemed to be in a state of panic around Bowen.

No one said a word in the few minutes it had taken them to get to the restaurant. Once the car stopped, Meckenzie jumped out and headed inside the restaurant. To her disappointment, Ty was not seated at the table they had occupied.

Meckenzie asked the hostess if she had remembered him leaving. The hostess said Ty had seemed drunk so they had called him a cab. The problem had been that he didn't know where he was supposed to go so he sent the cab away. Ty had walked off. Meckenzie asked the hostess if she remembered in what direction Ty had gone. She pointed down the street back towards Meckenzie's house.

Meckenzie got back in the limo. She gave the limo driver directions to head back down west 72nd street and then to make a left onto Central Park West.

Meckenzie asked him to take it slow so that they could look for missing member of their party.

Meckenzie positioned herself on one side of the car, while Isabel took the other and looked for Ty. He was nowhere to be seen on 72nd street. They had traveled several blocks before Meckenzie spotted Ty walking next to the park. He was talking to himself and looked extremely agitated.

"Ty." Meckenzie shouted from the car. The driver pulled over and Meckenzie jumped out of the car. Bowen was close behind her and stepped between her and Ty to protect her if Ty decided to strike out.

"Ty, we can help you. Get in the car." Meckenzie pointed to the limo idling on the curb.

"You did this to me." Ty said as he took two very aggressive steps towards Meckenzie. "I can't think straight. I can't figure out what I'm supposed to be doing but I do know that you are not here to help me."

"Isabel reverse the spell. He is never going to go with us if we don't take away the confusion."

Isabel stepped out of the limo. Ty stepped back, preparing to make a run for it, when she quickly uttered the reversal spell.

Ty stopped in his tracks. He shook his head trying to remove the fog. His hands dropped to his sides and his mood changed from defensive to aggressive. The anger that flashed in his eyes made Meckenzie take a step back. She couldn't believe she was about to ask him to get into a car with her. Ty would probably rather kill her right on the sidewalk of Central Park then bargain with her. Meckenzie took in all the courage she could muster.

"Ty get in the car. We need to discuss your brother and sister. We have a proposal for you."

Ty stood thinking about his next move. A hundred thoughts flashed through his eyes. He didn't like not having the upper hand. He was trying to figure out how to reverse their roles.

"Did they succeed in taking your brother and sister? We will never give them back. They may already be dead." Ty said with a smile.

"I told you we should have killed them in the park." Bowen said with a hint of I told you so.

"They don't have Taggart and Kellan. Actually it is just the opposite." Meckenzie pulled out her phone. Thankfully she had made the decision to take a picture of the snoozing pair in the back of the limo before they seperated. Kellan had volunteered to be in the photo, she wanted to make sure that Ty knew that she had not been bested by his siblings.

"Here, take a look." She held the phone out for Ty to see.

His smile faltered for a moment, then it was back, bigger and scarier.

"What do you want?" He said.

"Get in the car. We aren't going to hurt you. We just want to talk about how this is going to end."

"It will end when you are all dead." Ty was not going to make this easy on Meckenzie. "They would never want me to bargain for their lives."

"Fine." Meckenzie pulled her phone back and punched Taggart's name on her contact list. She held the phone up to her ear and waited for the phone to ring. Meckenzie turned to Isabel while she waited for Taggart to answer.

"You might as well confuse him again, or paralyze him. I don't care." When she said the last part, Taggart answered.

"Who's getting paralyzed?"

"Ty is not cooperating. Activate plan b." Meckenzie had not actually made a plan b. She thought this would be enough to get Ty to get into the car. It worked, because the moment she said it, he spoke up.

"I'll go with you." Ty said.

"Cancel plan b." Meckenzie said into the phone.

"That's good, because I don't know what plan b is." Taggart was laughing. Meckenzie heard Kellan say "Plan B?" in the background.

"I'll call you back when we have come to a decision." Meckenzie hung up the phone and followed Isabel and Ty into the car. Bowen walked up to the driver's window and gave him some instructions.

The car pulled off into the night again. Meckenzie knew that she would have to approach this conversation with arrogance. Ty was arrogant and would not agree to a deal if he didn't think he was at least matched by Meckenzie.

"We obviously have your brother and sister. It was among the suggestions that we kill them now and be done with it, but I don't believe that will get us anywhere. I don't know enough about our history to know why it is that you think we should be dead, or why Bowen here thinks you should be dead, but I do know that doing this here in the human world will be anything but messy. So I propose a truce until we graduate. Then we will be going to Aquanis and we can pick up this pointless battle."

"Why would I agree to that?" Ty snarled.

"Because we beat you. We have your siblings and mine are still alive. If you try again, we will beat you again. I can't promise the second time around that there will not be casualties involved. You have a much better chance in Aquanis of achieving whatever it is you wish to achieve, here we will outnumber you. Unless you are planning on marching an army through the portal and up to our front door and I'm not sure you want to mess with New York's finest. They are still pretty jumpy after 9/11 and it wouldn't take much to convince them that you are terrorists."

Meckenzie paused letting all the information sink in. She reached over to the mini fridge that was provided by the limo company and pulled out a bottle of water. Meckenzie offered drinks to the others. She decided she would sit back and let him stew for a few minutes. Meckenzie would let Ty come up with a counter offer.

Ty sat staring at Meckenzie trying to figure out if she were bluffing. She took a particular interest in her finger nails and the wonderful color of polish that she had picked out to match her dress. Ty finally cleared his throat to speak.

"We will leave. I cannot promise anything else. We have spies all over the city and it will take weeks maybe even months to disperse the information that you are off limits till graduation."

"Fine, but if someone attacks our home, I will not hesitate to let Bowen here kill them." Meckenzie decided that was as good an offer as she could expect, so she picked up the phone and called Taggart again.

He answered on the first ring, with a bit of anxiousness in his voice.

"It's about time." He said. "We were just about to track you by your cell phone again."

"Meet us at Columbus Circle. We will exchange them there." Meckenzie didn't really want to discuss anything further so she hung up after she relayed the meeting point.

When they met up at the Circle, everyone piled out of both limos. Meckenzie indicated to Ty to look inside the other limo and he would find his siblings.

"Someone going to reverse the spell?" He asked as he stuck his head inside the car.

"Isabel will reverse the spell after we are all in the car. You can use the car to take yourselves home. And don't return to school. There is no reason for you to be there now."

Meckenzie and her siblings got into their waiting limo with Jeff. Bowen and Isabel waited till they were safely seated, then Isabel walked over to the other car to reverse the spell. Bowen was never more than a step behind her. When her work was done, they returned to the limo. Bowen gave the driver instructions again and slid into the seat beside Isabel.

Meckenzie was happy they were headed home. Her father would be worried sick if they didn't get there soon. She knew there was more business to discuss. They had to make a plan for training and they would have to figure out a way to convince their dad that they need to quit school to keep themselves safe. They were also going to need a few more people around the house for protection. Ty's threat about the other spies coming after them, now that their identities were compromised, had her worried about her dad's safety as well.

"Bowen," Meckenzie had an idea. "How would you like to come to work for us? We need protection and training. It seems you have some gifts and knowledge that would be helpful to us if we are going to make it through this."

Isabel appeared to almost fall out of her seat. She started to object, but Meckenzie held up her hand indicating it wasn't up for discussion.

Bowen laughed, "She really is just like her mother."

CHAPTER 21

When they had finally made it home, there was a consensus that Bowen would be a much needed addition to their team. Meckenzie knew that her night was nowhere close to being over though. There was her father to deal with for one. She was also going to try and contact the Morrigan at some point. Meckenzie consoled herself with the fact that tomorrow was Saturday and there would be some sleeping occurring in her future.

The trips' father was waiting for them in the kitchen. He looked ten years older from the stress of just this one night. Meckenzie toyed with the idea of performing the calming spell on her father, but she decided that using magic to change his current emotional state, would probably only make him angrier. Somehow, they were going to have to protect him. Between his ability to worry about them and the possibility that someone would come for him as leverage, Meckenzie had to devise a plan to get him to Aquanis with them.

"It's about time you three got home. I was worried sick. Meckenzie if you ever hang up on me again, I will ground you till the end of time." He was ready to lay into them good when Bowen, Jeff, and Isabel came in behind them. "Who is he," their father gestured to Bowen, "and what is he doing here?"

"Dad that is Bowen. He knows mom and apparently Isabel as well. He helped us resolve the problem we were having tonight. We want to tell you all about it, but I didn't actually eat and Taggart is going to need something too. He did some healing tonight."

"Who did Taggart heal? Who is hurt? What happened?" Lawrence Desmond was sending himself into some kind of panic attack.

"Lawrence as you can see all three kids are fine. They were actually great tonight. We'll all sit down and talk about it. Let's just get them something to eat first. Why don't we all go to the dinner table and I'll make some sandwiches." Isabel was trying as best she could to calm him down.

Taggart decided he needed to do something about it before their dad had a heart attack, so he gave him a hug and held on a little longer than necessary. The healing power of Taggart's touch calmed their dad down immediately. Taggart led them into the dining room and everyone took a seat at the table. Meckenzie hung back in the kitchen and grabbed some bottled water out of the fridge. She got out a couple of serving trays and started to help Isabel get stuff ready for sandwiches.

Meckenzie didn't have a plan for this. How would they make it all work? She really wanted to go take a long shower and cry. Meckenzie had been so caught up in making sure everyone was safe that she hadn't taken any time to think about herself not being safe.

"You don't have to do this all on your own." Isabel said as if reading her mind. "You have a brother and sister to help you. You have me. We can get through this. Your mother would be so proud of you right now."

"I know that you're saying that to reassure me, but all it does is remind me that so many people know my mother more than I do." Meckenzie had been told too many times today that she reminded people of a woman who had abandoned her and her siblings. She wanted more than anything to have a relationship with her mom. Meckenzie just wished people would stop reminding her that she didn't have one.

"How are we going to convince dad to let us drop out of school? How are we going to convince him that we have to leave at the end of the school year? How are we going to convince him to hire Bowen?"

"That last one is all on you. I didn't suggest you hire him." Isabel seemed upset about the situation.

"What happened between the two of you?" Meckenzie thought she might have an idea. Love is the only thing that causes that kind of reaction in a woman.

"We were lovers. We were to be married actually. When I got the call to come here and help your mother, I tried to get him to come with me, but he felt he was of more use there. It just ended. That is all I'm going to say about that." Isabel had finished preparing the trays of meat and cheese, so they moved everything into the dining room.

As they entered the room, Taggart was shaking his head. Their father had a look of determination on his face. Something had him upset. Meckenzie knew the list of things was too long, so she decided she would just wait for him to voice his problem. It didn't take more than two steps before it happened.

"Taggart tells me you want to hire this man to help train you and guard you. Am I not still the father in this relationship? Shouldn't I be consulted about these things? You call and demand two limos on short notice none the less and then you bring home a stray that you want to hire. What happened tonight?" His face was cherry red, which meant his blood pressure was up.

Meckenzie sat down at the table and took a deep breath. This was going to take some finesse. She recapped the evenings events, allowing Kellan and Taggart to fill in the blanks were necessary. Meckenzie explained how the date had gone wrong, but that she had escaped unscathed. There was a brief moment when Kellan's being burned almost sent her father over the edge. He wanted to take her to the hospital and have her checked out by a real doctor. It took everyone in the room to convince him that Kellan was better than before. Kellan finally had to let him look her over with a fine tooth comb. He could find no signs of trauma so he let it go.

When the story had been completely recapped and he had all of his questions answered, he returned to the subject of hiring Bowen.

"So what is it you can do that will be beneficial to my children?" He asked skeptically.

"Well sir, if I wanted to, I could convince you to hire me without the help of your children. I have a way, a magical way of convincing people to do what I want them to. I am also trained as Isabel is in self-defense and fighting techniques. I have a way with herbs, so I can teach Taggart how to mix potions that will help him in healing. I have what is called a mind gift, so I can help Meckenzie understand some of her gifts. Kellan's gift is better served by Ardan, but I make a good punching bag as well."

"Ardan, who is Ardan?" Their dad asked confusedly.

"I am sir." Jeff responded. "Jeff is my human cover story. My Fae name is Ardan, and since we are past the pretense of hiding my heritage, you can call me Ardan."

"Well that is going to be confusing. Okay, so you will train with them." He said to his children. "Then what?"

This is the part that Meckenzie was dreading. She wasn't ready for another fight, even if there wasn't going to be any bloodshed. Though it was entirely possible her father would come to blows over their education.

"Well dad, we need to leave school." Taggart took the lead. He had a way with their father. It must be the father-son bond. "We won't be safe there. We will ask the headmaster to let us test out of the rest of the year. We will need to learn to control our powers and cast spells and we will need to learn how to fight and defend ourselves."

"Then we will have to leave to Aquanis. We were thinking at the beginning of summer. We will still have our birthday party and be here for a couple of more months, but we are going to have to leave." Meckenzie added, expecting a fight from him.

Their father didn't protest. He simply sat back in his chair. Rubbing his temples, he looked as if he was going to cry. They were leaving and it broke his heart. He had spent so many years protecting them, loving them and now he was losing them.

"I understand." It was like all the life had left his body. "I will need to tie up some loose ends around the office, but I think I should stay home as much as possible. I don't want to miss a moment with you kids while I still have you. I knew that you were going to leave to go off to college this year, but I thought I'd at least have holidays and summers with you. This, however, is a different scenario all together. You will be in another world, another plane. When will I get to see you? When will you come visit?" Tears were running down his face.

Meckenzie began to cry as well. She couldn't stand the heartbreak this was causing. She had to figure out a way to get her father to Aquanis with them. Isabel stood and began clearing the table. Ardan and Bowen took their cue and left to the kitchen. Kellan got up and wrapped her arms around their father.

"Dad if you could come with us, would you?" Meckenzie knew the answer to that question before she asked it. He would go anywhere to be with his children.

"Of course." He sat up in his chair. There was hope that he wouldn't lose his children forever. "Would your mom allow that though?"

"Mom asked about you. I think she would. She owes you that much." This is what Meckenzie was hoping for. She knew that it was a risky gamble promising him something she didn't know if she could deliver. Her dad was part Fae, so it would make sense that he could travel to Aquanis.

"I think that we should all just sleep on it and we can start finalizing plans later. I know I could use a good night's sleep." The strain of the day was evident in Taggart's eyes. He needed sleep. Even Kellan looked worn out.

"Yes, we should sleep on it. I think that we should set up a place for Ardan and Bowen to sleep. I don't want them leaving the house tonight. I still don't know if Ty will honor our agreement. Kellan can you find that air mattress we got a couple of years ago and some sheets. Taggart, maybe grab them some sleep clothes. We can put them in the gym. There are showers and a bathroom down there. It might be worth it to find a place for them to stay permanently. What do you think dad?" Meckenzie turned to her father.

"Sure, we can fix up a place in the gym. There is room in the back corner where we have the storage room. I even think there is a bed in there."

Everyone went off to do their assigned tasks while Meckenzie went to ask their guests to stay. She found them all in the kitchen sitting around the island. They were deep in conversation, which stopped as soon as Meckenzie entered the room.

Meckenzie ignored the abrupt end to their conversation. Frankly, she didn't have the energy to be curious. "I was wondering if it wouldn't be too much trouble, if the two of you would stay here tonight. I don't want to risk Ty not observing the truce and breaking in when we are weak. We would also like to invite you to move in for the next couple of months. We have a space in the gym that we can convert into a room for the two of you. There is a full bathroom down there because of the pool and gym."

"We were actually discussing how we were going to protect you three at night. This solves the problem. We can go get what we need from our places tomorrow." Bowen answered for the both of them. Ardan still hadn't really said much to Meckenzie since he had been knocked out at the restaurant.

"Kellan's getting an air mattress for tonight and Taggart is going to bring you some sleeping clothes. I'll show you downstairs if you'd like."

"Sure." Ardan got up to follow her. Bowen remained sitting.

"I think I'll have Isabel give me a tour of the house so that I can familiarize myself with it." Meckenzie knew that Bowen probably wanted to talk to Isabel alone about the new living situation. This could get touchy, so Meckenzie turned to head downstairs with Arden.

"How are you feeling?" Ardan asked.

"Tired. Sad. Scared. Mad. I'm a little bit of everything right now, except happy." Meckenzie felt so much that it was almost numbing.

As they reached the garden level, Arden reached out and grabbed Meckenzie's hand. He led her over to the garden. His touch was electrifying. Pulling Meckenzie into him, Ardan brushed the hair from her face. His breathing was shallow and quick, there was no mistaking the attraction he felt for her.

"I was so afraid that something had happened to you. I would have never forgiven myself if you had been hurt. I know that we have to work together and Isabel threatened to send me away if I was distracted by you, but I just need you to know that I will always be there to protect you."

The events of the evening melted out of Meckenzie's mind. There was only Ardan, standing in front of her, holding her close. She wanted his lips to touch hers, to erase the first kiss that she had experienced with Ty. Ardan's hands were playing with her hair, touching her neck. Meckenzie was bursting with electrical energy running throughout her body at his touch.

"That date was the hardest thing I've ever lived through. Him holding your hand, it was all I could do not to punch him. You were laughing with him and flirting. Did you like him? Did his betrayal hurt you?"

Meckenzie was having trouble finding her words. She wanted to scream out that Ty was nothing to her, but Meckenzie's mind was reeling with so many thoughts; she couldn't make any of them come out of her mouth.

Before she could answer him, they heard Taggart and Kellan talking as they came downstairs. Ardan pulled away from her. The cold of the night struck Meckenzie for the first time. Ardan's body had been providing warmth that was now missing. Her brother and sister headed down to the gym. Leaving them hiding in the shadows of the garden unseen.

"We should probably get down there. I'm sorry if I have offended you. I know that you are a princess. I just," Ardan paused looking for the right words. "I guess I just thought you liked me. I won't bother you again."

Meckenzie did like him. She wanted to tell him, but finding the words was not something she was able to do right now. Too many people's lives were in Meckenzie's hands. Isabel had said that Ardan would be a distraction. He would be sent away if Meckenzie didn't let her feelings go. She also knew that Ardan would be in danger from her enemies if she openly loved him. Seeing him lying in the alley, brought a reality to her that Meckenzie might lose him before she ever got a chance to love Ardan. So Meckenzie said nothing. Ardan turned and headed for the stairs leaving Meckenzie behind in the cold night air.

What had she done? She thought to herself. Ardan had given her the opportunity to tell him that she liked him. The whole day collapsed upon Meckenzie. She found herself on the cold tile floor of the garden crying into her hands. There was so much happening, so much hurt and pain that would come from all of this. Was she really meant to be with Ardan? Meckenzie allowed herself to cry for a few minutes more, but that is all she would allow herself to do for now.

Sleep was going to be her healer this night. So Meckenzie collected herself and left the garden, left it with the secret of Ardan's confession and left her tears upon the tile. Meckenzie's feelings for Ardan, the warmth of his touch, the quickening of her heart, left behind. Meckenzie left it all there so she could fight a battle that she had not known about a week ago. She left and went to bed.

CHAPTER 22

Meckenzie slept hard. There were no dream messages. There were no dreams. When she awoke, there was a soreness in her muscles, but moreover there was soreness in her heart. Meckenzie wanted to hide in her room all day, hide away from the world. It was already mid-morning, so she pulled herself out of bed and threw on an exercise outfit. Meckenzie didn't know what today would hold, but she knew there would be running in her future.

Everyone was up and about already. Kellan was working out with Ardan. Taggart and Bowen were setting what looked like a lab table in one corner of the gym area. There were all kinds of jars full of liquids, leaves, and other oddities. Meckenzie had passed Isabel in the kitchen preparing some kind of creamy looking salve. Her father was the only person missing. Meckenzie assumed he had gone to the office for a bit.

Meckenzie mounted the treadmill with her headphones on and ignored the activity that was bustling about her. She thought she would try to burn all the pain out of her body through exercise. Ardan didn't even acknowledge her when she came down the stairs. He continued to focus Kellan back to his instruction without even a glance in Meckenzie's direction. Taggart said something witty about her being a sleepy head and Bowen wished her a good morning.

Meckenzie did five miles on the treadmill and headed back upstairs. As she rummaged around in the fridge, Isabel cleared her throat like she wanted to have a conversation. Meckenzie wasn't in the mood, but she would let Isabel have her say.

"You are being too hard on yourself." Sadness touched the edge of Isabel's voice. "Everyone is safe and home and that is a best case scenario."

"It's just that so much is happening so quickly. I'm sad about everything I'm losing. No more school or friends. I can't tell Jeff, I mean Ardan how I feel. This is all so complicated and frustrating. I think I've done pretty good with it so far, so if I want to pout for a day, I don't see what the problem is."

"You're right; you have the right to mourn your old life. There just isn't a lot of time for you to do it right now. So take today, do whatever you need to; get it out of your system. Then, we will start training tomorrow."

"We need to talk about my dad. I want him to come with us when we go to Aquanis. We can't leave him like mom did. At least when she left he had us, we can't leave him alone."

"Taggart already talked to me about it. We sent a runner to your mother this morning with all the information about last night. I told her that you wanted to bring Lawrence. She will have the final say in it. She is the queen."

"I just think we would focus so much better not worrying about whether something is happening to him here. He would be safer with us."

Isabel knew she wasn't going to be able to give Meckenzie the answer she wanted. Diedra would have to make the decision.

"I can't say yes Meckenzie. I understand your concerns and I agree for the most part, but your mother will make the decision."

"Okay. I know." Meckenzie needed a subject change, this was just depressing her more. "We should fix up the storage room for Ardan and Bowen. Have they gotten their things from their houses yet?"

"Yes they went early this morning. Is Arden going to be a problem for you?"

"No, nothing will happen." Meckenzie had been trying not to think about last night's garden moment. There was nothing she could do about it now. "Can we just go make a living space for them? I don't want to talk about it."

Isabel agreed and the two of them headed back down to the gym area. The storage room was actually as wide as the room that held the pool and gym. You could fit three bedrooms in it if you wanted to. They went through the furniture that was in the room, furniture that had been in their family since her grandmother built the house.

They found two bed frames but no mattresses. There would have to be a call made to a mattress store to get some delivered. Meckenzie found a couple of bedside tables and an old chair. They enlisted the help of the others and set about making a living space suitable for their guests. Taggart and Arden went off to find some mattresses with the kids' emergency credit card.

Kellan and Bowen did most of the heavy lifting. Isabel had run upstairs to grab some cleaning supplies, since a fine layer of dust had settled over much of the furniture. Stuck back in one corner, there were four sets of bookshelves that were requisitioned to work as room dividers. They placed them two by two back to back so that there was some privacy. They were even able to set up an old dining room table in one corner to act as a place for eating, writing, or playing games.

When they had finished, the room looked like a studio apartment. In order to stay busy, Meckenzie went on a hunt for pillows and sheets. She gathered up all the materials she thought might make the room comfy. Meckenzie even grabbed a vase out of the kitchen and cut some fresh flowers in the garden.

Arden returned to find Meckenzie dusting the bookshelves by herself. Isabel had gone to finish getting lunch ready, and Bowen was probably hanging around Isabel. Kellan had disappeared when it became evident that all that was left to do was clean.

Ardan stopped at the door, trying to decide whether to enter the room, or to leave. Since Ardan had his belongings that he had retrieved earlier with him, it made no sense for him to walk back out. Meckenzie stopped dusting and turned toward Ardan. She felt like they should talk, though she had no idea what she would say to him.

Ardan began putting away his clothes in the chest of drawers that had been moved into his side of the room. Meckenzie put down her cleaning materials and went to him. She touched his back, wanting him to turn and put his arms around her again. He froze in mid-action at her touch.

"We should talk." Meckenzie said. "Last night..."

"Forget about it." Ardan's voice betrayed him, the emotion in it was overpowering to Meckenzie. She wanted to hold Ardan and comfort him, but her sense of duty stopped her.

"I think you got the wrong idea." Meckenzie explained. "It's not that I don't like you. It's that there are too many people counting on me. There is too much at stake for me to get distracted. When you were lying in the alley and I had no idea whether you were alive or dead, I knew that I couldn't risk your life. If I publicly love you, you become a target for my enemies. I would never forgive myself if you were killed because of me."

"I'm here to protect you; it is possible that I might die for you anyways." Ardan pleaded.

"That is a possibility," Meckenzie wanted to send him as far away from this as possible to save him, but she couldn't make that decision. "My mother sent you here to guard all three of us; I can't send you away, even if I want to."

"I know." His shoulders dropped as the sadness flowed through him. "I need to be able to protect all three of you. I don't know that I can protect anyone but you with what I'm feeling." He turned around and took Meckenzie in his arms.

Meckenzie's mind spun into pure joy. Warmth rushed through her limbs and she melted into his embrace. Meckenzie felt she could spend the rest of her life here in his arms and that was the problem. She pushed back from Ardan, missing him before he had even let go.

"We have to be able to work together. Ardan, I can't stand you ignoring me, but we can't be together. Not yet. Can we do this? Can we work together and fight together?" Meckenzie begged him to say yes with her eyes.

Ardan smiled at her, "You will make a wonderful queen. You care so much for others. You put them before yourself. I can do this. I can be your teacher and soldier and someday this will be over."

Meckenzie loved him already. There was no mistake, he was meant to be hers. And someday, she hoped, he would.

CHAPTER 23

The weeks flew by, Meckenzie, Taggart, Kellan and their father had gone down to the school on the following Monday with a cover story about finding their mother and needing to focus on her for a while. They convinced the head master to let them test out of their classes and still receive diplomas at the end of the year. The headmaster wasn't very happy about the situation and informed Taggart that he would have to forfeit his valedictorian status.

Taggart, like the wonderful man he is, explained that in life sometimes family is more important than being number one. The headmaster was made to look a fool for implying that they would choose school over their mother.

Kellan was still moody and uncooperative about leaving. She had on several occasions taken her anger out with Ardan on the sparring mat. Ardan was a good sport about it; he never complained, or got angry with Kellan for it. Meckenzie found so many wonderful things in his personality when he was dealing with Kellan. Kellan would disappear for hours during the day to pout, usually preceded by some kind of outburst. Isabel had actually had some luck teaching her to be able to use her growth ability. On one occasion Kellan had grown on command, but she was still having problems shrinking back down to her normal size. Isabel seemed to think it had to do with her inability to practice patience. Meckenzie thought it was because Kellan just wanted to be difficult.

Bowen was more than impressed with Taggart's ability to learn. He was the most proficient at spell casting and potion mixing. Taggart remembered everything. Bowen had an impressive library of books that he brought over from the place he had been staying. Taggart devoured everything he could get his hands on, and most of his free time was spent in Arden and Bowen's room reading and studying.

Meckenzie had the most problems with potion making. She had never been good at chemistry, or cooking, which Isabel compared it too. There were so many ingredients that were foreign to her. Dragon scales, pixie dust, wolves bain, and the sap of a tree person, all these mystical items sat on the shelves of the potion area. Meckenzie couldn't even imagine how you would get a scale of a dragon, or sap from a tree person, for that matter.

Spell casting came easy for Meckenzie, if she could remember the words. Her natural ability had actually knocked out everyone in a twenty foot radius when she cast a sleeping spell. Luckily Bowen was not there and was able to help her revive Isabel, Taggart, and Kellan.

They had met with the party planners twice over the past few weeks and finalized all the birthday plans. The invitations had been sent out and it was the bright spot in Kellan's future, because every time they talked about it she got excited and seemed to smile for hours afterwards.

Morgan and Meckenzie talked twice a week in the dream state. The first meeting between them had been intense, but it had been nothing compared to the meeting after their fight with Ty. Morgan had been worried and their mother had wanted as many details as Meckenzie could remember. It had been a long meeting and when Meckenzie awoke from it, she was more tired than when she had gone to sleep. Taggart had the wonderful idea of putting an audio recorder on the bedside table so that Meckenzie's half of the conversation could be recorded and reviewed by the others.

Their mother had not made the decision yet as to whether their father could come with them. Meckenzie asked every time she met with Morgan. Isabel told her to be patient, but time was running out. Their father had started making arrangements to leave. He had promoted a new partner and started turning his assets into money that he was stashing all over the world. He had met with his lawyers several times to develop a trust to take care of the house and other areas of their lives. Meckenzie didn't have the heart to think about the possibility that all of his actions may have been for nothing.

It was the week before their birthday that Meckenzie decided that it was time they went to the safety deposit box and retrieved its contents. She convinced her dad that it was time, so she Kellan, Taggart and their father headed to the bank. Bowen had insisted on going with them for protection, but had stayed in the car when they had arrived at the bank.

The ride over to the bank was intensely quiet. They all new that the necklace was in the box, but there was a letter for their father as well. Meckenzie was sure that this would be highly emotional for him; no one mentioned its existence.

The bank manager was very helpful and led them into a private viewing room while the box was retrieved. As they sat waiting for the box, their father paced the small room. Meckenzie grabbed his hand as he circled the room and gave him a big hug.

He smiled, "What was that for?"

"You have been the best father any of us could have asked for. Whatever is in that box, just know that there is no scenario in life that would not lead us back to you."

Taggart and Kellan agreed. Since their mother had left, it had only been their father and the trips for eight years and he had done the best job he could do raising three kids. He had loved them and spoiled them, and taught them the value of a dollar. He had given them discipline and showed them joy. There were trips to see the world and demonstrations of how being at home is sometimes the best vacation that anyone can ask for.

While most kids in their school who had two parents only saw them on rare occasions, they had their father every night for dinner. He had made choices in his life that always put his kids first, and they were not ever going to leave him behind because the parent that ran away said they had to.

"You will be the grandfather to our children." Taggart added. "Whether we are here or there, they will know you."

"She has to let you come with us, she owes us that much." Kellan was still so angry with their mother.

Just then an attendant came in with the box. They all sat around the table staring at it, dreading the contents. Finally, their father took out the key and opened the box. Inside was a velvet bag, which had to hold the necklace. There was a letter underneath it addressed to their father. Under that was a photo, it surprised them that there was something else in the box. It was a picture of their mother and father in the hospital, holding the three of them as newborns. On the back were the words, "the happiest I've ever been." It was their mother's handwriting.

In the photo they were wrapped in blankets. Their father was holding Taggart with his little blue blanket. Meckenzie and Kellan were snuggled into each of their mother's arms. Everyone was smiling and content. The photo managed to capture the love that Diedra had for her children. It radiated right out of the picture and Meckenzie felt in her heart. Even Kellan softened as she beheld the photo.

Finally, all attention turned to their father. He held in his hand the letter addressed to him, but he had not opened it. He was struggling with what to do; a hundred different emotions played out on his face. Their father tucked the letter inside his jacket and stood.

"Well, I think we should get this home." He held up the pouch with the necklace inside. "We can discuss the letter after I read it in private, if I feel it needs to be discussed."

With that they left the bank and headed home. Their father had retired to his study with the letter, leaving the necklace pouch in Taggart's hands. The triplets took the bag and headed for the gym that had basically become training headquarters. There they found Isabel and Bowen laughing and talking. It seemed that the spark was not gone between these two.

They gathered around the table in Bowen and Ardan's makeshift room. They knew the velvet bag Taggart placed in the middle of the table was last touched by their mother. The last person to wear the necklace inside was their mother.

"Well, someone's got to take it out." Kellan said as she reached for the bag, no one stopped her. She untied the string that held the bag closed and slid it open. As Kellan turned the bag over, the necklace slipped out into her hand.

It looked like a three leaf clover. Each leaf sparkled with a beautiful jewel. Kellan spread the bag out on the table and laid the necklace on top of it so everyone could see it.

"I don't see what the big deal is all about." Kellan said unimpressed. "It's just a necklace."

"It's not just a necklace; it holds all the power of your ancestors." Isabel impatiently interjected. "You don't understand the sacrifice that went into this necklace. Powers were surrendered into it and a life was taken to bind those powers there. Our powers are there within those shiny stones. Legend says whoever wears the necklace has all that power at their control. So it would reason that it amplifies powers. Each of you will wear a piece of it; therefore each of you will be stronger because of it."

She picked up the necklace and slid the chain off of the charm. She twisted the stem of the clover and slid it up. The three leaves of the clover slid off. Each a beautiful formed heart pendant. There was a green stoned heart that Isabel handed to Kellan. The red one was given to Taggart, and the blue one to Meckenzie.

Meckenzie slid her fingers across the stone's smooth surface. A shiver of warmth emanated up her arm into her head. She turned the pendant over and found a tiny loop on the back meant for a chain. Kellan had already retrieved the chain from the necklace and was threading it through her charm. She put the necklace on and the green stone sparkled against her skin.

"Whoa." Kellan exclaimed. "This is freaky."

"Did you feel something?" Isabel curiously inquired.

"Yes it's like warmth spreading all over my body. I feel lighter and heavier at the same time."

Isabel reached for the velvet bag. Tucked away in a small pocket inside the bag were two other chains. She handed one to each Taggart and Meckenzie. They slid the chains in place and put on their charms.

The warmth hit Meckenzie in the middle of her chest and spread outwards. She felt it most potently in her head. It was like she had a fire burning in her brain warming her from the inside out. Without even trying Meckenzie could hear everyone's thoughts. She didn't even have to concentrate; the words just came streaming in. It would be very nerve wracking if she couldn't figure out how to control it, but as soon as she thought of controlling it, the words were gone and it was quiet again in her head.

Taggart was smiling from ear to ear. He had his hand over the charm sitting on his chest. There was something very calming in his manner.

"This is amazing. I feel like my heart is warm." Taggart's hand was still resting on his chest.

"My whole body is warm." Kellan added.

Everyone turned to Meckenzie. "My mind is toasty." She said laughing. "I guess the stones warm the part of you associated with your powers."

"It's not really warming you." Isabel explained. "It is producing an amplification of your powers. So the area that your powers come from feels warmer because more energy is being produced."

They were all marveling at their charms when Ardan came into the room with a box. "Your masks for your birthday party have arrived." He said sitting the box down on the table. They opened it up and found costume masks decorated in bright colors. Meckenzie's looked like a fairy princess which was ironic. Taggart had a wolf mask done in white, gold and silver. Kellan's mask was a butterfly with wings that flowed from the side. Everyone would wear masks to the party, so there were some extras in the box for their father, Isabel, and the two guys.

"Are you starting to get excited?" Bowen asked.

"About our birthday, yes, about leaving, no. We need to know about dad." Meckenzie responded.

"Your mom will make a decision soon." Said Isabel.

Kellan was frustrated with that answer, "What in the world could she be considering? She wants us there, she wants us to be happy, then she wants dad there too. She can't run off and then expect us to leave him as well."

They had been having this argument for a couple of weeks and Isabel was finally done.

"I can't make her answer you. This is not the life she would have chosen for you three. It is not the life she would have chosen for herself. Do you think she wanted to leave you? Do you think she wanted to leave…" Isabel paused

From behind them, their father finished her sentence, "the man she loved."

Everyone turned to find him standing in the door holding the letter they had retrieved earlier. He looked haggard. His eyes were red and puffy from crying.

"She loved me, I know she did. The picture in the box showed our love. The letter says she had to leave but that she never wanted to. She had always hoped that we would be together forever. Living our little lives with our three beautiful children. If she hasn't made a decision yet, then it is because she is worried about me. I think it is best if we stop questioning her decision until she makes it. Isabel can't fix it and no amount of complaining about your mother will take away the last eight years, so it's time for you three to grow up. She also told me some super-secret fairy stuff in that letter. If these people who are waging a war against your land win, they will come here next. They plan on using their magic to enslave all of mankind. When your mother went back she went to hold them at bay so you could grow up with as normal a childhood as could be expected."

Their father paused and took in a deep breath as if steading himself for what he was about to say.

"Your mother is afraid that I will obstruct you in some way. If there comes a time where you have to give your life to preserve peace, she knows I would never allow it. She knows I would protect you with my own life which in turn would put your life in danger. If you are trying to save me all the time, then who will be watching out for you. It might be necessary for me to be somewhere else while all of this is going on, hiding somewhere else in this world. Your mother has asked me to do as much in the letter. She has asked me to leave you and not try to find you. I think she thought I would remarry. In her letter she indicates that I should save myself and my loved ones and let you do your duty. This is why she hasn't answered. She was waiting for me to read the letter and tell you that I wasn't going to go."

"But dad you can't leave us." Tears were flowing down Kellan's face. This just might push her over the edge. "I won't go if you don't."

"This is the last time we are going to talk about this until your mother responds." He said. "If she says no, I will go away. I have everything in place to leave, so no one will be able find me here. I have some ideas of where I'd like to hide if I have to. It will be like an early retirement. There is enough money to last a lifetime. Actually there is enough to last my lifetime, your lifetime, and your children's lifetime. So I will start making plans for that option. If I have to leave, we will find a way for you to contact me. I will leave word with my lawyer and set up a mailbox somewhere for correspondence. Then it can be forwarded anywhere in the world."

"That I love you three enough to walk away should tell you how much I respect your mother. I know she is trying to do what is best for everyone in this world and in hers. So it's time you forgive her. You will need her if I'm gone. You will need to trust her. If I can ask you three for one thing, then I ask you to forgive her, for me." Their father left the room and his three children to think about what he had said.

CHAPTER 24

The garden had been transformed with long flowing linen curtains and plush couches. The ballroom was filled with linen clothed tables set with fine china and silver and a stage had been erected in one corner of the dance floor in which a DJ had begun setting up.

It was the evening of the triplets' eighteenth birthday party and the day had been filled with last minute emergencies and overlooked details. Everything had come together beautifully in the end. Their party planner Doreen had out done herself with the food that was being delivered at this moment. The house smelled of delicious hors devours, roasted chicken, prime rib, and various other foods that would be available this evening.

Meckenzie had finished getting ready and was searching the house for anyone who actually lived there. There were cater-waiters milling about in the ballroom listening to the DJ test his sound equipment with a little Katy Perry. Adam, the party decorator, was in the garden adding last minute decorating touches.

"Have you seen any of my family?" Meckenzie surprised Adam. He had not realized she had entered the garden.

"Oh my gawd girl, you look fantastic?" Adam rushed over to Meckenzie and spun her around. "Is this Vintage?"

Meckenzie was wearing a dress that she had found while going through some trunks in the storage space downstairs. It had been her mom's dress. It was a classic sweetheart floor length gown of a shimmering gold fabric that flowed behind her like a river of honey. Meckenzie's mask matched it perfectly. Kellan had found a dress to wear as well and had it taken out for an emergency fitting. She was broader than Meckenzie and their mom, but the seamstress had been able to alter the dress and Kellan had looked gorgeous in it. It had a rainbow iridescence that matched her butterfly mask.

"Yes, it was my mom's dress." Meckenzie twirled as Adam shrieked with delight. "Have you seen Taggart or Kellan?"

"No, but that aunt of yours was through here a minute ago adjusting cameras and talking on her cell phone. I swear I saw her moving rocks around too, but it's been a long day and I could have been seeing things."

"Thanks Adam. I'll see you later." Meckenzie headed downstairs where she assumed everyone had gathered. Sure enough, she found Isabel, Bowen, Taggart, and Arden assembled around the potion table. Ardan was wearing a tuxedo and looked absolutely dashing. His hair had gotten a little longer so it was curling up over his collar. There was a place inside of Meckenzie that wanted to run her fingers through that hair. Twist her fingers into his beautiful locks and pull his mouth down to hers. Meckenzie cleared her head of these thoughts. They had done a great job of working together without letting their feelings find their way into it.

"Hey guys, what are we doing in our secret spy lab?" Meckenzie was feeling great this evening and her sense of humor had started coming back the last couple of days.

They all turned in Meckenzie's direction. Ardan's eyes met hers and she could see the desire spark in them.

"You look beautiful sis." Taggart smiled.

"You look handsome too, bro."

Meckenzie rubbed his hair so that Taggart would have to fix it before the party. Everyone's mood seemed to be on the happy side this evening.

"We are putting some extra precautions into place. With all the people flowing in and out of the house, it is best if we are cautious. Here," Isabel handed Meckenzie a couple of vials, "keep these in your purse. One is a smoke bomb that your brother came up with; it should be thrown on the ground. It will cause a dense fog. The other is a paralyzing potion. Throw it on the person you want to paralyze. This will help you avoid paralyzing everyone on Central Park West." They all laughed at Meckenzie's ability to project a spell in a large radius.

"The magic alarms are set. Anyone with fairy blood will be able to feel it when they go off. It will buzz you like an electric fence. It won't hurt, but you will feel the vibration." Bowen had upgraded the magical alarms when he had first moved in. "We will be monitoring the party from down here. We set up a viewing station for the many cameras around the house in the corner of our room. We have brought a couple of extra people over for security. They will be here any minute. Ardan will be in the ballroom with you three all night. Isabel and I will come and go, as we will be monitoring the perimeters as well as communicating with the others."

"Has anyone seen Kellan?" Meckenzie was wondering where her sister had gotten off to.

"I thought she was getting ready." Taggart said absently as he mixed another potion.

"I'm right here." Kellan came down the stairs looking lovely.

"You look amazing." Meckenzie rushed over to give her a hug. "You ready to turn eighteen?"

"Technically we are already eighteen."

"Okay, ready to blow out some candles?"

"As ready as I'll ever be." Kellan was very aloof. She seemed to have something on her mind, but Meckenzie didn't have time to ask because Bowen began to go over the security measures for the evening with Kellan. Isabel gave Kellan the same potions to keep in her purse.

The trips and Ardan headed upstairs to the party. Guests would start arriving at any minute and it was important that they were there to greet them. Their father was already in the sitting room on the first floor with two gentlemen dressed in all black. They were discussing the cameras positioned over the door and in the entry.

Bowen entered and greeted them as old friends; they must be the extra security detail Meckenzie realized. As Bowen introduced them, they bowed to the triplets. It was the first time someone had addressed them as royalty. Meckenzie felt uncomfortable and Kellan snickered. Before it got uncomfortable, Bowen took them down to show them the ballroom and garden.

"I'm glad I get to see you three before this shindig starts up. I have something for you." Their father pulled out three small ring boxes from his pocket. He handed the red one to Taggart, the green one to Kellan and the blue one to Meckenzie. "I hope you like them."

The triplets opened the boxes to find they each had been given a ring. Taggart's was inset with a ruby and eight small diamonds in a large square platinum setting. Kellan's had a large princess cut diamond set off by two emeralds in a platinum setting. Meckenzie was amazed that he had taken the color of their necklaces into designing these rings. Meckenzie's ring was the most beautiful thing she had ever seen. There were a half a dozen sapphires and diamonds sprinkled through a platinum band. It sparkled from every angle.

"Thank you so much, this is so beautiful." Kellan hugged their father tightly.

"Now they don't have any magical powers, but I thought no matter what happens, that you would always have a piece of me with you."

"Thanks dad." Taggart gave him a hug.

Meckenzie was on the verge of tears. She knew she couldn't cry though, she didn't have enough time to fix her makeup. She hugged her father; she buried her head in his chest and breathed in deep. Her dad smelled as he had always smelled, sandalwood and citrus. It was some cologne that he had worn since the 70's. Meckenzie loved the smell of it.

"Well, there will be guests arriving soon." As if on cue the doorbell rang and everyone went off to greet the first guests.

People began pouring in and were shown down to the ballroom. The masquerade ball was a huge success; everyone was drinking, eating and laughing. The triplets' friends from school had asked about their absence. The trips just confirmed the story that they were dealing with a personal family matter and needed to be home.

When it was time to cut the cake, the lights were turned off as a huge cake was wheeled in. The triplets circled around with their father to blow out the candles as everyone sang happy birthday. Meckenzie got ready to make her wish, but the only wish she could think of was that this would all be over soon so that they could get on with their lives and be near their father.

Applause erupted as they blew out the candles and the lights came back on. Meckenzie saw her first at the back of the room. She was standing next to the door holding a mask to her chest. Her blond hair was pulled away from her face and she looked a little older, but it was her.

Meckenzie must have stopped breathing because Taggart touched her shoulder, but Meckenzie couldn't take her eyes off of her; she might disappear if that happened. So when Taggart followed her eyes to the back of the room, his hand dropped back to his side.

"Mom." He whispered.

M C Moore

CHAPTER 25

For the first time in eight years, they were in the same room as their mom. Doreen was urging them to cut into the cake so that they could start serving it. Taggart numbly took the knife made a slice and handed Doreen the knife to begin serving the guests. The triplets made their way through the crowd accepting congratulations as they went, but never taking their eyes off their mom. Kellan's breathing had accelerated the moment she had spotted their mother. She was getting angry, which could spell trouble if she was unable to control her powers.

Their mother smiled at them as they approached her. Meckenzie still couldn't believe she was really there. Their father had followed them to the back of the room and was the first to speak.

"Diedra you don't seem to have aged a day, you are lovelier than I remember." He was mesmerized by her smile. "Maybe we should go somewhere more private."

"I think that would be best." She led them out of the room and headed for the stairs. Bowen was standing outside the ballroom and led the way up the stairs. He seemed to be aware of their mother's desire for privacy and he led them to Lawrence's study.

Everyone took seats and Bowen closed the door as he stepped back outside to guard it.

"You girls look beautiful. I do believe those are my old dresses. I can't say that I ever looked as lovely in them as you do." The smile that played across their mom's face was enchanting.

Kellan was not enchanted. She was angry.

"You just waltz back in here and think that everything is going to be okay because you showed up for our eighteenth birthday party. What about the seven you missed? What about the Christmases and the school plays? What about everything else? You run off and then you expect us to jump for joy and come with you. So you have showed up to fetch us have you?" Kellan was sobbing, her body trembling with anger.

"I'm sorry Kellan. I really am. Life doesn't always go the way you want it to. Sometimes when all you want in the whole world is to be a mom, you have to be the Queen instead." Their mother's face was filled with sorrow.

"You didn't have to go back. You could have stayed. You didn't have to leave us."

"Yes Kellan, I had to leave. I had thousands of people depending on me to lead them. I needed to be there to protect them. I needed to be there in order to protect you."

"But it didn't protect us did it. They came here and attacked us. They burned me, and if Taggart wasn't a healer what would have happened? I'd be in a hospital right now, or dead." Kellan was visibly turning red in the face. Meckenzie was afraid that she would do her she-hulk routine right here in the middle of the study.

"Kellan calm down. You're going to change into your larger self if you don't." Taggart placed his hand on her back trying to relax her. It had the opposite effect. Kellan jumped to her feet.

"I'm not going to sit here with her. You guys can do what you want; I'm going back to the party." With that she stormed out of the study.

"Do you two feel the same way she does?" Diedra asked them. The smile was gone from her eyes; it had been replaced with eight years of pain and distance.

"I'm not going to say I completely understand how you left, but I do understand why." Taggart's level headedness was one of his best features.

"I could say the same thing as Taggart. I'm happy you are here though and I am happy that you cared enough to come back." Meckenzie stood up and went to hug her mother for the first time in eight years.

Diedra held on tight. There were all those years to make up for. Taggart joined them and they had a good family hug.

"Well, there is much to discuss, but I think it can wait till after the party. If you don't mind I would like to talk to your father alone and I think someone should go find Kellan and make sure she is okay."

Meckenzie and Taggart left their mother and father in the study. Meckenzie was curious if they were discussing where their father would be spending the next few years. It really involved all of them, so she was a little frustrated that they had not been asked to join the conversation. She toyed with the idea of eavesdropping with her mental gifts on the private conversation, but decided it was probably more important to take care of Kellan.

Bowen was positioned outside the door still. He must be guarding the Queen. Meckenzie thought he had probably seen which way Kellan had gone.

"Did you see Kellan leave?"

"Yes, she went up to her room, I think." Bowen smiled knowing Kellan's temper.

Meckenzie turned to Taggart, "I'll go get her. You go to the party and make sure that people don't start wondering where we all have run off to."

There wasn't much that Meckenzie could say to Kellan that would ease her anger. This was a suicide mission and Meckenzie knew she was going to have to take the fall and be the bad guy to get Kellan back to the party. She knocked on Kellan's door, but there was no response.

"Kellan, its Meckenzie. Can I come in?" There was still no response. "Kellan I'm coming in."

Meckenzie opened the door, but the room was dark. As she flipped on the light switch she noticed that the room looked like someone had riffled through all of Kellan's clothes and belongings. Stuff was scattered all over the room and some of Kellan's things were missing. The photo of the family that she kept beside her bed was missing. Kellan's laptop was gone as well, the cords hanging all over her desk.

Meckenzie walked over to the desk. Set against the speakers was an envelope addressed to Meckenzie and Taggart. Just as she was sliding her finger in the envelope to tear it open, her body started buzzing. It was just as Bowen had described it, an electrical fence without the pain. The magical alarm was going off.

Meckenzie took the envelope and ran down the stairs. As she hit the second floor her mother, father and Bowen were coming out of the study. They all moved towards the stairs, someone was in the house but they didn't know where.

"Did you find Kellan?" Bowen was taking the stairs two at a time as he yelled back to her.

"No, she wasn't there. There was this note." Meckenzie held up the envelope so everyone could see it.

Meckenzie's father had put himself in front of their mother and was headed cautiously down the stairs. Meckenzie fished the potions out of her purse and prepared to paralyze anyone who might be coming up behind them.

There were so many things happening at once, that Meckenzie didn't know where they should go, but Bowen obviously had a plan. When they reached the landing of the first floor, he was headed to the front door to check with the guard. Unfortunately, the guard was not there and there were no signs of anyone forcing their way in. The sounds of the party still going echoed up the stair way into the foyer. The DJ was encouraging people to dance as he started playing Party Rock by LMFAO. Meckenzie couldn't help but think of how much Kellan loved this song, which made her hope that Kellan was downstairs safe right now.

"I think we should get the Queen to the gym, we can protect her better down there. Meckenzie try and find Kellan and Taggart."

The magical alarm was still rattling through Meckenzie's body as they started down the stairs. They met Taggart, Ardan and Isabel at the foot of the stairs. Kellan wasn't with them, which meant she was still missing. Meckenzie pulled the letter out of her bag and tore into it.

Dear brother and sister,

I know that you think we should run off and fight this war. I know that you have forgiven mom, but I have not. I am going to run away. I have saved up a lot of money and have a friend that is going to let me stay with her. I won't come back until this war is over. Don't try and find me. I will just run again if you do.

Tell dad I'm sorry. I really didn't want to leave him, but I had to choose myself this time. Stay safe.

Love

Kellan

Meckenzie was shocked. Where had she gone? She needed to tell everyone.

As they started to discuss what to do next, Meckenzie yelled it out. "Kellan's run away."

Everyone stopped and looked at Meckenzie. She held out the letter she had just read. Her father took it from her hands and read it aloud for everyone to hear. Now they had two problems, there was someone in the house who wanted to hurt them. And Kellan wasn't in the house anymore. At that moment the magical alarm stopped buzzing Meckenzie bones. Everyone noticed it at the same time.

"Whoever was here is gone." Ardan stated. "We should try to find Kellan."

"Let's go to the gym first and look at the tapes. We need to know when and how Kellan left. Plus we might be able to see who was here." Bowen led them downstairs to his room, the makeshift security room. Their father excused himself to find Doreen so he could end the party.

Meckenzie realized she hadn't even gotten a piece of her own birthday cake. It seemed like such a trivial thought considering her sister had just run away and someone had broken into their house. They say just before you go crazy, your mind starts to think of mundane things. Meckenzie thought maybe she was going crazy.

CHAPTER 26

When they reached Bowen and Ardan's room where the video equipment was set up, there was only one special ops fairy there. He was scanning all the cameras looking for the intruder. He was running the dvr back to when the alarm went off.

"Where's Johan?" Bowen asked him.

"I'm not sure; he stepped outside the front door and out of the range of the camera there. He never came back. I have been here the whole time trying to figure out who was in the house. I haven't seen anything that would indicate anyone came in the front door."

"Well, we have another problem that is more important now, Kellan is missing. Did you see her leave the front door at any point?" Bowen took control of the situation. He moved a chair up beside special ops fairy and started directing him to which times and cameras to watch.

The main screen suddenly filled with the image of the study door with Bowen standing outside of it. A few seconds later Kellan came out. She was crying and ran towards the stairs. The camera then switched to the third floor as she ran by and continued up the stairs. On the fourth floor camera you could see Kellan exiting towards her bedroom. The view switched to a view of the sitting area between Kellan and Meckenzie's rooms.

"How many cameras are in this house now?" Meckenzie realized there were a lot more than she initially thought.

"About 40." Taggart responded. "We had to cover all the exits, the stairs, the common areas, and the elevator."

As soon as he said it, Meckenzie realized what Kellan had done.

"The elevator." Meckenzie shouted. "She took the elevator to the fifth floor and exited the roof. There is a service ladder that goes to the building next door."

Sure enough Kellan was seen coming out of her room with her bags. Tears still stained her face. Her hair was pulled back and she had changed into street clothes. She hit the elevator button, the doors opened and to everyone's surprise, there on the elevator was Ty. He whispered something and Kellan fell to the ground.

Ty had not honored their agreement and he had come back and taken Kellan. He had been in the house, and the alarm was not triggered, not even when he cast the spell. Ty pulled Kellan's body onto the elevator along with her bags, and they rode up to the fifth floor. Meckenzie watched as Ty's brother, who had apparently been waiting for him on the roof entered the house. As soon as he stepped in the house, you could see the reaction of the Fae to the magical alarm sounding, on one of the monitors, you could even see Bowen run into the study to protect the Queen. Meckenzie realized that Ty had not triggered the alarm. It remained silent until his brother had entered the house.

"Why didn't Ty trigger the alarm?" Meckenzie asked.

"I don't' know, he must have used a shielding spell, or an amulet, or he could have a shielding power." Isabel answered.

On the monitor Ty and his brother stood there having a conversation in the elevator. It was obvious that his brother was not entirely happy with the situation. In a bit of rage, Ty struck his brother across the face. The brother, though obviously larger and stronger than Ty, slumped his shoulders and reached down to carry Kellan out onto the roof.

The roof camera showed, a third guy came up the service ladder. They talked for several minutes, it looked like Ty was trying to convince the guy to do something. Then the guy stepped away from them. Kellan's lifeless body was lying on the roof. She wasn't moving, it was hard to tell if she was even breathing.

"Is she alive?" Meckenzie wasn't sure she wanted to know the answer to that question.

"I think so." Isabel put her arm around Meckenzie. "I don't think they would be taking her if they killed her, they would have just left her for us to find. I am sure they plan on using her for leverage."

The third guy was waving his hands about and speaking. A fog was surrounding him; the air seemed to be swirling all around him. A small light appeared in the midst of it all, it began to grow in size as his movements became more frantic. Within a moment the light was the size of a door. Ty indicated to his brother to grab Kellan.

Everyone in the room had stopped breathing. They watched raptly as Ty stepped into the light and disappeared. His brother followed, hauling Kellan over his shoulder. The third guy stepped through and as soon as he disappeared, so did the light. It was all over in a matter of minutes. They had kidnapped Kellan.

"They have a rifter." Bowen turned and addressed the Queen. Tears were welling up in her eyes. "We'll need to notify the Air and Earth kingdoms. With a rifter they can go anywhere."

"What's a rifter?" Taggart asked.

"We haven't seen one obviously in over eight hundred years, but what we have learned from history books is that a rifter is someone who can tear a rift between the planes. They allow travel without the use of a portal. They basically create their own portal. So they can go anywhere at any time. We have to travel through the portals that only work between two specific points in the worlds and only at dusk and dawn."

"So we can't even go after Kellan till tomorrow?" Meckenzie was dismayed to realize that Kellan was on her own for the night with Ty and his cohorts.

"We can't go after her at all right now." Their mother said. "We will go back to Aquanis in the morning and wait for them to contact us. Then we will devise a plan. There is no way that I'm jeopardizing you two right now. So you will have to be ready to go in the morning. We can guard you better at the castle."

"Castle?" Taggart asked.

"Yes you'll live with me at the castle." She responded.

"What about dad?" Meckenzie had to know what was going to happen to their father.

"He will hide here in the human world. We have already discussed it. He knows that it is what is best for you. If we finish this, we will send for him. Someone should tell him what has happened, I'll do it. You two need to go get ready to leave in the morning. Don't bring too much stuff. Travel light. Anything you need will be provided for you." Their mother turned and headed to find their father leaving Taggart and Meckenzie standing there staring at the empty roof on the TV screen.

So that was it. They were going to Aquanis. Kellan had been kidnapped. They were moving to a castle. And they were going to war. Meckenzie was pretty sure this was the worst eighteenth birthday ever. She only wished that she and her siblings would make it to their nineteenth.

ABOUT THE AUTHOR

M C Moore lives in Southern California where she writes young adult fiction. Her first novel, 'Trefoil', is being met with rave reviews. The second book in the Trefoil Trilogy will be 'Aquanis' due out December 2011.